EGGSECUTIVE ORDERS

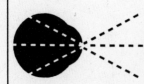

EGGSECUTIVE ORDERS

JULIE HYZY

WHEELER PUBLISHING
A part of Gale, Cengage Learning

GALE
CENGAGE Learning

Detroit • New York • San Francisco • New Haven, Conn • Waterville, Maine • London

GALE
CENGAGE Learning™

LIBRARY OF CONGRESS CATALOGING-IN-PUBLICATION DATA

Hyzy, Julie A.
    Eggsecutive orders / by Julie Hyzy.
        p. cm. — (Wheeler publishing large print cozy mystery)
    "A White House chef mystery"—T.p. verso.
    ISBN-13: 978-1-4104-2603-1 (alk. paper)
    ISBN-10: 1-4104-2603-3 (alk. paper)
    1. White House (Washington, D.C.)—Fiction. 2. Women
Cooks—Fiction. 3. Easter egg hunts—Fiction. 4. Washington
(D.C.)—Fiction. 5. Large type books. I. Title.
PS3608.Y98E33 2010
813'.6—dc22   2010003202

Published in 2010 by arrangement with The Berkley Publishing Group,
a member of Penguin Group (USA) Inc.

Printed in the United States of America
1 2 3 4 5 6 7 14 13 12 11 10

For my daughters,
and in memory of my mom

ACKNOWLEDGMENTS

Sincere thanks to the great people at The Berkley Publishing Group, especially Natalee Rosenstein and Michelle Vega. And to copyeditor Erica Rose. And to the folks at Tekno, especially Marty Greenberg, John Helfers, and Denise Little.

A big and special thank-you to my daughter Sara, who always reads first.

It's great to have experts to turn to — and my sincere gratitude to Diane Springer who — between VJA marching band competitions — helped me come up with an efficient way to kill a character. Any and all errors with regard to this method, and its subsequent discovery, are mine.

Thanks to reader Barbara Czachowski for her catch in *State of the Onion.* Ollie greatly appreciated Barbara's kind correction and made note of it in this adventure while she and her family toured the National Mall.

Thanks to Mystery Writers of America,

Sisters in Crime, and Thriller Writers of America for camaraderie and support, and thanks especially to wonderful readers who take the time to let me know what they think of Ollie's adventures.

CHAPTER 1

The phone rang while I was brushing my teeth. Phone calls at four in the morning usually mean one thing: bad news.

I quickly swished water in my mouth to clear away residual foam, and hurried to my bedroom to stop the unnerving jangle.

As executive chef at the White House, I make it a point to get to work every morning before the sun comes up, so I reasoned that this might be one of my staff catching me at home to call in sick. Either that, or my mom and nana were having trouble getting to the airport. Despite the fact that our kitchen had a lot to do before the Easter Egg Roll next week, I sorely hoped this was, indeed, a staffer calling in. I didn't want to think that my mother and nana might cancel their plans to visit me.

I reached for the handset. A split second before I answered, I glanced at the Caller ID.

Not my mom. Not a staffer.

The display read simply: "202."

The White House was calling *me.*

"Olivia Paras here," I said as I picked it up.

"Ollie, it's Paul." Paul Vasquez, the White House chief usher, wouldn't call me at home unless it was a dire emergency.

"What happened?" I asked.

"There's a car waiting for you downstairs."

"Downstairs, here?" I asked. Although I'd been awake for nearly an hour, my brain was slow to comprehend. "Downstairs where I live?"

"That's right," he said slowly. "Two agents will escort you to the residence today."

"Why? What happened?"

"You'll be briefed when you get here. Just hurry. They're waiting for you now. Follow their lead."

"But —"

"Ollie." His tone forced me to focus.

"Yes?"

"For God's sake, don't say *anything* to *anybody.*"

He hung up before I could ask what he meant.

Two Secret Service agents were waiting for me in the lobby when I came out of the elevator. Both male, both large, they were clad in nearly identical outfits of navy pants and gray sport coats, and wore similar buzz-cut hair. In a more chipper situation, I may have asked them if they were Tweedledee and Tweedledum, but I didn't recognize either of these guys, and neither wore an expression that encouraged levity.

The one closest to me nodded solemnly. "Ms. Paras?"

I nodded back.

"This way," he said. He started for the front doors, gesturing for me to walk directly behind him. I couldn't see around his broad back, and was about to step aside when his twin came in close behind, effectively making an Ollie sandwich.

I started to ask, "Why all the —"

But shouts from outside drowned out my question. "There she is!"

I still couldn't see much, but just as the damp morning air hit my skin, the sound of agitated scuffles reached my ears. A crowd rushed up, encircling us. Stark bright lights silhouetted the agent in front of me. I winced at the intensity and at the sharp shouts: "Ms. Paras, Ms. Paras!"

In an effort to see better, I started to move around Agent Number One, but Number Two placed a restraining hand on my shoulder. "Keep moving."

Half-turning, I started to ask what was going on, but the agent gripped harder, urging me forward.

Someone thrust a microphone into my face — and kept up with our brisk pace until the agent behind me strong-armed him away.

A woman's voice, shrill and plaintive: "Ms. Paras! What went wrong at dinner last night?"

Instinctively I turned. The agent tightened his grip on my shoulder, but that didn't stop me from hearing another voice boom: "What was in Carl Minkus's food?"

My right foot bumped the agent in front of me and I stumbled. Tweedledum's hold prevented me from falling on my face.

"She fainted!" someone yelled.

"No I didn't!" I shot back.

"You didn't?" someone shouted. "You're saying this wasn't your fault?"

A female voice this time: "Then what killed Carl Minkus?"

That stopped me. "What?" Carl Minkus was dead?

The two agents trundled me forward into the waiting car. A third agent held open the big black car's rear door as Tweedledee stepped to one side. The enormous men formed a wall on either side of me, with only one path open for me to go. I scrambled to safety.

Media mongrels clambered around the open door until the agents bulldozed them back. Amid all the shouting, I heard one high voice ring out: "What was in his food? And who prepared it?"

One of the Tweedles lowered himself next to me. I scooched to the other side, where reporters peered in the side windows. Armed with microphones and manic inquisitiveness, they banged on the glass, straining to be heard.

The agent next to me pulled his door closed, effectively hitting the mute button on the craziness outside. I was bewildered by the sudden realization that we were in one of the agency's bulletproof vehicles. We pulled away slowly, then picked up speed as the gaping pack of news guerillas fell away.

I resisted the temptation to sink into the vehicle's soft leather seats and make myself small. Instead, I perched forward, facing the agent next to me. "Carl Minkus is dead?"

His twin was driving, the third agent next to him in the passenger seat.

Agent Number Three was a little younger than his counterparts — smaller, too. And while the Tweedles remained stone-faced,

Number Three blinked at my question.

I focused on him. "What is going on?"

With his defined jawline and classic profile, Number Three reminded me a little of Tom. Younger though. He had the look of a newbie Secret Service agent.

When he blinked again, and started to turn, the agent next to me spoke up. "You will be briefed when we arrive," he said.

The agent in the passenger seat licked his lips and shifted his eyes front.

I sat back, trying to piece things together. Carl Minkus was a big shot with the National Security Agency. I didn't remember his exact title with the NSA, but I knew he was as much admired as he was feared. He'd been a bulldog fighting terrorism. Alone, he'd been responsible for the prosecution of more than a thousand suspected terrorists. Lately he'd turned his sights inward, accusing American citizens of terrible deeds. He'd gone after several high-profile celebrities, and had ruined more than one career. Some people called him the Joseph McCarthy of terrorism. Last night he'd been among the president's guests at dinner, but I didn't know whether the president had invited him to chastise or to congratulate.

Minkus, in his mid-fifties, was a vibrant,

outspoken defender of the republic. My shoulders jerked in an involuntary shiver and I tried to suppress the wave of panic shooting up my chest. Good thing it was dark in the car — I felt the heat in my face and knew it was as red as a beefsteak tomato. Minkus had been at dinner last night, now he was dead, and the press was already blaming me and my kitchen.

But . . . it wasn't our fault. Was it?

Rubbing my temples, I reviewed last night's menu. Except for Minkus being a recent convert to vegetarianism, he had no other dietary restrictions. No allergies. Minkus wasn't vegan. Which meant that dairy and eggs were allowed.

Did we serve him an item we shouldn't have? I stopped myself. How ridiculous! The White House kitchen was freakishly conscientious about our guests' dining preferences. Minkus would not have been served anything that conflicted with his needs. And, even if he had accidentally ingested a meat product, it certainly wouldn't have killed him.

No, I reasoned, even as my knee bounced a panicked tempo, he must have had an aneurysm or something. That had to be it. Or maybe an undiagnosed heart condition. Something unpredictable. Maybe his recent

15

switch to vegetarianism was to help combat high cholesterol. Maybe he was on doctors' orders to lose weight. It couldn't have been anything he ate. At least, not something we had prepared.

I looked at the three men accompanying me on our race to the residence. Not one of them returned my gaze. "I'll be briefed, you said?"

One of the guys in front nodded.

My voice kicked up an octave, despite my attempts to keep calm. "And they think Mr. Minkus died because of something we served last night?"

No reaction this time.

"Well." I folded my arms and sat back, striving for control. "As soon as I'm done being briefed, I'll be sure to run a complete investigation of my kitchen."

The agent driving the car met my eyes in the rearview mirror. "Already underway."

I should have guessed, I thought. With a frown, I leaned back in the very comfortable seat, although at the moment I was anything but.

CHAPTER 2

I wished we would just get to the White House already. Despite the car's speed, I felt like we were moving in slow motion. I wanted to get there — and get everything settled. Now. But no matter how hard I willed it, I couldn't make the limo move faster.

Still dark at this hour, the streets were wet from heavy overnight rains. Our tires sliced through deep roadside puddles, hammering dirty water against the side of the sedan every time we took a turn. I touched the thick window and hoped the storms hadn't delayed incoming flights. My mother and nana were coming to visit me — for the first time. I'd been begging them to make the trip, almost since my first day at the White House, but they'd come up with excuse after excuse. I knew my mother was a reluctant flyer, and my nana had never been on a plane. Fear of the unknown kept them in Chicago, and now that I'd finally convinced them to come visit me, I should have been ecstatic.

I wasn't. I was panicked. Today was now in turmoil. I had planned to get breakfast finished and lunch started before heading to the airport to pick up my family. Instead, I was racing along the streets of D.C. in a specially armored limo because one of the guests I'd fed last night was dead.

I leaned toward the bulletproof glass and tried to see the sky. God, I hoped their plane wasn't delayed. It might be all the reason they needed to cancel the trip.

"My cell phone!"

The agent next to me startled at my exclamation.

I grabbed at my purse. Even as I pawed through its cavernous pockets, my heart dropped. The early morning call from Paul had thrown me off and I'd left the cell phone charging at home.

How would my mother get in touch with me?

I gripped my hands into fists and shut my eyes against the frustration of it all. Now she wouldn't be able to reach me.

"We have to go back," I said.

The agent next to me shook his head.

"My cell phone," I said again, in case he'd

missed my distress. "I forgot it."

"You'll have to do without."

"But my mother is —"

"Sorry, Ms. Paras. Our orders are to bring you in as quickly as possible."

Oblivious to my concerns, the agent in the passenger seat spoke into a microphone. I couldn't make out what he said, but I wasn't focused on him as much as I was on my own irritation. Great. Of all days to leave my cell at home, I'd picked the absolute worst. Not only did I not know what was in store for me, I wouldn't know how Mom and Nana were progressing on their trip. I would be incommunicado until these agents saw fit to set me free. I would have to make other arrangements for my family, but at this moment, I couldn't quite figure out how.

Lost in my ruminations, I didn't catch what the driver said, but the next thing I knew bright lights surrounded us and a crowd of news media swarmed the car. They glowed like ethereal monsters clawing and reaching, shoving cameras and microphones at the bulletproof glass. I shrunk down in my seat as spotlights swept the car's interior. For the first time, I wished it was still storming. Then maybe these vultures would disappear. Dissolve on the ground like a hundred Wicked Witches of the West. But instead of stealing their brooms and handing them off to the Wizard of Oz, I'd be content to grab their microphones and crush them beneath my heel.

I hadn't had the happiest relationship with the press since my promotion to executive chef. They liked to portray me as a lucky bumbler. It didn't matter that I'd won awards, or that my menus were respected by prestigious culinary experts. What mattered was that I'd gotten myself in the middle of an assassination plot, and followed that up with a disastrous — though ultimately laudable — holiday spectacle. In order to sell newspapers and magazines, they'd portrayed me as either a good-luck charm for this administration, or as a fumbling cook who fed the First Family and, between courses, fought off assassins.

The press didn't know the real me. But the First Family did. What I wanted, more than anything, was for my mom to see me in my element. To understand that I was not just a cook, but a respected member of the White House staff.

I rubbed my forehead as we pulled through the security gates. This wasn't what I'd hoped for when my mom came to visit.

For a chef, this situation — a dead dinner guest — couldn't be worse.

CHAPTER 3

Two agents accompanied me to a utilitarian office on the second floor of the East Wing. Although it was no larger than ten by twelve, the area felt cavernous with its high ceilings and spartan furnishings. Blue-draped windows, white walls, and a man at a desk, scribbling. Two other agents flanked him.

I was hoping to see Tom there. No Tom. Not a single other Secret Service agent I could call a friend.

My escorts left me there, and the large man behind the desk gestured me forward. He glanced at his notes. "Ms. Paras?" He didn't smile. "Sit," he said, pointing. "Please."

I sat.

Jack Brewster kept his gaze on the papers before him, as he massaged his wide-set nose. "You know who I am?"

"Yes." I had met the assistant deputy of

the Secret Service a long time ago, but he probably didn't remember.

He frowned. "Your name comes up in my files with increasing regularity." Still without looking up, his scowl deepened and he shook his head, as though he'd just smelled fish left out overnight. "You know why you're here?"

"Is Carl Minkus . . ." I stumbled over the words, "really dead?"

Bulging eyes finally met mine. His were bloodshot and yellowed — from lack of sleep, or lack of happiness, I couldn't tell. Maybe a combination of both. Brewster cleared his throat, but it came out like a growl.

"That is correct. Agent Minkus is dead. His body was taken from the White House last night."

"But I was here last night. Why didn't anyone tell —"

"Why should anyone tell you?"

I blinked. "Because . . . I mean . . ."

"Ms. Paras, contrary to your apparent belief, you are not the hub of information here in Washington."

That stung. I bit my lip as he continued.

"You obviously came to that conclusion due to the press's interest in your antics here at the White House." Under his breath he murmured, "If it were my decision you'd be out on your —"

"Mr. Brewster," I said sharply.

He looked up.

"I don't think of myself as a 'hub of information' as you put it," I began, anger bubbling up. "I'm only suggesting that if I'd been notified last night that Mr. Minkus had collapsed, maybe I could have started looking into things *last night.*" I emphasized the words. "And by now we would have determined the kitchen's role — or lack thereof — in Mr. Minkus's demise."

He leaned toward me, thumping meaty forearms on the desk. "They told me you were a handful."

I bit the insides of my mouth. "I prefer to think of myself as proactive."

"Call it what you like." He massaged his nose again. No wonder it was so wide. "I've assigned a group of agents to determine your staff's culpability in this situation. You are to cooperate with them. Fully. Do you understand?"

"Of course," I said, bristling. "But I can guarantee that Mr. Minkus did not die as a result of anything that came out of my kitchen."

"That remains to be seen."

Brewster asked me a few questions about

my employment at the White House — information he could have easily gleaned from my personnel file. Then he asked me about the meal we had prepared for Agent Minkus at last night's dinner. Whenever I tried to add commentary, he held up a hand and reminded me to "just answer the question."

When he finally finished, I wiped fingers along my hairline, and grimaced at the perspiration there. Brewster had that effect on me — he probably had that effect on everyone he met.

As though silently summoned, one of the matching-bookend agents came in.

"Agent Guzy," Brewster said. "Ms. Paras is ready for her interrogation with the Metropolitan Police. Take her downstairs."

My interrogation? What had *this* been?

I had turned when Agent Guzy arrived. Now I twisted back to face Brewster. "I don't have time to be questioned right now," I said, pointing to my watch. "I have to get breakfast ready for the president and the First Lady."

Brewster blinked. Like a bored cow.

"And my staff," I continued. "They won't realize why I'm not there. I need to talk with them." I was perched at the edge of my chair, leaning in toward the desk, as though the proximity of my speech would make my words more meaningful to Brewster. "You don't understand —"

"No, Ms. Paras," Brewster said slowly. "It is you who does not understand. Until we know what caused Agent Minkus's unexpected death, there will be no food coming out of the White House kitchen. Especially not to be served to the president or his family."

I sat back. "You can't actually believe that —"

Still speaking slowly, he licked fat lips. "You will cooperate fully with the team assigned to you."

I wanted to argue, but I couldn't decide what to say.

Brewster fixed me with an impatient glare. "Now, I will ask you again. Do you understand?"

I rubbed my forehead. "I'm beginning to."

Brewster turned to Guzy. "Have your brother bring in Buckminster Reed from the other room."

Bucky. My second-in-command. One by one, they would bring in everyone from the kitchen. Probably the sommelier and the butlers, too.

Suddenly I felt the weight of it all. Someone had died on our watch. This had never happened before. Although I understood the need to find out why — and how — I knew no one on my staff would have made such a tragic mistake with food. Minkus could not have died as a result of our preparations. He must have died naturally, or in some non-food-related way.

Brewster brought his face close to mine, interrupting my chain of reasoning. "You're dismissed."

As Guzy and I headed out the door, I remembered something.

I rushed back to Brewster's desk. "We had guests yesterday."

The way Brewster raised his eyes made it seem as though his lids weighed a thousand pounds. Each. "Yes," he said. "And one of them died. We have established that."

"No, I mean in the kitchen." The man's bored expression urged me to talk faster. "I can *prove* that no one in the kitchen did anything wrong. We had cameras rolling yesterday. All day. We had guest chefs in the —"

He held up his hand. "Guest chefs?"

"A TV special," I said. "Suzie and Steve." I wanted to make the point that I could prove that nothing had been handled improperly. We could get this whole thing cleared up if only someone would take the time to review yesterday's recordings.

"Suzie," he repeated without interest. "And Steve."

"You know, the SizzleMasters."

He rubbed his nose, then scribbled a few notes on the pages before him. With another impatient look at me, he turned to Guzy. "Get me everything you can on this Suzie and Steve. And round them up, too."

"Round them up?" I asked in horror.

Guzy tugged my elbow.

"You misunderstand," I said. "I'm not saying they did anything wrong. I'm saying I have proof that —"

"Lot of that misunderstanding going around here today, wouldn't you say, Ms. Paras?" Brewster pointed to the door. "Thanks for the tip. You think of anyone else who might be suspicious, you let us know."

CHAPTER 4

Looking small and scared, Cyan was seated on a white plastic folding chair when Agent Guzy brought me into the next room. "Cyan!" I said, rushing toward her.

She jumped to her feet. "Ollie."

"No talking."

We stopped, startled — feeling like criminals. Did they really believe we killed Minkus?

Taking a seat next to Cyan, I realized, belatedly, that that's exactly what we were up against.

Agent Guzy walked to the far end where his twin stood, staring straight ahead. Brewster had mentioned they were brothers, so I hadn't been too far off when I assigned them the monikers of Tweedledee and Tweedledum. Guzy One spoke in low tones to Guzy Two, and the second man left the room.

My chair wobbled. I tried to sit very still

to prevent it from making noise in the silence. *Hard to do in such a chilly place,* I thought, suppressing a shiver. White unadorned walls prevented me from finding anything of interest to focus on. The only thing in the room I could watch was the agent, who stood unmoving, except for the occasional blink.

Cyan and I shared a look. She shrugged. Since we were forbidden to speak, there wasn't much else to do except try to put together what I knew. Carl Minkus's death was unfortunate, and I felt bad — the way you feel bad whenever you hear that anyone has died — but I didn't have any particular affection for the man. In fact, I don't think I'd actually ever met him. The closest I'd gotten was when he'd been a guest at the White House. And that had only been maybe twice before.

Third time's the charm.

Ooh. Bad thought.

"How long are we going to be here?" I asked.

Guzy One directed his gaze to me, but didn't speak.

Cyan whispered, "Isn't your mom arriving today? And your grandmother?"

I nodded. "I sure hope we're out of here by —"

"No talking."

Just as Guzy One said that, the door opened again and Bucky was ushered in, accompanied by Guzy Two. Brewster must not have had very many questions for my assistant chef. "That was quick," I said to Bucky.

He yanked himself out of the agent's grasp. "What the hell is going on here?" Bucky asked.

Guzy Two pointed. "No talking."

Bucky, Cyan, and I shared a look that spoke of our disbelief at the way we were being treated. I'd never met either of these Guzy brothers. They clearly hadn't been on the Presidential Protective Detail for very long. Then again, they might have just been brought in for the day. After all, it wasn't every day that a White House soiree ended with a dead guest.

The third agent from this morning's car ride came in. The weak link. I fixed him with a smile before he had a chance to join his comrades. "Hi," I said. "What's your name?"

He looked perplexed by the question, but answered. "Snyabar."

The Guzy brothers exchanged a look as I stood up. "Agent Snyabar," I began, "I think we've gotten off to a bad start here."

31

Snyabar moved closer to the Guzy brothers, who stepped apart to allow him into their midst. I advanced, noting that the little chef was causing the big Secret Service agents to circle their wagons.

"Please return to your seat, Ms. Paras," the first Guzy said. "You will be summoned by the investigators soon."

"Really, is all this necessary?" I asked.

The way the three men stared straight ahead, without even acknowledging that I'd spoken, scared me most of all. We were trusted White House staff members. At least, we had been yesterday. Right now I felt vulnerable — and guilty. I even started to doubt myself. Could there have been some combination of spices, foods, or beverages that was toxic to Carl Minkus? Was there some way I could have known this?

I was about to try breaking the Secret Service barrier again, when the door opened, and Peter Everett Sargeant III strode in. "Ah," he said. "Here you are."

I found it unlikely that he'd been looking for me for any valid reason. Peter Everett Sargeant and I had never gotten along. I'd say that we didn't see eye to eye, but I believed the fact that we were almost the same height was exactly the problem. Peter was an incredibly short fellow, obsequious and ingratiating to everyone in power, but condescending and obnoxious to those below him, and especially staffers who were shorter than he was. Which was . . . me.

"Is there something you need, Peter?"

Our Secret Service guards, surprisingly, didn't scold me. Apparently talking among ourselves was verboten, but conversing with the angry chief of cultural and faith-based etiquette affairs was not.

Sargeant paced in front of Cyan and Bucky, his hands clasped in front of him. "Well, well, well," he said. "How the mighty have fallen."

I folded my arms. "Care to explain?"

The agents shifted their weight, in sequence. Guzy One stretched his neck, then glanced at the door.

Sargeant's little eyes narrowed as he came close. "Do you have any idea the trouble we're dealing with out there?" He gestured vaguely toward the residence. "The trouble you've caused?"

That got my back up. "I don't believe it's been proven that the kitchen had anything to do with Carl Minkus's death. And until that time, I'll thank you to stop pointing fingers."

One corner of his mouth curled up. "Just wait, Ms. Paras. I've heard things."

I must have reacted, because Sargeant's smile got a little bigger. "Yes, it seems Agent Minkus commented about his meal, right before he collapsed."

We were talking about a person's death here, and yet Sargeant seemed almost gleeful in his explanation as he continued. "Something was most definitely wrong with the meal and it won't be long before every finger points at you." He sniffed, glancing as he did at Cyan and Bucky. "At all of you."

I couldn't stop myself. "What did Minkus say?"

At the far end of the room, the door opened and someone called for me.

Sargeant didn't reply, but before I could ask him again, Guzy One stepped between us. "Ms. Paras, you've been summoned."

"But . . ." I sputtered.

"Now," Guzy said. He nipped my elbow between his thumb and forefinger and guided me toward the door.

I wasn't done with Sargeant. Even though I was sure he was baiting me, I couldn't stop myself from asking again. "Minkus said something about the food?"

"He most certainly did." Sargeant's eyes glittered.

What kind of person found enjoyment only when someone else was suffering?

He raised a hand and gave me a little finger wave. "I'll fill you in later. I'll be here," he said. "And with any luck, *you* won't."

CHAPTER 5

Guzy One shuttled me out of the East Wing into the main residence and up to the first floor. The walk through the majestic entrance and cross hall — which I'd done hundreds of times — should have felt comforting and familiar. But all I could concentrate on were the echoing squishes of my shoes against the marble floor and Agent Guzy's brisk clip-clip-clip beside me.

I'd assumed we were headed to Paul Vasquez's office, but instead wound up in the State Dining Room, where it appeared the authorities had set up a command post. The prior evening's dinner had been served in the adjacent Family Dining Room. That, to me, was a misnomer because when the First Family dined together, they tended to congregate upstairs in the private quarters. This Family Dining Room was on the main floor and the Campbells often used it for intimate business dinners, like last night's had been.

There were dozens of Secret Service agents in the State Dining Room. Several folding tables had been brought in and computers set up. There were uniformed agents as well as PPD agents, and I quickly scanned the room, looking for Tom.

Being short is a major disadvantage because I was lost in a sea of broad shoulders and hurrying clerks. Tom is tall, and I aimed my gaze upward, but Guzy tugged me toward the northwest corner of the room, near the pantry.

"Paul!" I said when I saw our chief usher.

Urgency must have been apparent in my voice because he left a group of agents, and hurried over to me. "Ollie, how are you holding up?"

I managed to squirm out of Guzy's grip. "I don't know."

Paul winced. "This is a bad one." He turned to Guzy and nodded. "Thank you."

Guzy seemed perplexed by the dismissal, as though not quite sure how to take the directive from Paul. As chief usher, Paul didn't control the PPD, but there was an understanding between him and veteran agents. Paul controlled the residence, and if he was taking responsibility for the executive chef, then Agent Guzy needed to find something else to do.

"Sir, I —"

"You're free to go."

Raising his voice to be heard above the din, Guzy tried harder. "But, sir —" He reached out a hand, as though to ensnare my elbow again. I sidestepped him.

From behind us, a familiar voice. "It's okay. I got it."

We both turned.

"Tom!" I said. Paul Vasquez rolled his eyes. Although Tom and I had tried to keep our relationship quiet amongst the White House staff, it was getting to be a joke that the only people truly unaware of the situation were the president and the First Lady themselves. And apparently Agent Guzy, too.

He looked dumbfounded. Which was quite a sight from this expressionless behemoth. "Agent MacKenzie," he said, his tone deferential.

Tom stepped between us. "I'll take it from here."

I leaned up to whisper: "Bucky and Cyan."

Tom smiled down at me, then addressed Guzy again. "Would you please see that Ms. Paras's assistants are escorted to the Library?"

Guzy nodded. "Right away."

When he left, Tom turned to me, asking the same thing Paul had. "How are you holding up?"

I started with my topmost concern. "My mom," I said. "I forgot my cell phone at home. In all the excitement —"

Paul looked confused.

Tom ran a hand through his hair. "They're arriving today?"

"They're supposed to touch down at eight fifty this morning."

He looked at his watch. It was just after five our time, which made it four in Chicago. "Early. Are they at the airport now?"

"They should be." I shrugged. "But I have no idea."

Paul cleared his throat. "The investigators need to talk with Ollie."

Tom shepherded us toward the pantry, where I'd expected it to be quiet. Instead, there were paper-booted, latex-gloved technicians taking apart every inch of my workspace. They were covered, head to toe, in Tyvek jumpsuits and wore masks over their faces and shower caps over their heads. I could only imagine that the scene downstairs in my kitchen was worse. I groaned.

"It's standard operating procedure, Ollie," Tom said. "They have to examine everything."

We both knew that before this episode was over, my kitchens would be turned inside out and upside down. Which was exactly the state of my stomach at the moment.

The door between the pantry and the Family Dining Room had been propped open and I could see more technicians in full protective gear. President Campbell stood at the doorway leading to the stairway and Usher's Room. He was having an intense conversation with Agent Craig Sanderson.

At that moment, the president looked up and made eye contact with me. His mouth was set in a grim line and I thought I could detect disappointment, even across the crowded room. I was sorry to see it there, even if I had done nothing to cause it. He nodded in acknowledgment, then turned slightly away from me, to continue his conversation.

"What is going on?" I asked.

Paul urged me back into the center of the pantry, then called for quiet. The busy technicians stopped what they were doing and turned to face us. I was glad to have Tom behind me.

"This is Executive Chef Olivia Paras," Paul said in a clear voice. "If you have any questions, she will be available in the

Library."

From behind their obscuring getups, I could make out that three of the technicians were male, two female. One of the men wore glasses behind his safety goggles. Why were they dressed so protectively? Did they think Minkus died as a result of an airborne contaminant? If so, then wouldn't the other guests have been affected? Wouldn't we all be at risk? I wanted to get out of this room with its suddenly close quarters and heavy, stale air.

"You'll be happy to cooperate, right, Ollie?" Paul said, nudging me forward.

"Yes," I said. I caught his hint and spoke assertively to the group. "I know you have a job to do and I'm here to help in any way I can. My staff and I are at your service."

Paul nodded, then moved us back out the door, through the State Dining Room, where activity had grown to fever pitch. I wanted to stop, but Tom and Paul kept moving me forward.

"We've got to get you out of here," Tom said under his breath. "They've got Metropolitan Police here and we can't be sure of leaks."

"Leaks?" I asked, as the two men escorted me to the stairs adjacent to the East Room. "But what could be leaked?"

41

"That's the thing you learn in the world of politics," Paul said. "You never want to give out information you don't need to share. Anything that *can* be misconstrued, usually is."

I'd expected our path to take us to the Library, where Tom had told Guzy to take Cyan and Bucky, but as we reached the bottom of the stairs we walked across the hall to the China Room.

The door opened as we approached. The third agent from this morning, Agent Snyabar, was there, as were two Metropolitan Police detectives who proffered their badges for my inspection. A male/female team, their names were Fielding and Wallerton. Tom and Paul escorted me in and led me to one of the wing chairs. I declined, not wanting to be the only seated person.

Just then, the door opened and Craig Sanderson came in. Craig was a tall agent, handsome and crisp. As Tom's supervisor, he was aware of our relationship, but had enough regard for Tom that he preferred to remain "officially" uninformed.

Craig and I were cordial to one another. There were times his Appalachian drawl sent shivers up my spine. This was one of them. "Ms. Paras," he said slowly. "Why am I not surprised to discover your involvement

42

in this terrible tragedy?"

"Hi Craig," I said, striving for informal. The less formal, the less intense our conversation would be. At least, that was what I hoped.

"Please, have a seat, Ms. Paras."

This time, I sat.

Craig took the wing chair opposite mine and the two detectives came around to flank him. They both held open small notebooks — a lot like the one Craig now held poised, waiting for me to speak. But what could I possibly say?

Tom and Paul stood on either side of my wing chair, and I twitched against the nubby fabric. I didn't want to stain the armrests, so I wiped both hands on the front of my slacks. I'd thrown on white canvas pants, a white T-shirt, and a light gray hoodie this morning. Although the day was cool, I was itching to remove my sweatshirt. The fireplace next to me wasn't burning, but I felt what it was like to sit in the hot seat.

"Agent Brewster talked with me this morning," I said to break the silence. Too late, I remembered the old adage "He who speaks first, loses."

Craig arched his brows. "And what did Agent Brewster have to say?"

"Not much," I said, wondering why I'd

even brought it up. "He seems to think my kitchen — or I — had something to do with Agent Minkus's death."

"Did you?"

I blinked. "Of course not."

Craig's mouth twisted sideways. He wrote nothing, but the two detectives scribbled furiously. The forty-something woman — Wallerton — was tall and thin to the point of emaciation. I'd characterize her features as skeletal, and her wispy blonde hair did nothing to contradict that observation. The other detective, Fielding, was older. He had the look of a man who'd seen a lot in his day, but rather than fit the stereotype of paunchy veteran detective, he was trim and good-looking, with dark hair that was just beginning to go gray at the temples. Neither of them smiled.

Craig eased back in his seat, slightly. "We have a preliminary report from the medical examiner," he said.

I held my breath. "Already?"

Dumb question. This was the White House. Everything was done expeditiously. When something was needed, all stops were pulled out until it was accomplished.

"What did they say?" I asked, inching forward. "Do they think it was a heart attack?"

Craig's mouth turned down in a way that made my own heart drop. "It was not a myocardial infarction."

I swallowed.

The two detectives glanced up at me, then continued to write.

"What was it?" I asked.

"We expect to have more information within a day or two."

I wanted to scream, "Just tell me!" but I pulled my hands together on my lap and clasped my fingers, hard. "My kitchen is clear, right?"

Craig did that thing with his mouth again. When he fixed me with a stare, I felt my insides turn to jelly. Hot, slippery jelly. Like the kind Polish bakers fill their *paczki* with every Fat Tuesday. "No," he said.

My voice came out in a whisper. "What do you mean, 'no'?" I felt a hand on my shoulder. I didn't know if it was Paul's or Tom's. My vision telescoped, focusing solely on Craig's angry stare, and after the whoosh in my head silenced, all I could hear were pens scraping against notepaper.

"The medical examiner believes that Carl Minkus ingested something at dinner that killed him."

I sucked in a gasp. " 'Ingested something that killed him'?" I repeated the words, but my brain couldn't accept the meaning.

Craig continued. "The medical examiner is doing very in-depth toxicology screenings today. They're waiting on results, but we won't have answers for a while."

I shook my head. This wasn't happening. "But that doesn't mean it was something he ate . . . something we served. Couldn't he have eaten something at lunch that did this?"

Craig wasn't budging. "Doctor Michael Isham is one of the finest pathologists in the country. We will have to wait and see what he says."

"But . . ."

"Until we can prove that food served at last night's dinner was not responsible for Carl Minkus's death, you and your staff are banned from the White House kitchen."

"But the Easter Egg Roll," I said. "It's a week from today."

"The Easter Egg Roll is not my concern."

"We have a lot of work to do. I mean . . . this is a big deal. Surely the president and First Lady understand that. How can we prepare for the Egg Roll if we aren't allowed in the kitchen?"

Craig licked his lips, but I interrupted before he could answer.

"And what about preparing regular

meals!" I was growing indignant. I knew we could probably keep the house running by utilizing the family kitchen on the second floor, but that would certainly not give us enough space to prepare for the entire Egg Roll extravaganza. "We need the kitchen," I said pertly. The cafeteria on the basement-mezzanine level was an option, too, but I much preferred working in the kitchen I called home — the main kitchen on the ground floor.

"Until you are cleared, you won't be preparing any food at all."

"But the other kitchens . . ."

"You don't understand," he said. "It isn't just the kitchens we're investigating. We're investigating all of *you*."

My mouth dropped open. Again I felt a hand on my shoulder. I was pretty sure it was Paul. "You can't be serious," I said.

"When the safety of the president of the United States is at stake, I'm dead serious."

I pulled my lips shut — tightly, to prevent an outburst. Then: "What about the other guests?"

My question seemed to take Craig aback; the two detectives, too. They stopped writing long enough to send me quizzical looks.

"So far, the other guests are unaffected," he said. "But I understand you prepared a separate entrée for Carl Minkus. He was served food that the other guests did not touch."

"That's true," I said. "Mr. Minkus is vegetarian, and we made sure to follow his dietary guidelines exactly." I raised a finger and shook it for emphasis. "I made certain to personally oversee everything that went out that night." I knew such a statement put me at higher risk for investigation, but it was true. Nothing went out without my approval. "But if he had an allergy that we were unaware of —"

"His medical records indicate no such allergy."

"Maybe he recently developed one."

"Maybe you're grasping at straws." Craig consulted notes for a brief moment, then met my eyes. "You told Jack Brewster that you had two guest chefs in the kitchen yesterday."

"Suzie and Steve," I said. "The Sizzle-Masters."

The female detective shot a questioning look at the handsome older detective. He supplied the answer, and I heard his voice for the first time. "It's on the Food Channel," he said. "Suzie and Steve are big into steaks and barbecue. They have their own show." He shrugged. "It's pretty good."

Craig didn't look at him. "Why were they in the White House kitchen?"

"This is what I was trying to tell Agent Brewster," I said. "We were filming a segment for the *SizzleMasters* show. It's kind of like one of those challenge cooking shows where the TV personality shows up and challenges the competitor. We were working on the filets for last night's dinner and the network planned to air the segment about three weeks from now."

Paul interjected. "I approved this because Mrs. Campbell was very much in favor of giving viewers an intimate look inside the White House kitchen."

Craig looked confused, so I said, "We were not only being challenged by the Sizzle-Masters, we were serving the food prepared during the challenge." I waved both hands in front of me to ward off an anticipated argument. "But we weren't filming the guests actually enjoying what we'd prepared. We made extra for our judges."

"Judges?"

"We enlisted a couple of the butlers to sample the steaks. It's part of the schtick for the TV show."

Craig held up a hand. "I do not care about 'schtick.' What I do care about is the fact that we have a dead guest on our hands. A very prominent, very dead, guest. And I believe we are trying to find out what he may have ingested that took his life. Carl Minkus was a vegetarian, correct?"

"Yes, but —"

"Then I do not see the relevance in discussing this television challenge. I do not see what bearing any of this has on our investigation."

Exasperated by the slow deliberation of his cadence, I rushed to get my words out. "We had cameras rolling the entire time. They were supposed to send me a copy. I'm sure if you contact the production company, you'll be able to get one, too."

Craig glanced up to the female detective. She nodded, and Paul accompanied her out of the room.

Chalk one up for me.

"Did anybody else have a vegetarian meal at dinner yesterday?" Detective Fielding asked.

"No," I said. "We made Mr. Minkus's dinner especially for him."

My stomach dropped when I realized what I'd said. Why not just take out a full-page ad, announcing that the White House kitchen killed Carl Minkus?

Fielding flipped a page in his notebook. "What about side dishes? Salads? Desserts?

Was there anything that all the guests ate?"

"Sure," I said. I rattled off the prior evening's menu, and told him that in addition to Carl Minkus's sesame eggplant entrée, he'd been served a lemon-broccoli side dish, a salad with homemade dressing, and he'd shared in one of Marcel's spectacular desserts. "That you'll have to get from Marcel. I know it involved spun sugar and ice cream, but beyond that —"

Craig interrupted. "He is being questioned as well."

"But no one else has gotten sick, right?" I asked hopefully.

"As of this moment," Craig said, "that is correct."

"You have the entire guest list?" I was pushing it, I knew, but I wanted to be sure they knew I was willing to help in any way I could. "We added Philip and Francine Cooper at the last minute yesterday."

"We have the entire list," Craig said.

Fielding grimaced, but dutifully wrote it down. "I didn't have that."

Craig didn't like to be one-upped. He went through the entire guest list with Fielding, ticking off names as he spoke. "Ruth Minkus was in attendance with her husband. Additionally, we had Philip Cooper; his wife, Francine; and Alicia and

51

Quincy Parker," he said.

At the mention of Alicia Parker's name, Craig winced. Everyone knew our fiery defense secretary.

"Don't forget the president and First Lady," I said. "They were there, too."

Craig gave me a lips-only smile. "Yes, we are aware of that."

Detective Wallerton returned, and together with Detective Fielding and Craig they questioned me about everything that went on in the kitchen yesterday. I remembered almost every detail, but told them I needed to consult my files for a few of the ingredients used to prepare Mr. Minkus's meal. After listening to my exhaustive recitation and taking plenty of notes, the detectives seemed satisfied with my answers.

Craig surprised us all by turning his attention to Tom. "Agent MacKenzie, how long have you been on duty?" Before Tom could answer, Craig continued, "You have been here for over twenty-four hours. More than thirty, in fact. Am I correct?"

Tom nodded. "Yes, sir."

"Go home, Agent."

Tom started to argue that as a ranking Secret Service agent during a crisis, his place was at the White House, but Craig cut him off. "You are relieved. Get some sleep.

And don't come back until you do."

Tom left without further comment, but I knew how disappointed he must be. I was disappointed as well. His silent presence had been a comfort.

By the time they were done asking me everything fourteen times each, I was sticky and clammy and wished I could race home and shower. Then I remembered Mom and Nana.

I glanced at my watch. Eight thirty. I'd never make it to Dulles in twenty minutes. Even if I were cleared to leave right now.

"Are we keeping you from something?" Craig asked.

Drained from the nonstop queries, I didn't even bother to explain. "No," I said, hoping that when I wasn't there to meet them, my mother didn't hustle Nana on the next flight back to Chicago.

Finally dismissed, I was led to the door. "So who will take care of the First Family's meals?" I asked.

Craig sniffed. "Several of our agents have agreed to take on that responsibility. They are working out of the second floor kitchen and the Mess."

My face must have telegraphed my disbelief, because he added, "Some of our agents are quite talented in the culinary arts. One of them was a full-time cook in college. He knows what he's doing."

I closed my eyes. This was worse than I thought. "What about us?" I asked. "Should I just stay home and twiddle my thumbs until you guys give me the all-clear?"

Craig's face remained impassive. "Do whatever you like, Ms. Paras," he said. "But plan on doing it here. You aren't going home anytime soon."

CHAPTER 6

When I got to the Library, Bucky and Cyan were waiting for me. Bucky stood up. "How long do we have to stay here? We've got work to do."

"No," I said, "we don't."

Cyan opened her mouth to question, but I held up a hand. "We're out of the kitchen until further notice."

"What?"

"Here's where we stand," I said, lowering myself into the wooden armchair Bucky had just vacated. "Until it can be absolutely proven that Carl Minkus didn't die as a result of our kitchen's negligence, we are forbidden to prepare food in the White House."

Bucky paced. "We couldn't have done anything. I mean . . . there's no way. We read his dietary requirements." He dragged the back of his hand against his forehead. When he turned to me, his face was pale and his voice cracked. "This has never happened before."

I stood and placed a hand on his shoulder. Surprisingly, he didn't move away. "We did nothing wrong."

Bucky shook his head. "This is terrible."

For the first time, I actually let the truth sink in. A man was dead, possibly as a result of something we'd fed him. Although we'd followed every protocol, the fact remained that our kitchen could be guilty of negligence. I'd been adamant about our innocence, but what if we *had* been negligent? Then Carl Minkus was dead prematurely. And, as executive chef, blame fell squarely on me.

Bucky practically choked his next words out. "Did you think about botulism?"

I was about to answer when he pushed me aside. He covered his mouth and hurtled himself through the adjacent door.

Cyan jumped to her feet. Disregarding the fact that he had disappeared into the men's lounge, the two of us followed Bucky in. He'd made it to the lavatory and into one of the stalls just in time. The sound of retching carried through the door. I tapped on the wood paneling. "You okay?"

We heard him cough and spit. "Yeah."

"Bucky," I said, "this wasn't your fault."

He sniffed, noisily. "I know."

I held up my hands in a helpless gesture. Cyan shrugged. "Then come out."

There was a long moment of silence, where we heard nothing but the faint rushing of water through nearby pipes.

Finally, Bucky said, "This is my life."

I leaned toward the stall door, not knowing how to answer that.

"We're always so careful," he said, his voice plaintive. "I've never worked anywhere with such stringent guidelines. And I like it that way. I want to stay here."

"Nobody's kicking us out, Bucky," I said, trying for levity. "Yet."

When he spoke again, his voice was a whisper. "What if they let us all go? What if they say we were negligent — even if we weren't? Then I'll never get a job anywhere. My entire career will be down the tubes."

To punctuate his words, he flushed the toilet. Cyan and I exchanged a glance, and stepped a little farther away from the door when we heard the lock turn.

Bucky emerged, looking less sweaty and pale. He wiped a handful of bathroom tissue across his forehead and offered a wobbly smile. "I've worked my whole life to get here," he said. "When I think of how easily it can all be lost . . ."

Bucky's eyes glistened and he turned away from us toward the sinks, where he turned on the tap and avoided looking into the mirror.

"Listen," I started to say.

He shook his head. "The two of you don't understand. You can't. I worked hard to get here. I put in the best years of my life — before either of you came to the White House. And I thought I would be named executive chef someday."

I stood behind him to his right, and in the mirror I could see the weak smile turning sour. He gave me a quick glance. "Instead, they gave it to you."

There wasn't much for me to say. This position wasn't a "gift." I knew I had earned it and I knew exactly why Henry had chosen me as his successor over Bucky. But I couldn't say that. Not now.

"Being the first female White House chef is a coup," he continued. "I get that. I understand that the First Lady had a point to make. But now I see the writing on the wall." This time his glance was for Cyan. "Ollie is grooming you to take over when she gets rid of me, isn't she?"

Cyan looked to me for answers. I had none. It was true that Cyan had really come into her own over the past year, but Bucky was a valuable member of my team. I said so.

"I'm not planning to let you go, Bucky. We're a team."

"After this fiasco, maybe we're all gone."

His face went pale and damp again and he looked like he wanted to make another mad dash for the stalls. Squeezing his eyes shut, he held tight to the countertop for a moment before splashing cold water onto his face. He turned off the water, then patted himself dry with one of the nearby linen hand towels.

Once he calmed himself, I asked Cyan to excuse us. She left the men's lounge and I waited until I heard the door close.

"Bucky, I have no intention of 'getting rid' of you. None whatsoever."

He stared down at the draining water. "Henry favored you from your first day on the job. And now you favor Cyan." I watched his hands flex. "I'm a middle-aged white guy. Nobody wants me. Maybe I should resign. But . . . where could I go?"

With Bucky's talent, and his White House résumé, he could go almost anywhere he chose. Instead of saying that, however, I assured him, "You're not going anywhere."

"You just keep me on because you haven't figured out my replacement yet."

"Not true," I said. "Bucky, damn it, look at me."

When he did, my heart broke for him. Bucky, my acerbic, temperamental, yet brilliant assistant was terrified of losing his life's work. I'd never seen him this vulnerable, and for possibly the first time, I understood that Bucky wasn't ornery because he wanted to be. He made things difficult because he felt he didn't fit in with the rest of us. And it was true. His personality kept us distant. But for him to think that he didn't belong in our White House family was anathema. He was as much a part of the team as anyone, and more so than most.

In that split-second I realized I hadn't been as effective a leader as I'd hoped to be. Henry had tolerated Bucky's occasional tantrums and quick criticisms, and I'd been trying to emulate Henry since I'd been promoted. But maybe this was an opportunity to do even better.

"What?" he said when several seconds passed and I hadn't said anything. "Feeling good about yourself now that you made me admit my failings?"

I kept my voice low, but strong. "You want a guarantee that you're not going to be fired? I can't do that."

If he had expected me to speak soothingly

and to bolster his ego, he was mistaken. I read the surprise on his face. Bucky knew my need to keep people happy as well as he knew that his prickly nature kept most people on guard. But I decided the best way to get through to my first assistant was by speaking the language he knew best.

I continued. "Every four, sometimes eight, years all of us have to be prepared to be released by a new administration. That's the way this particular job works. And that's what we all signed on for. And if that happens, it happens. It isn't because we aren't the best chefs in the world — it's because the new family has different preferences. And if we tender our resignations to a new First Lady and she accepts them — there's no shame in that."

Taking a breath, I plunged on. "There *would* be shame in our being fired because a guest died. Huge shame. But we would all be in the same boat. We would all be faced with such a damaging mark on our records that we couldn't go anywhere and hold our heads high. It would be like starting over."

"But you're younger —"

"Not by all that much." That was a stretch. Bucky was at least fifteen years my senior. But aging — like seasoning — was often a good thing. "And if we go down, we go down together. You know that none of us would ever endanger one of our guests."

He nodded.

"And I believe the First Family knows that as well. I'm convinced that no matter what the medical examiner finds out, we will not be held up for ridicule on our own. I do not believe that the president or the First Lady will throw us under the bus."

He grimaced.

"Listen. You are my second-in-command. If you try to sneak out of here before all this gets settled —"

"Sneak?"

"The way you're talking, you're planning to put your résumé out on the market as soon as they let us out today."

"I'm being practical. If somebody's head is going to roll, I know it'll be mine."

"Bucky," I said, and waited for him to look at me again. He was afraid that *I* would throw him under the bus. But telling him that he was the most valuable chef I had on staff would be pointless now. He wouldn't believe me. He'd think I was just trying to be nice. "Pick yourself up. Nobody is going to be fired today."

He gave a snort. "Until they decide we poisoned Carl Minkus."

"And if they do, then you know exactly

whose head will roll. Mine."

He said nothing, but I could tell by the look in his eyes that I was finally getting through.

"I'm the one on the chopping block here," I said. "I'm the executive chef and, by definition, everything that is served is done so with my approval. Until they find evidence that we had nothing to do with Carl Minkus's untimely demise, I can't even access the kitchen to help prove that we're innocent. But I'll be depending on you and Cyan to remember every single detail from the dinner preparations last night."

"Can't you figure out some way to get insider information from the Secret Service?" he asked. "I mean, can't Tom help you out a little bit here?"

I shrugged. "He was ordered to go home. I have no idea what's coming next from them."

Bucky wasn't his normal self again yet, but he did seem to be mulling over the problem. "I'll write down some notes."

"Careful," I said. "Make sure nobody has access to them except you. You never know what can happen when things are taken out of context."

He rubbed the corners of his mouth downward, kept his hand there as he asked,

"What about Suzie and Steve?"

"They're already on the list to be investigated."

"You think there's any chance one of them did something wrong?"

"I certainly doubt it." My hand covered my mouth as a thought occurred to me. "You don't think someone did this on purpose?"

"Oh, hell. I never thought of that."

The door banged open and the two Guzy brothers came in, taking up more than their fair share of space in the small room. Their jaws dropped as they took in Bucky's startled glance, both our hands over our mouths, and the fact that we were standing in the men's lounge.

Guzy One looked a little confused, but his voice was brusque as ever. "When you two are finished being sick, we need you out here."

The two agents pivoted and left the bathroom.

If the situation hadn't been so miserable, I might have found it funny.

After another interminable wait, followed by questions from every possible branch of law enforcement, Cyan, Bucky, and I were released. I glanced at my watch and my stomach bubbled. Two fifteen. My mom and nana's plane had touched down hours earlier. I berated myself again for forgetting my cell phone at home. I could just picture them sitting on hard airport seats, dialing me at home, dialing me on my cell, and getting frustrated by the unending shifts to voicemail. They would have given me the benefit of the doubt until about ten in the morning. By now, they would have just felt sad and forgotten.

As we started for the East doors, the Guzy brothers swarmed us. Even though there were only two of them and three of us, their size and authority made us feel small and surrounded.

Guzy One held up a hand. "Not so fast."

The day's frustrations had taken a toll and my tone was less than accommodating. I was, in fact, snippy. "They told us we could go."

"Too many reporters outside."

"What, you expect us to hang around here all night?"

Guzy Two shook his head. "We're driving you back."

"What about Cyan and Bucky?" I asked.

"We're taking all of you."

I turned to my crew. Bucky shrugged. Cyan forced a smile. "At least we won't have to wait for a train."

As we made our way to the black limousine, we heard shouts from beyond the White House fence. I wanted to shroud my head so that the cameras couldn't exploit my face on the evening news, but I didn't. Neither did Cyan or Bucky. The three of us followed one Guzy agent, and his brother brought up the rear.

Cyan had been keeping tabs on my family issues and now she addressed Guzy Two. "You should drop Ollie off first," she said. "She needs to get home."

"No ma'am," one of them said. "We have orders."

"Orders to take us all home," Cyan persisted. "But not what order to drop us off, right?"

"No ma'am," he said again. "We have a specified route. Ms. Paras is our last dropoff because we have another stop to make in her vicinity after that."

So much for that idea. "Thanks for trying, Cyan," I whispered.

As Cyan and Bucky loaded into the limousine's cushy backseat, I realized that was the most either of the Guzy brothers had said to us. I was beginning to see the brothers' differences rather than just their similarities. Number Two had slightly darker hair, a slight lisp, and, apparently, more willingness to converse.

"What's your name?" I asked before I got in. "Your first name, I mean."

"Jeffrey."

"And your brother?"

Jeffrey looked to his sibling for approval, but Guzy One had already slid into the driver's seat and didn't acknowledge my question. "Raymond."

For some reason I expected them to be named Mark and Michael, or Dan and Don, or John and Joe.

"Is there any way at all you can get me back to my apartment quickly?" I asked. "My family is in town. That is, I hope they still are. I haven't heard from them and I need to grab my cell phone."

When Raymond half turned and cocked an eyebrow over his recently donned sunglasses, Jeffrey gestured me into the car. "No."

They'd confiscated Cyan's and Bucky's cell phones during the interrogation. Now, using Cyan's recently returned cell, I dialed my mom's phone about a hundred times on the ride back. No luck. I wanted to ask Raymond Guzy what his affection for the brake pedal was all about. The drive this morning had been at lightning speed. The trip back this afternoon was so slow, I swore I could watch roadside cherry blossoms blooming.

I'd never been to Cyan's or Bucky's homes and I was surprised and dismayed that Cyan lived so far outside of D.C. proper. To save time, I was half tempted to invite them both back to my apartment and then worry about getting them to their respective homes later. Tempting as it was, that wouldn't have been fair to them.

When it was finally just me in the backseat of the limo, I tried once again, this time in vain, to get Jeffrey to talk.

I sat in silence for the long ride back toward Crystal City, watching the world pass me by — slowly — unable to find beauty in the burgeoning spring just outside my window. Of course, poor Carl Minkus wasn't appreciating the fresh greenery either.

I thought back to my conversation with Bucky and wondered if someone had done Mr. Minkus deliberate harm. I had to believe the Secret Service and the Metropolitan Police were asking the same question.

I should let it go.

I had enough on my plate figuring out how Carl Minkus died. I had to worry about the Easter Egg Roll on Monday, the welcoming event afterward, and about my mom's and grandmother's welfare. Where were they? The fear of not knowing overwhelmed me.

The morning's weather had shifted and the storms had moved out of the area. Skies were clear without a cloud. Clear enough for takeoffs.

I watched a southbound plane traverse the solid blueness above and gave silent thanks. At least I knew they weren't on that one. With the direction this one was going, it was probably headed for Atlanta, or Orlando. I allowed myself a small smile. *Find blessings where you can,* I reminded myself.

And then the plane turned. Headed west.

I stared at the back of the driver's head and tried not to think about missed opportunities.

CHAPTER 7

Mrs. Wentworth was coming out of her apartment just as I made it to my door. One of her hands was wrapped, claw-like, around her cane; the other held a covered plate. "Ollie!" she said. "I'm so glad you're home."

As neighbors went, Mrs. Wentworth was pretty great. She paid close enough attention to my comings and goings to know when something was wrong, but was shrewd enough not to poke her nose in when it wasn't needed. Well, not too often.

"Sorry," I said, holding up my keys. "Can't talk today, I —"

My door was open. Just a crack. But enough to startle me speechless. I knew I'd pulled it closed behind me this morning. I remembered working the deadbolt, thinking that I'd yanked the door too loudly and that I might wake Mrs. Wentworth up. Although from what I could tell, the woman never slept. Had someone broken in?

I took a step back, putting my hand up to silence whatever Mrs. Wentworth might say next. But she didn't take the hint. "Ollie," she began.

"Shh," I said, then crept forward.

There were voices coming from inside my apartment. A quick laugh. Familiar voices.

Mrs. Wentworth tapped me with the foot of her cane. "They're here. Your mother and your grandmother." Still behind me, she called out loudly, "Ollie's home!"

A thousand questions flew through my mind at once. I knew I'd never given Mrs. Wentworth my key — although that was an oversight I'd meant to correct for years. I also knew that James, the doorman who knew me best, was out of town this week. I couldn't imagine anyone contacting the building supervisor to allow my family in. They didn't know my mom and nana, but they all knew I worked for the White House. Nobody would have been allowed in without my approval.

I didn't have any time to think because just then the door swung completely open and my mother stepped out, wrapping me in a bear hug. I hugged back, surprised, relieved, and completely joyful, all at once. Heat threatened to close my throat, but I managed to croak, "Mom."

She squeezed tighter, then let me go long enough to hold me at arm's length. "You look wonderful," she said, her wide eyes taking me in. "You are even more beautiful than you were last time I saw you."

I opened my mouth and told her that she looked beautiful, too. And she did. But she was shorter, and older than I remembered. Her hair was cut differently, and she'd let it go gray. The contrast between it and her olive skin gave her an overall wizened appearance. There was still the quiet strength that I remembered in her bearing — for all her disdain of flying, she was one of the most fearless women I knew — but today she looked more vulnerable than she ever had in my life. I'd joined the White House as a Service by Agreement — SBA — chef during the prior administration, and I hadn't been home in all that time. Sure, it had been a while. But to me, it looked like my mother had aged.

"Ollie?"

The second most fearless woman I knew grabbed me with both hands, pulling me away from Mom. "Nana," I said, bending down to give her a hug. A tiny woman, Nana was always wiry, always gray-haired. She hadn't changed so much. Her bright eyes sparkled and her face blossomed with wrinkled glee. "You didn't tell us," she said, shaking a finger at me.

"Didn't tell you what?"

Mrs. Wentworth knocked me with her cane again. "Move over, honey," she said. "I'm bringing my biscotti. Your family's never tried it."

My confusion was profound. "How did you get in?"

Instead of answering, my mother took me by the arm. "You must be hungry."

I was, but until that moment hadn't noticed. "I tried calling you," I said. "Over and over."

Nobody seemed to pay me much mind.

I stopped walking and placed a hand on my mother's arm. "Why didn't you answer your phone?"

"I turned it off."

That took me aback. "Why did you do that?"

"We knew you were busy," she said with a perplexed look, "and we were already here."

Mrs. Wentworth had tottered over to my kitchen table and was uncovering the dish while Nana looked on. They were two elderly women, separated in age by only a few years, and they seemed to be entirely too comfortable with one another to have only just met.

"How did you get here?"

Nana held a chair out for me, which seemed ridiculous. I was by far the youngest person in the room, I should be holding out a chair for her. But she pointed with authority. "We ate. You make yourself comfortable and we'll warm something up."

Mrs. Wentworth settled herself across from me and sampled one of her biscotti. She smiled as the dry cookie snapped between her teeth. "My favorite," she said.

"More tea?" Nana asked her.

"Please."

"Somebody please tell me what's happening here," I said, exasperated. "I've been worried sick about you all day and I'm thrilled to see you here, but . . . how?" I looked to Mrs. Wentworth, who had taken another dainty bite. "Did the super let them in?"

My mom half turned from reaching into the refrigerator. She locked eyes with Mrs. Wentworth and then with Nana. Like a shared joke.

Mrs. Wentworth chewed, then swallowed, as Nana poured hot water over a new teabag. "Why don't I let your mother tell you?"

"Mom?"

With her back to me, my mom shook her head. Her voice was a playful scold. "Why didn't you tell us?"

How *could* I have told them? I'd been debriefed in meetings all morning. But that didn't mean they hadn't seen it on the news. "Tell you?" I asked. "You mean about the dead guest?"

The three of them stopped. My mom turned. "What dead guest?"

"The one at the —" I stopped myself. Living with my mom and nana as I had for years before striking out on my own had prepared me for such disjointed conversations. But it had been a long time and I was out of practice. With my fist against my forehead and the other hand raised to halt further talk until my brain could catch up, I grabbed the floor before anyone else could beat me to it. "First things first. Tell me how you got here, and how you got in."

The alarm in their eyes at my "dead guest" comment hovered a moment, but they read my anxiety and decided to let the matter drop, for now. Their faces relaxed into tiny, conspiratorial smiles.

My mom set a plate of food in front of me, but I didn't even notice what she'd prepared because her eyes met mine and held tight. "Tom," she said.

"Tom?" I felt slow and stupid. My mother and nana had never met Tom. I'd mentioned him a few times, sure, but I'd held back on waxing too poetic on our relationship. I'd had serious boyfriends before and sometimes I thought Mom took the breakups harder than I did. I wasn't about to put her through another one, although I held out hope that this particular relationship would continue to evolve. "Tom let you in?"

Nana settled herself in the chair to my left. She reached over and clasped my forearm. "Why didn't you tell us he was so tall? And so handsome?" She laughed. "Tommy is a serious beau, isn't he?"

Heat shot up my face. "Tommy?"

My mom laughed. "Nana started calling him that on the ride over here. I think he likes it."

"The ride over here?" Again, I tried to stop my mind from reeling. "Start at the beginning," I asked again. "Please."

Nana pointed. "Eat."

I dug my fork into the heaping food on my plate. Homemade meat loaf. Whipped potatoes with a pat of butter swimming in the crater's center. I used to pretend my mashed potatoes were a volcano and the butter its lava. Green beans. Standard fare in homes around the world, this meal offered a savory taste of memory in every bite. My mom watched me from across my kitchen, beaming.

I forked off another small portion of meat loaf and watched the tender ooze before I took a bite. "Okay," I said, almost unable to contain my joy at eating favorite homemade foods that I hadn't prepared myself, "I'm eating. Now, all of you, tell me what's been happening here."

Mom set a glass of Pepsi in front of me, and the chilled can next to it. I was usually a water fanatic, but today I needed the treat. I took a long swallow and thanked her.

"Can I get you anything else?"

"Just sit down, please," I asked. "And talk to me."

As my mom took the chair to my right, I again noticed the group's conspiratorial air. It was disconcerting to sit in one's own kitchen and to be the only one not in on the whole story. I waited, firmly committed to staying mum until I got the answers that, despite their attempts to be coy, the three of them were clearly bursting to tell me.

"Our plane touched down right on time," my mom began.

Nana added, "You know we were scheduled for eight fifty."

I nodded.

Mom took up the story again. "We tried to call you while we were waiting for the plane to unload, but there was no answer. We tried again — quite a few times."

"My fault," I said. "I got called in early and forgot my cell phone at home." Putting my hand up to forestall further conversation, I ran over to my bedroom and rescued the little gadget, noting on my way back that I had seven missed calls and two messages. Undoubtedly all from Mom.

Back in my seat, I dug into my meal again. "Go on."

She exchanged a glance with Nana before continuing. "We were making our way to the baggage claim when we saw this really handsome young man —"

"In a suit," Nana added.

"Tom?" I asked.

Mom nodded. "Tom."

My heart swelled. When I told him my dilemma, he'd gone down to Dulles himself to meet my family. And after being on duty for so long. He must have been exhausted, and yet he still did this for me. What a sweetheart. I bit my lip. What a guy.

"In a suit," Mom continued, "holding a big white card that read 'Paras Family.' As soon as we saw it, we headed his way. It was funny, because even though we saw the sign, it seemed like he'd picked us out of the crowd and he was headed right for us."

"I must have described you both very well."

"Or we were the only two women 'of a certain age' disembarking together," Nana said with a wink. "Looking lost."

"Tom brought you here?"

"He did. Drove us the whole way in a big black car that had a phone and a TV in the back seat."

Almost finished eating, I sighed, feeling relief settle over me. "I'm so glad."

Nana tapped my forearm. "I noticed he had keys to your apartment."

I chanced a look at Mrs. Wentworth, who had grabbed another biscotti and seemed to be in her own little world.

My face flushed again. Having my mother and grandmother know that my boyfriend had keys to my apartment was a small price to pay when that little fact had saved them from being stuck at the airport for several long, boring hours. Mom and Nana had always been go-to-church-every-Sunday-and-sometimes-more-often Catholics. They attended rosary meetings, baked for fund-raisers, and brought casseroles to grieving families. The church — and in particular, our parish — fed their need to be needed. I expected them to chastise me — sharply — for what those shared keys represented. "As a matter of fact . . ." I began.

Nana stopped tapping and now gripped my forearm, hard. "Good," she said. "I worry about you alone out here. It's a big city and there are dangers everywhere. I'm glad you have Tom to keep an eye on you."

I turned to Mom, who gave me "the look." "Yes," she said. "I'm sure he keeps a very close eye on you."

Blood flushed upward into my face, again. "He and I are —"

I couldn't say we were just friends, because that was patently false. But we were more than just lovers. We'd reached a level of comfort and intimacy that I wasn't quite ready to share, but felt compelled to defend.

"Ollie," my mom said, mercifully stopping me, "he's a very nice young man."

"You think so?"

Mrs. Wentworth saw fit to chime in. "He knocked on my door and asked if I would mind spending a little bit of time here. He said something about having to get back because of a situation." She glared at me. "He wouldn't tell me what it was."

I rose to his defense. "You know he's really not supposed to talk about anything that goes on at the White House."

Nana hadn't let go of my arm. "Is he really in the Secret Service?"

I nodded.

"Are they all as handsome as he is?"

I grinned. "Just about. And they're all really, really nice." I remembered my recent interrogation with Craig, then I thought about the recalcitrant Guzy brothers before amending, "Well, most of them, at least."

"Any of them my age?"

"I want to know about the dead guest," Mrs. Wentworth said, interrupting. "I haven't had the TV on today, and I haven't been online either."

All eyes were on me. I took a deep breath. "He was one of our dinner guests at the White House last night. Carl Minkus."

Mrs. Wentworth slammed her hand on the table. Biscotti crumbs went flying. "I don't have the TV on for one day and I miss all the good stuff. What happened? Somebody shoot him on the way home?"

Since the news of Carl Minkus's death had brought thousands of reporters to swarm the White House, I had no reservations discussing what I knew. I'd just started explaining how we all had to undergo questioning, when the doorbell rang.

"That'll be Stan," Mrs. Wentworth said. "I told him to come around when he was done working."

I went to the door. "Hi Stan," I said, letting him in and wondering exactly when I'd lost control of my apartment. Probably just about the time Tom brought my family in and put Mrs. Wentworth in charge.

I followed the elderly electrician into my kitchen, where I offered him my seat. "No, no," he said, backing up to lean against the counter. "Ladies, sit. I've been on my back all day fixing a problem in the basement and I could use a chance to stretch."

As he passed behind Mrs. Wentworth, he grabbed her shoulders and gave them an affectionate squeeze. The two of them had been an item for a while now, and seeing them together never failed to make me smile. He greeted my mom and nana in a way that let me know they were not strangers either.

"We had lunch together," Mom told me. "Tom stayed long enough to grab a bite to eat."

Nana added, "He said he could see where you got your cooking talent."

"We had a wonderful time," Mom said. "He really cares about you."

Were we talking about the same Tom? While I never doubted his affection for me, he'd been Mr. Let's-keep-our-relationship-low-key from the outset. I was speechless.

Mrs. Wentworth didn't want to let go of

the day's scoop. "He told us you were tied up today and that you'd be late. Why were they questioning you, Ollie? Did you know Minkus?"

Before I could answer, she boosted herself from the table and grabbed for her cane. Stan was at her side immediately. "What do you need, honey?" he asked.

She pointed a gnarled finger toward my living room. "Turn on the TV. We'll get the story there and Ollie can fill us in during the commercials."

Within moments we were tuned into the all-news station and sure enough, beautiful anchor people were providing updates. The White House served as backdrop for their solemn expressions and somber tones.

I settled myself cross-legged on the floor, allowing the elderly folks to take the couch and chairs.

"As we've been reporting, Special Agent Carl Minkus died earlier today, of undetermined causes. We are keeping a close watch on the White House, where he was a dinner guest last night and where the investigation into his unexpected and untimely death is being conducted."

The screen changed to a photo of Minkus and his wife, Ruth. Minkus had been a ruddy-faced, overweight man, fifty-three years old. The picture showed the couple at a recent government sponsored event — Minkus in a tux, with his petite, strawberry-blonde wife next to him. Minkus had his arm around her waist and she smiled up at her husband, apparently unaware of the camera, into which Minkus beamed.

The news anchor continued. "The couple has one child, Maryland State Representative Joel Minkus."

Stan gave a low whistle. "Look at them. That there's what's known as a trophy wife."

Next to him on the couch, Mrs. Wentworth arched an eyebrow. "They've been married for years. She doesn't count. Anyway, trophy wives are tall. She's tiny."

"Trophy is trophy," Stan said with a shrug. He waggled his eyebrows. "But I'd rather have you on my shelf than her, any day."

Mrs. Wentworth slapped him playfully.

I focused on the television, where the scene changed again. Ruth Minkus stood behind a gaggle of microphones. I couldn't figure out where she was until the cameras pulled back enough for me to see the hotel logo on the lectern. She was talking, but we couldn't hear her. The news anchors were giving updates as a lead-in. "Ruth Minkus has agreed to make a statement and to bring us up-to-date on her husband's death. She's

84

speaking to us from a local hotel to keep camera crews and reporters away from the family home."

Ruth's voice now joined with her image. "Joel and I . . ." She paused to compose herself. A couple of people behind her placed comforting hands on her shoulders. "We wish to thank everyone who has been so supportive at this difficult time."

Reporters shouted questions at the weeping widow.

My mom made an unladylike noise. "Vultures."

Joel Minkus leaned sideways, toward the microphone. The man was about my age and tall, but otherwise took after his mother. From what I'd heard of him, he was a strong proponent of environmental issues, and despite his relatively young age, he inspired cooperation between opposing factions. He was a golden boy, and apparently deservedly so. "Please," he said. "Can't you see how hard this is for us?"

My mom shook her head. "They should leave the poor woman alone."

"My husband," Ruth continued, "would have been overwhelmed by all this attention. He was a determined man who loved this country very much. If there was one thing he always told me, it was that he

85

hoped to die in the service of the United States." Tears streamed down her face. "I . . . I suppose he got his wish."

The tension in my living room was tight. No one spoke.

An off-camera voice shouted: "Do you think he was a target because of his investigations?"

Ruth's eyes widened as she turned to her son. "Target?" she asked.

Joel stepped up to the microphone again. "Please. Let's wait until the medical examiner gives his report." He licked his lips and made pointed eye contact with audience members. "Have some compassion. My father just died. He was the finest man I've ever known. He was strong, well-loved, and most of all, patriotic. Let's not make assumptions until all the facts are in."

The news anchor interrupted to resume commentary. "The White House has prepared a statement." With that, the scene whisked away from the grieving family to a press conference in the Brady Briefing Room. White House Press Secretary Jodi Baines stepped up to the microphone. I felt for her. There wasn't a rule book for this situation. As she expressed the White House's condolences for Special Agent Minkus's demise, the elderly people in my living room fidgeted. Caught up in the story, myself, I'd almost forgotten they were there.

Jodi said: "Medical Examiner Dr. Michael Isham just finished briefing President Campbell and will now take questions."

Slim, though not particularly tall, Isham had a long, pleasant face, and dimples so deep they looked like implanted studs. The dimples stayed prominent even though he didn't smile. Another somber face in a day of sad solemnity. He blinked several times, canting his head slightly to avoid the bright lights' glare.

"He *looks* like a morgue doctor," Mrs. Wentworth said.

I turned, wanting to ask what she meant, but thought better of it. Stan patted her on the knee. "Shh."

"Good afternoon," Dr. Isham said, with a deadpan gaze into the audience. "As you all know, Special Agent Carl Minkus was declared dead at approximately one fifteen this morning. His body arrived at the morgue shortly thereafter and we immediately initiated an autopsy. The cause of death is undetermined at this time. We are waiting for test results."

"What kind of tests?" a dozen reporters shouted.

Isham held up his hands and both rooms fell silent — the briefing room and my living room.

"At this time," Isham continued, "we cannot share that information."

An explosion of questions: "Could Agent Minkus have been a victim of bioterrorism?"

"What do you expect to find?"

"Is the president at risk?"

Jodi leaned toward the microphone. "Ladies and gentleman, please. One at a time." She pointed. "Charles, go ahead."

The reporter stood. "We've heard conflicting rumors about Carl Minkus's behavior just before medics were summoned. Do you believe he might have suffered a heart attack?"

Isham licked his lips. "Again, we have not determined cause of death at this time."

A voice piped up: "Didn't Minkus complain that something was wrong with his food?"

I sat forward.

Isham answered, "I can't answer that."

Jodi sidestepped toward the microphone. "Mr. Minkus did not say anything specific about food," she said. She raised her hands when the group began to protest. "Witnesses did report that Mr. Minkus's speech became slurred. Before he collapsed, he said that his lips were stinging and that his tongue was numb."

As she stepped away, the shouts rang out again for Dr. Isham: "Could a poison have done this?" And following up: "Is there a danger to the president?" "Is there danger to the general population?"

Isham held up both hands. "The problem with certain poisonous substances is that they are very difficult to identify. While we test for several known toxins, there are many we can't identify unless we know what to look for. At this time we've done preliminary tests, but we can't even speculate until the specimens we've sent out to special labs have come back."

"How soon can we expect results?" a reporter in the front asked.

"It may be a couple weeks."

After another eruption of questions, Isham held up his hands again. "This isn't *CSI*," he said. "We work in the real world. This is a painstaking process and we need to be patient."

The man in the front stood up. "Was it something Agent Minkus was served at dinner last night?"

Isham licked his lips. I held my breath. "As I said, we cannot speculate until we receive certain test results."

The front-seat reporter stared at the medical examiner, still pushing. "Did the White House kitchen staff kill Special Agent Carl Minkus?" He tilted his head for the follow-up. "Inadvertently, or on purpose?"

Isham shook his head. "It is much too early to make that determination. We will be looking into . . ."

The television screen changed and again we were treated to the grave face of the news reporter. "The White House has only commented to express its sorrow at the passing of one of its most dedicated citizens. When questioned regarding the kitchen staff's responsibility in this terrible tragedy, the White House had no comment." The news anchor raised an eyebrow. I hated him for it.

"We have footage of Executive Chef Olivia Paras, who was brought in to the White House for questioning in this matter." His gaze shot off-screen and the scene shifted.

"Ollie, that's right outside our building," Mrs. Wentworth said.

"Yeah." I knew what was coming.

The handheld camera lent an air of panic and immediacy to the dark, early morning scene. Guzy One — Raymond — emerged from the front of my apartment building, his right hand raised in a way clearly meant to stave off reporters. Instead, the microphone- and camera-wielding crowd clamored around his side where I had a hand up to block the bright glare. The garish lighting made it look like they were bringing out Public Enemy Number One. Our little threesome moved in relative silence — the network didn't broadcast the angry shouts from the piranha-like reporters who dogged our every step — and the television news anchor, in a voiceover, said, "When asked by our news crew if she'd inadvertently served a toxin to Special Agent Minkus, the current executive chef had this to say." His voice faded and they brought up the sound on the scene outside my building's front door.

My face was an angry glare. "No, I didn't!" I heard myself shout.

In my living room, I winced. Taken out of context, my indignant exclamation made me look like the bad guy.

"Ms. Paras refused to answer any of our questions," the news anchor said, "before being taken away in the custody of government security agents."

"Taken away in custody? They made it sound like I was arrested!"

Everyone in my living room said, *Shh.*

91

The anchor was finishing up. "There you have it, the latest update in the shocking death of Special Agent Carl Minkus. Please stay tuned for updates as we find out more about the White House kitchen's role in the unexpected death of one of our most revered public servants."

"Oh, Ollie," my mom said.

I got up. "Turn it off."

Someone did.

The news anchor had referred to me as the "current" executive chef. As though there was another chef waiting in the wings for my head to roll. But I knew I couldn't have been responsible. I knew no one on my team could have been responsible. We were too careful, too determined for that.

My home phone rang. I started for it, but stopped myself when I didn't recognize the number.

"Maybe it's Tom calling you," my mom said.

I shook my head. "He would use my cell phone."

As though wakened by my words, the little phone buzzed. I checked the display. Another number I didn't recognize.

"Are you going to answer that?" Mom asked, then amended, "I mean, either one of them?"

"I have a feeling . . ."

The house phone silenced, waited a few beats, then rang again.

This time the display read "202."

I shoved the vibrating cell into my pocket and picked up the home phone. "Olivia Paras."

"Ollie, it's Paul."

I nodded. I'd figured as much.

"How are things going over there?" he asked.

"As well as can be expected," I said, glancing around the room at the four sets of concerned eyes staring back at me. "My family is here and that's helping take my mind off things." That was a lie, but I was determined to sound strong. The sadness in my mom's face almost made me falter. "What's up, what can I do for you?"

"Don't answer your phone if you don't know who's calling."

"Got that," I said. "The calls have already started coming in."

"You may still be hounded in the morning, so try to stay home as much as possible."

"What about coming in to work? Can I take the Metro?"

Paul's tiny delay in responding caused my stomach to flop. "Ah," he said slowly — too slowly, "let's hold off on that for now. We'll let you know when the time is right to come back."

That hurt. "Understood," I said as bravely as I could muster.

His voice was tight. "This is a bad one, Ollie. But, believe me, it will be over soon. And you and your staff will be back in the kitchen before you know it."

"I hope so," I said. But for the first time, I detected insincerity in Paul's tone.

The minute I hung up, the phone rang again. Another unfamiliar number. I waited, but the caller didn't leave a message. Two seconds later the phone rang again. As did my cell. Again.

I hit "ignore" on my cell, and unplugged my house phone. My mother, Nana, Mrs. Wentworth, and Stanley stood looking as helpless as I felt. "It's okay," I said. "We're still not allowed in the kitchen for now, but the chief usher says that we'll be back to normal in no time."

The looks in their eyes told me they didn't believe my halfhearted cheer. That was okay; I wasn't sure I believed it, either.

"What about Easter dinner at the White House?" Mom asked. "Don't you have to prepare for that?"

"And that big Egg Roll the day after,"

Nana added. "How are you going to boil all those eggs in time if you can't get back into the kitchen?"

Good question, I thought. Too bad I didn't have an answer.

CHAPTER 8

I guess I shouldn't have been surprised by the headlines the next morning: MINKUS DEAD AT WHITE HOUSE, followed by an in-depth examination of his life from his boyhood home in rural Maryland to his exalted position as a Special Agent with the NSA, where he excoriated terrorists like St. George slew dragons.

As I read, I wondered how they gathered all this information so quickly. It occurred to me that newspapers and television networks must keep fat dossiers on every public figure in anticipation of the day that figure's obituary comes due. There was a lot here about Minkus. More than any normal person would care to know. His whole life, starting on page one and continuing on pages eight and nine. Complete with pictures.

My mom came in from her shower, poured herself a cup of coffee, and helped herself to one of my still-warm honey-almond scones. "Why are you putting yourself through all that?" she asked, gesturing toward the newspaper.

"Can't help myself, I guess." I pointed to the picture of Carl Minkus as a prodigious ten-year-old. "He was kind of cute as a little kid." I looked at the most recent shot they published. "I wonder what happened."

"Good morning," Nana said, then looking at us, asked, "What's with all the glum faces? I figure that we should look at Ollie's mandatory time off as a vacation. Maybe we can do something today."

Leave it to Nana to find the silver lining.

She came over to stand behind me, reading the newspaper over my shoulder. "He was an angry man," she said. "You can see it here." She pointed to the small space between his eyes. "He made a lot of people angry, too." As she took a seat at the table, she made a *tsk*ing noise. "They compared him to Joe McCarthy. He died young, too." She fixed me with a look that said he deserved it. While I appreciated the support, I didn't feel as though that was an appropriate outlook, particularly today.

"He was trying to combat terrorism," Mom said as she poured a mug of coffee for Nana. "Minkus, that is. I don't really remember McCarthy."

"*Pffft.* A poor excuse to invade a person's privacy if you ask me."

Mom and I made eye contact. I wondered what had caused this outburst. As though I'd asked the question aloud, Nana licked her lips and leaned toward me. "Look, I'm sorry this Minkus guy is dead. Not for his sake, mind you, but because of how it's affecting you. I saw what Joe McCarthy did to this country, and this Minkus guy was doing the same thing — all in the name of national security. He was making a name for himself by making other people's lives miserable. That's a hell of a thing." She reached out to grab another section of the newspaper as she gestured to mine. "I'll take that when you're done."

"Gladly." I started to close the paper when I caught sight of another article on page two. This one by Howard Liss in his *Liss Is More* daily column. "Uh-oh."

"What?" Mom asked.

To me, Howard Liss always looked like an aging hippie. His picture stared up at me, his salt-and-pepper hair pulled tight into a ponytail, which draped forward over his right shoulder. Whatever that signified. He wore one hoop earring, and a cocksure grin. "Liss," the caption read, "is always more."

"This guy." I snapped my finger against his face. "He's covering the Minkus story. And if I'm right, he's going to blame it on some right-wing conspiracy group."

I was wrong. He blamed it on me.

I'm not suggesting the president hire a professional taster, as monarchs did in the olden days to prevent assassination by poisoning, but I am asking the question: How safe is the food we serve to our administration? What real safeguards are in place? Who watches the chefs? Is our president's security really left up to the woman who has made a name for herself by allegedly saving the president's bacon, not once, but twice? Could our current executive chef, Ms. Olivia Paras (whose name you will recognize from prior action-packed features), be getting bored with her day-to-day cooking responsibilities? Could her taste for excitement have pushed her over the edge to take unnecessary chances with Sunday night's dinner?

How dare he!

"What's wrong?" Mom asked.

"This . . . this . . ." I couldn't find the words to express my fury. "He thinks I did this. He thinks I did this on purpose!"

Carl Minkus's untimely demise may serve as a valuable wakeup call. If we act now, we have a chance to save others from preventable disasters. Let's not be so quick to assume that Minkus was targeted by someone he was planning to investigate. Let's take a closer look at our own house first — the president's house. Maybe a little negligence? Maybe a strong need for attention? Maybe things just got out of hand? Perhaps someone added more than an extra teaspoon of salt to the soup.

"This is ridiculous!" I said, standing up. "What is he thinking? I'll sue him for libel. Or slander. Or whatever it is you sue for when people make up lies."

My mom read where I pointed. "He puts it all in question format," she said. "He isn't saying you're guilty. He's asking, 'What if?' "

I headed to the phone to call Paul, then belatedly realized I'd unplugged it. "Aaah!" I said when I picked up the dead receiver. Mom and Nana stared at me with twin looks of pained confusion. They didn't know what to do. Neither did I.

"How do I fight something like this?" I asked.

Nana picked up the paper. "This guy is a nutcase."

"That doesn't make it any easier for me."

Mom shrugged. "No one will pay his article any attention."

"I thought this guy was a liberal," Nana said.

"I thought so, too. Why do you ask?"

She pointed. "Here, further down he talks about what a great guy Minkus was and what a blow this is to the country. He says Minkus was respected by heroes and criminals alike."

I came to stand behind her. "What an odd thing to say. I would have thought someone like Liss would never support someone like Minkus."

"I'm telling you, honey, that's why nobody will even remember this come tomorrow."

My cell phone vibrated and I looked at the number. Tom. "Hello?" I said. I caught myself smiling. Mom and Nana exchanged knowing glances.

"How are things?" he asked.

"I've been better."

"Did you read today's paper?" he asked.

"How could I miss it?"

"I'm sorry you have to go through this,

Ollie." After a moment he asked, "How's the family settling in?"

I walked into the living room. "Pretty well. Things aren't going quite the way I'd hoped. Did you get my message?" I'd left him an effusive voicemail the night before, thanking him for taking care of my mom and nana and bringing them safely to my apartment. "I really appreciate all you did for me yesterday. If you hadn't picked them up . . ."

"Ah," he said, deflecting. "I was happy to do it. Hey, what do you have planned today?"

"My mom and nana want to go to Arlington."

"Visit your dad's grave?"

"They haven't been here since he died, and now that I happen to have so much free time on my hands —"

"Do you have any time this morning?"

"What did you have in mind?"

I could almost see him shrug. "I don't have to be back until noon, so I figured maybe, if you wanted to go for coffee or something . . ."

"You want to come up here?"

"No," he said, almost too quickly. "I think you and I need to talk."

I swallowed. "That sounds ominous."

He gave a half-hearted laugh. "Sorry. I just meant it would be better if we could meet one-on-one." He quickly added, "Not that I don't want to see your family. They're great. I just would rather we have a chance to meet alone."

When I got off the phone and returned to the kitchen, Mom and Nana were waiting expectantly.

"We're meeting for coffee," I said.

"He doesn't want to come up here?"

"Busy day. He's got to get to work," I explained. Being part of the Presidential Protective Detail — the elite of the Secret Service — meant that more often than not, our relationship came second to his schedule. I was used to it. Often, my responsibilities took precedence over our relationship, too. That might change over time; it might not. "He only has an hour or so."

"As long as we're not holding you back," Mom said.

I put my arm around her and gave her a kiss on the cheek. "You could never hold me back."

Tom was already at the restaurant when I arrived. We'd been coming to this out-of-the way place almost since we'd started seeing one another. Although it came up short in romantic inspiration, Froggie's offered all-day breakfast and endless cups of coffee, served by a staff that still hand-wrote receipts and called customers "hon."

We settled ourselves in an aqua vinyl booth, a framed photo of artfully arranged scrambled eggs on the wall next to us. "You hungry?" I asked.

Tom pushed the laminated menu away with a grimace. "Nah."

"Just coffee," I said to the waitress who appeared at our table.

"You got it." She turned both our mugs upright, poured, and collected our menus.

"So, what's up?" I asked when she was gone.

Tom stared down at the dark brew in his mug, like the coffee had said something nasty to him.

Uh-oh, I thought. I didn't like the feel of this. The look on his face made my heart pound faster, and my neck sweat. I thought if I came up with a witty comment I might relieve the tension, change the subject. But I couldn't come up with anything.

In the three heartbeats it took him to raise his eyes again, I thought how odd it was that I'd been singing his praises yesterday, so confident that his helping my mom and nana was proof he was willing to take our relationship to a new level. I was so sure we were moving forward. And now it felt more like he was about to break up with me.

"This is going to be hard, Ollie."

I didn't think my heart could stand it another moment. It banged so relentlessly I put a hand to my chest to keep Tom from hearing it thud. What had happened? What had changed since yesterday? His eyes provided no clue.

"What's going to be hard?" I managed to ask. My voice cracked. I hoped he didn't notice.

He opened a little creamer and poured its contents into the mug. I kept mine black because I didn't trust my hand not to shake when I grabbed a creamer for myself. I swallowed, my throat starchy-dry. "What are you trying to tell me?"

His brow furrowed and he stared down at the coffee again. Neither of us had taken a sip yet, and when the waitress breezed by with pot in hand, she didn't even slow at our table.

"Craig," he said.

"Craig?" My heart skipped. Had I misheard him? "Craig Sanderson?"

He nodded.

"What does Craig have to do with us?"

"Us?" Tom looked up. "Nothing."

Now I was confused. "Explain."

"Craig put me on this Minkus death investigation."

"That's a bad thing?"

"We've all been assigned a specific angle."

I waited.

"He's assigned me to you."

I didn't understand why Tom was so upset. "You know I didn't do it, right?"

That got the first smile of the day. "Of course."

"Well then, your job is done. Whatever you need from me, you've got. I'm going to be the most cooperative subject you've ever known."

As I spoke, my smile grew. Tom's didn't. "You don't see the problem, do you?"

I shook my head.

"Craig has made me responsible for keeping you *out* of the investigation."

"That doesn't make sense. If they think Minkus died because of something I served him, then I'm part of this investigation already. How can he keep me out of it?"

"Okay, maybe I misspoke. You can't exactly be kept out of it, but he wants your efforts controlled. That's my job. I'm supposed to make sure you don't get involved in this investigation yourself."

"Now, why would I do that?"

Tom shot me a look of exasperation. "Ollie, look at your track record."

"I never intended —"

"Uh-huh," Tom said, interrupting my lame attempt at defense. "That's exactly the point. You make us believe you're all innocent and out of the loop and then — *bam* — you're at the very center of a major conspiracy."

"That was an accident."

"Both times?"

We were silent a moment. Tom took a breath. "We will be asking for your help. There's no way we can proceed without your cooperation."

I made a "Duh," face, but didn't say anything.

"Craig's exact directive is that I'm to act as liaison between the Secret Service and the kitchen. I need to be aware of every single thing you do."

I started to speak, but Tom held up a hand.

"The reason he picked me," he said, reading my thoughts, "is because he thinks that if I'm in charge of you, you'll actually cooperate this time."

The waitress came by, pot in hand, again. She eyed our untouched cups. "You two positive you don't want something else?"

We assured her we didn't and as soon as

she turned away, I added cream to my coffee and took a sip. It was something to do. And it gave me a moment to think.

Tom drank his, too. Bolstered, either by the interruption in what had become a tense conversation, or by the coffee, he sat up straighter. "Craig knows you had nothing to do with Minkus. We all know that. But that doesn't mean we can skate when it comes to your investigation. We have to follow every lead, have to take every step — just as if you were a true suspect. If we don't, we'll get raked over the coals." He held the mug in both hands and stared at me. "But the real reason Craig is doing this is because he doesn't want you involved."

I nodded.

"I mean, not at all."

"Okay," I said. "Done."

He waited a moment, then took another sip of coffee. "You promise?"

"Of course," I said.

"Do you have any idea what this means to my career if you don't stay out of it?"

I didn't understand why Tom was getting so worked up. He and Craig were friends. "I'm sure he wouldn't —"

"Craig has made it clear that if you get involved in this — like you have in the past — I will be dropped from the PPD."

"He can't do that."

"The hell he can't. He's my immediate supervisor."

"I mean, he can't make you responsible for someone else's actions."

Tom slowly shook his head. "Yeah, well, tell him that."

My fists were bunched and I saw Tom's gaze stray past them, before he met my eyes. "I know you don't *mean* to get into trouble . . ."

"I haven't gotten in trouble," I said, my voice rising. "In fact, I'd say I've helped when no one else could. And I've even saved a few lives along the way, too."

His hands came up, but my anger refused to be abated. "Just how, exactly, does Craig think to keep me out of this? For crying out loud, Tom, I work in the kitchen at the White House. And when a guest dies after eating one of my meals, you bet I'm involved."

Tom grimaced. *"Shh!"*

I lowered my voice. Too late, people around us had perked up. An avid eavesdropper myself, I recognized the body language. "All I'm saying is that Craig would be an idiot to refuse to use me as a resource."

"I told you. He intends to do just that."

"Now I'm confused."

"It gets complicated."

"Because officially" — I raised my hands to make quotation marks in the air — "I'm a suspect?"

"That's right."

"That's a crock."

We both took long sips of coffee. The waitress waited across the room, pot in hand, eyebrows raised. When I looked at her, she turned away and set about filling mugs at another table.

After a few tense moments of silence, I asked, "What about Suzie and Steve?"

Tom blinked. "Who?"

"The SizzleMasters. Remember, they were in the kitchen that day."

"You suspect them?"

I thought about it. "Not really. But my point is that we had a camera rolling most of the day. It would be enormously helpful if I could review it."

"Not gonna happen."

I waited for him to say more, but he didn't. "This is so wrong," I finally said.

"It's only temporary."

"It's still . . . wrong."

When he looked at me, I was taken aback by the alarm in his eyes. "Ollie, don't get involved. Unless the directive comes from me. Or Craig. Please. I know how you are. I know how you want to fix things. You think you're helping, but —"

With an almost palpable snap, hot anger shot furiously into my chest and spouted out my mouth. I couldn't stop myself. "I have helped. I *do* help."

Tom looked around the room and raised his hands. "Ollie, please."

"Please what? Please let the Secret Service do its job by itself? Is Craig so insecure that help from the chef unnerves him?"

Tom glanced around. "I think it's time we leave." He motioned for the waitress. Mistaking his call for more coffee, she poured eagerly.

When he asked her for the check, she pursed her lips. "Okay," she said. "Be right back."

I bit the insides of my cheeks tight, trying hard to hold on to my temper. As much as I wanted to help this investigation — both to clear my kitchen and to satisfy my curiosity — the fact that I'd been banished from doing so wasn't what was getting under my skin. It was Tom. He wouldn't admit that I'd been key to preventing some major disasters in the White House. Disasters that, for one reason or another, the Secret Service could not have anticipated. Naturally, the media continued to speculate about what a busybody, amateur-sleuth wannabe I was.

I expected more from Tom.

The lines on his face were deeper than they had been. He seemed to hold himself too tightly — too wound up. A small part of me softened when I looked at him. This had to be hard for him, too. Craig issuing the edict that Tom was responsible for me was mean-spirited. Not to mention unnecessary.

Tom didn't even look at the waitress when she dropped off the check. He mumbled a "Thank you," and stood next to the booth, waiting for me.

Tom hadn't asked for this assignment and I knew, clearly, that he wasn't happy with it. If we were to get through this, I needed to keep our lines of communication open. I got up and touched his arm. "By the way," I said, "thanks again."

He looked at me with total confusion.

"For picking up my mom and nana from the airport," I said. "For getting them safely to my place."

His cheeks reddened and he looked away. "They're nice ladies. I was glad to help."

"It means a lot to me."

Still not moving toward the cash register, Tom looked at me. "I don't want to fight about this."

"Neither do I."

He shook his head. "But I know how your mind works."

I nodded slightly. I had to give him that.

"I'm afraid that you *will* get involved, Ollie," he said. "You'll think that you're just asking a simple question — just checking the veracity of a small fact — but before you know it, you'll be in the center of everything." He shook his head. "Again."

"No one complains except Craig and the newspapers," I said. "Doesn't that tell you something?"

He seemed to consider that, but a moment later shook it off. "Let's go."

Outside he walked me to my car. "Do me one favor," he said. "If something, anything, comes your way that's even remotely related to this investigation — tell me."

"I would always —" The sentence died on my lips. There had been a few instances — more than a few, if I were totally honest — I hadn't remembered to alert Tom to my plans. I forced a smile. "I will."

The pain was in his face again. "I've worked hard to become part of the PPD. This is it — this is all I've ever wanted. You know that, don't you? There's nothing more prestigious than being part of the Presidential Protective Detail. Not for me, anyway. I don't know what I would do if Craig dropped me from his team —"

I ran my hand along his shoulder. "I promise," I said. "Anything comes my way — anything at all — I will tell you."

"And if I ask you to back off of something?"

"I'll back off."

"Thanks."

We shared a moment of quiet camaraderie, but then I had to ask, "Do you think there's any chance of my team getting back into the kitchen soon?"

His shoulders slumped. "Didn't you hear anything I said?"

I hadn't wanted to hurt him, but he didn't seem to understand. "This isn't about the investigation. This is about our commitments. We have Easter on Sunday, and then the big Egg Roll on Monday. I need to get back."

"A man died at the White House after eating there. You think they're not canceling everything as we speak?"

Exasperated, I stared at the sky. "Something needs to be done."

He waited until I looked at him. "But not by you. Right?"

I wanted to argue, but that would only cause him more anxiety. "No worries. I promise."

He leaned forward and kissed me on the forehead. Like an uncle or kindly grand-father might do. Not exactly a clear signal of how things would be between us, going forward.

"I'll be in touch," he said.

Yeah. Sure.

CHAPTER 9

"Back so soon?" Mom asked when I returned to my apartment. She must have read the expression on my face, because when she turned away from the sink, her smile withered. "What's wrong?"

"Nothing." That didn't appease her, and I knew it wouldn't. So I came up with a white lie. "With this investigation, Tom is under a lot of stress. He and I can only meet if it's official business."

"The impression of impropriety?"

I nodded. "Something like that."

The way Mom studied my face I could tell she wasn't buying my story. Of course she wasn't. She knew me too well. "And I hate being banished from the White House," I said, dropping into one of my kitchen chairs. "The whole point of you coming out here was so that I could show you around the president's mansion. Now I'm not even allowed in myself."

She made reassuring noises, the kind she always made when I was disappointed or frustrated and there was nothing we could do about it.

I smiled across the table. "I bet you wish you had stayed home."

She patted my hand. "Of course not. Nana and I flew out here to see *you*. That's the whole reason we came. And you know that this problem will get worked out. In the meantime, it's nice having you all to ourselves."

"But the tour I promised you —"

"There will be plenty of time for that. If not this trip, then next time."

My mom always had a way of looking at the positive side of everything. Even when I didn't feel like it. I couldn't shake the sadness, but I wanted to let her know her efforts were appreciated. I traced a finger around on my table top. "Thanks."

"I *would* like to take that trip to Arlington, though."

I glanced up. "Of course."

"Now you have plenty of time to show us around Washington." Her eyes were bright and her smile just a little too fixed. She knew how much their trip meant to me. She sensed my disappointment and felt sorry for me. And that made me feel even worse.

Taking care of others always worked for getting my mind off my troubles. If I couldn't control the White House kitchen, I could at least take steps to improve my mood. "You got it," I said, standing. "Let's grab Nana and go."

Nana took that moment to come into the kitchen. Wearing blue jeans with turned-up cuffs, a black fanny pack, and a sweatshirt that read I ♡ WASHINGTON, D.C., she looked from my mom to me. "I'm ready. Where are we going?"

We took the Metro to the Arlington National Cemetery stop and made our way to the bright visitor's center. Sunlight poured in through the skylights, spilling onto the floor around us, and dappling the potted ficus trees. I was willing to bet they designed this place with extra cheer to help dispel sadness. It worked — to an extent.

"Let's take the Tourmobile," I said, grabbing an information brochure. "It's pretty reasonable, and we can get off and reboard wherever we like."

My mom placed a hand on my arm. "Will it take us near . . . ?"

I nodded. "I know just where Dad's grave is. We could probably walk to it," I said, "but I'm sure you'll want to visit some of these other sites as well."

"Don't think I can manage it, do you?" Nana asked. She smiled, but I sensed a tiny bit of hurt in the question.

I pointed in the direction of Arlington House. "I know you want to visit President Kennedy's grave, but that's an uphill walk," I said. "That, and the fact that there are more than six hundred acres to explore are just too much for me. But if you really want to walk it . . ."

Telling her I had a hard time making the trek up to Arlington House was stretching the truth a bit, but I knew we had a lot of ground to cover. Literally. The Tourmobile would allow us to enjoy the journey and maybe even learn a little bit from the narration as we traveled.

About fifteen steps away from us, a young man stood, staring out the windows by the front door. He worked his jaw. Handsome guy, from what I could see. Something about his profile seemed familiar, but I couldn't quite place it. I was very good with faces, but I knew that until I got a direct look at him, I wouldn't be able to make the connection. I wondered if he was here to visit a grave, or just to sightsee. I bit my lip. I sensed a familiarity, but at the same time, a vague negativity. Whoever he was, he reminded me of something unpleasant. I turned away.

Nana spoke. "No, we'll take that bus of yours," she said with a grin. "I wouldn't want you to overexert yourself."

My mother studied the pamphlet I'd given her and eyed the information desk in the center of the room. "Do you think they're having any funerals?"

"Arlington averages twenty-eight funerals per day," I said.

They both gasped. "That many?" my mom asked. "Will we be in the way if we take the tour? I don't want to intrude on anyone's grief."

"We'll be fine," I said. "Let's just not take any pictures of people visiting graves." I turned toward the east wing. "How about we hit the washroom before boarding?" I asked, moving that way. "There won't be any others on the tour except —"

I stopped short when a woman emerged from the washroom. She was instantly recognizable: Ruth Minkus. She made eye contact with me as she skirted past and I couldn't help but notice the hot, red rims makeup couldn't hide. Ruth gripped a paper tissue in one hand, holding it close to her heart, and I held my breath, hoping she didn't know who I was. Instinctively I turned to watch the young man who had been staring out the window walk up to her. He took her arm. "You okay, Mom?" he asked.

Joel Minkus and his mother looked exactly as they had on television last night — except yesterday they'd seemed smaller, and somehow less real, less flesh-and-blood. And as much as I had been worried about Carl Minkus's death, and felt for his family, I had been insulated — at home, away from the immediacy, the fierce reality of their grief.

My mom touched my shoulder. "Ollie," she said in a whisper, "isn't that — ?"

"Yes," I said, turning away from the twosome. "Let's move over there by the trees. We'll be out of the way."

Nana had bypassed us to disappear into the ladies' room. "Damn," I said, then addressed my mom. "You wait here for her, and I'll meet you . . ." I looked around, trying to decide whether I should say something to Mrs. Minkus. I didn't want to apologize, because I knew I wasn't responsible for her husband's demise, but as one of the players in this drama, I felt almost compelled to offer my condolences.

But what, exactly, should a person in my situation say?

My mom hadn't left my side. She whispered again, "I think she recognizes you."

I turned. Ruth Minkus was staring. The red-rimmed eyes now blazed with anger.

"Oh, God," I breathed, turning back. I gripped my mom's arm and guided her toward the washroom. "Go on," I said. "Take care of Nana. I'll find you."

I attempted to slink to out the side doors, keeping my face averted, but an exclamation behind me caused me to stutter-step. "You!" Ruth Minkus shouted. "You're the chef!"

Her voice echoed loudly, and I wasn't the only person who turned to see her pointing at me. I closed the space between us, hoping she would lower her voice — hoping the horde of tourists milling about the visitor's center wouldn't recognize us. Hoping they would turn their attention away from our imminent and, undoubtedly uncomfortable, conversation.

"Mrs. Minkus," I said, offering my hand. "I'm so sorry for your loss."

She backed away from me, horror-stricken. "You killed my husband."

I don't know whether I was more shocked by her accusation or more relieved that she'd at least spoken quietly. I answered fast. "No," I said. "That's not true. I didn't."

"Mom," Joel said, stepping between us and keeping his voice low, "Please."

Ruth whirled toward him. "She killed your father."

"Nothing's been proven yet." He shot an apologetic glance toward me, then placed his hands on her shoulders and made her look up at him. "Let's not make a scene. Please? Dad wouldn't want that."

Her posture slumped as her gaze dropped to the floor.

Joel stole a look at me. "I'm sorry," he said, shifting to stand next to his mother. He kept one arm protectively around her. "We've just come from visiting the site where my father . . . my father . . ." He faltered, then cleared his throat. "Where my father will be buried. My mother wanted to see it. To make sure . . ." He cleared his throat again, then shook his head slightly, as though berating himself for providing explanation. He turned to Ruth. "Come on, Kap is waiting for us outside."

Ruth grimaced, still looking at the ground. I couldn't tell whether she was reacting to Joel's mention of the grave site, or of "Kap." To me it seemed the latter. I was about to make a hasty exit, expressing condolences once again, when my mom and nana appeared, flanking me.

At almost the same moment, an older gentleman stepped up to take Ruth's free arm. He was tall and fit, with deep crow's-feet at his eyes, and a full head of white hair that picked up glints of light from above. While he was clean-shaven, he had the look of a man who probably needed to use the razor more than once per day. I put him at sixty-five, but good-looking enough to turn the heads of women of all ages. "You were in here so long, I was worried."

She recoiled from him, but he seemed not to notice.

"Hello," he said to us, a quizzical expression on his deeply tanned face. "Are you friends of the family?"

"No," I began, but Joel took charge.

"Kap," he said, relief in his voice. "Mom could probably use a little air. And I think it would be good if she sat down." At first I thought Joel was asking Kap to take charge of Ruth so that he could say something to me in private, but he surprised me by leading his mother away. "We'll be in the car," he said.

Kap nodded as they left. He turned back to us and flashed a smile.

"Well, it was nice to meet you," I said, even though we hadn't officially been introduced. I just wanted to get the heck out of there.

But Kap seemed unwilling to let us go. He raised an eyebrow. "You look familiar."

My face went hot. "I'm the executive chef at the White House."

"Ah," he said. I felt the weight of his comprehension. In the space of two seconds, his expression shifted from anxious to genial. "Today has been very difficult for Ruth, as you can imagine. We spent most of the morning at the funeral home, making arrangements. Carl, having been a decorated veteran, always wanted to be buried at Arlington, so we made those arrangements as well."

My mom had moved closer. I couldn't understand why. The last thing I wanted was to prolong this unexpected meeting. I desperately searched for a polite way to extricate ourselves, but Mom interjected.

"My husband is buried here, too."

Kap's awareness shifted. Where he'd been paying attention to me as though I were the only other living human being in the cemetery, he now turned his gaze toward my mother. "I'm very sorry to hear that," he said. "Has it been a long time?"

"Yes," she said. "Very long." And then she surprised me by adding, "Too long."

My jaw nearly dropped. What the heck

was this? My mom was flirting with a complete stranger in the middle of Arlington National Cemetery. While it had been more than twenty years since my dad died, and my mother had had a gentleman friend or two since then, it seemed odd to see her so flushed and eager. Like a teenager.

"I'm here from Chicago visiting my daughter." Mom cocked her head at me like I was a little kid.

I felt like one — left out of the adult conversation. Who was this guy, anyway? A brother? Brother-in-law? This Kap didn't look like either Carl or Ruth Minkus. He was older than both of them and looked to be Middle Eastern, or Greek, whereas the Minkuses likely came from Western European roots.

Kap smiled broadly. This was one handsome senior citizen and I understood my mother's instant attraction to him. Still . . .

Holding out his hand, he said, "Zenobios Kapostoulos. But everyone calls me Kap."

My mother placed her hand in his and smiled back. "Corinne Paras."

"I am delighted," he said. "And were we in different circumstances, I would very much enjoy continuing our conversation. But, as it is, I must tend to Ruth and Joel."

My curiosity got the better of me. "You're

part of the family?"

His smile still in place, he shook his head. "Carl and I worked together. He and I are — were — good friends. Business required my presence out of the country for many years and I've only recently moved back to the area. Of course, I had hopes of rekindling our friendship." His eyes tightened. "But, unfortunately, it was not to be. Carl and I had only a short time to catch up. And now this." He shook his head again. "It is very sad."

"Kap?" Joel called from the doorway. "We're ready to go."

Kap gave a little bow to us all, and held my mother's gaze for an extra few heartbeats. "It has been my pleasure, ladies."

Nana sniffed when he turned away. "How come nobody introduced me?" She fanned herself as she watched Kap leave. "My, my," she said approvingly.

Had my family gone nuts in the head?

"What was that all about?" I asked them. "I thought we were here to visit Dad's grave."

Mom still wore the remnants of a smile as she pinned me with a meaningful stare. "Don't chastise, honey. Opportunities to interact with charming men don't come around very often these days." She chanced

127

a look out the window, but the Minkuses were gone. She shrugged. "Just a little distraction."

I would have said more, but it seemed pointless. "We'll probably never see him again anyway."

"Probably not," Mom said. She sounded wistful.

We got off the Tourmobile at the stop for the Tomb of the Unknowns, but diverted from the rest of the group to follow the road that led toward my dad's grave site. I had been here plenty of times before. But not with my mom — at least, not when I was old enough to remember. I took Nana's arm as we stepped off the pavement onto the grass. "You okay?" I asked them.

Nana said, "Sure, sure," but she glanced nervously at my mom.

"Mom?"

She took in the expanse of green, all the identical white headstones. "I haven't been back here since . . ." Her voice caught. "I can't even remember exactly . . ."

I reached out and grabbed her hand, squeezing lightly. "I know where he is," I said.

We walked silently past rows and rows of headstones, our feet making soft shushing sounds in the almost-green grass. I came to visit my dad's grave from time to time because it gave me peace to do so. I thought about how I sometimes talked to my dad, but after noticing how tight my mom's face had grown, I decided not to mention that. This was going to be tough for her.

"Here," I said.

Nana stepped away from me to stand next to Mom. The three of us gazed at the white headstone, which read ANTHONY M. PARAS. SILVER STAR.

Mom looked around us. "The trees are a lot bigger now."

I nodded.

Nana patted Mom on her shoulder. "He was a good man, Corinne. And he loved you very much."

Mom covered her eyes and cleared her throat. She spoke, but I couldn't make out what she said. Not that it mattered. I got the feeling whatever she'd said wasn't meant for me or for Nana.

The three of us spent a long quiet moment there together. Finally, Mom looked up. "Thank you," she said throatily. "This was important to me."

I put my arm around her and hugged. "For me, too," I said.

From there we made our way back to the

Tomb of the Unknowns.

"Oh," Nana whispered when we positioned ourselves behind the brass railing at the top of the rise. "Look at that."

I'd been here many times but I understood my grandmother's awe. Stretching out eastward beyond the tomb was a green vista that overlooked hundreds of other graves. But it was here, at the tomb itself, under the sharp blue spring sky, that her attention was captured.

The sentinel walked twenty-one measured steps. He then turned and faced the simple, white monument for twenty-one seconds. Whenever he switched positions, he first kicked out one leg in a taut, well-practiced move, then smacked the active foot against the stationary one with an audible clack. Turning, he faced back down the mat upon which he'd walked, shifting his weapon to his outside shoulder, with another tight, structured move. He then took twenty-one more steps back the way he'd come. A brisk breeze made the three of us shiver, but the sentinel never flinched. When he turned to face the tomb again, Nana asked, "He does this all day?"

"They operate in shifts," I whispered. I gestured for us to leave and we made our way up the marble steps into the adjacent museum. There were no words to describe the solemnity I always felt in the presence of deceased veterans. Keeping my voice down seemed the only respectful way to talk. And I knew from prior visits that any loud conversation would result in the sentinel's chastisement of the crowd. "They change every hour."

"Handsome man," Nana said, glancing behind us. "Tall."

"They all have to be between five-foot-eleven and six-foot-four."

"Really? There's a height requirement?"

We were inside the small museum now, and although we spoke freely, we still kept our voices low. "There are a lot of requirements," I said. "You should look it up. They're a very dedicated group. And only about one-fifth of those who apply are accepted into their ranks."

"Look it up on the Internet, you mean?" Mom asked.

"You mastered e-mail. There's nothing scary about surfing the 'Net. Unless you're downloading from a questionable source, you really can't hurt your computer."

"Oh, she isn't afraid of that," Nana said. "She's afraid of becoming addicted to the thing."

I turned to my mom. "Seriously?"

"One of my girlfriends joined something called 'chatrooms' and now she never wants to come over for coffee or go out to movies."

"Who?"

I laughed when she told me. "You don't even like her."

"That's beside the point."

After strolling along the outer rim of the breathtaking Memorial Amphitheater and finishing our Tourmobile trek, we took the Metro back to my apartment, where Nana decided to nap for a little while. When she was out of the room and the place was quiet, I realized that I would usually have a phone call or an e-mail to look forward to from Tom. Not so today. My cell phone had been extraordinarily silent and when I checked my inbox, I had only two new non-spam messages. One from Bucky and the other from Cyan. Both were looking for updates. I wrote back, but confessed I had no news.

Speaking of news, I called Mom over to the computer in the spare bedroom — the room where I was staying while she and Nana used my queen-sized accommodations. "Here," I said. "Let's give you a quick tutorial."

She shook her head, but at least she took

a seat on the daybed behind me. "I don't see why it's so important for me to learn this," she said, pointing at the headline that described a double-assassination in China. "I can get this from watching the news."

"True," I said. "But the news simply projects the day's biggest stories — or what they deem most important. If you're interested in something that doesn't have to do with China" — I motioned toward the monitor — "you can search for whatever it is you need."

"What happened there, anyway?" she asked.

I scrolled down the article to find out that two upper-level Chinese government officials had been shot, execution style, in a restaurant in Beijing. According to "unconfirmed reports," the two Chinese officials had been buying United States secrets from an "unnamed insider." It appeared that the Chinese government, believing their conduit had been compromised, had sanctioned the double-assassination.

Their killer had been immediately apprehended and offered no resistance when taken into custody. He had, however, been killed himself shortly thereafter. Details were sketchy, but the Chinese police were claiming that he had grabbed for one of their officers' weapons in a futile attempt to escape. Political pundits were speculating that the police were covering up the fact that the gunman had been shot in cold blood after carrying out his allegedly government-sanctioned hit.

"Just like Lee Harvey Oswald," Mom said.

"If you believe the conspiracy theories."

Her gaze was glued to the screen. "I don't believe our government killed President Kennedy. But Jack Ruby's oh-so-convenient shooting makes me wonder who did." She made a clucking sound. "And I'll bet there are people all over China tonight wondering who was behind this one."

Still at the helm, I clicked the browser bar and said, "I love the Internet. It's like having the most comprehensive library available to me twenty-four hours a day." I typed in the name of an author I knew my mother liked. "Look. Lots of information. Biography, book descriptions, reviews. This is great stuff." I gave her a meaningful look. "But don't believe everything you read."

She moved closer and I let her have my seat. I showed her how to search. It took a few tries before she was willing to take control of the mouse and keyboard, but eventually I stepped away. "Have at it," I said. "Look up whatever you like. Just keep it clean, okay?"

She looked up long enough to catch my wink.

"You're going to be sorry if I spend my whole vacation sitting in front of this computer," she said.

"Don't worry. I won't let that happen."

She was already typing. "You'd better not."

CHAPTER 10

My breath caught the next morning when I opened the paper. With all the excitement yesterday running into Ruth Minkus at Arlington, I had almost forgotten about Howard Liss's accusations. Almost. But not completely.

The newspaper's headlines dealt with the Chinese assassinations, but I didn't stop to read the coverage. All my focus was on getting to page two to see what new mischief Howard Liss was up to.

Whatever Happened to Mean Minkus?

The media (and dare I say it — the government) is persisting with society's tendency to confer sainthood on an individual just because that person is dead. Have we so quickly forgotten the "Mean Minkus" appellation bestowed on our recently departed compatriot? I'm sure others aren't so forgiving. In fact, I would be willing to bet that several high-profile celebrities are sleeping a little easier tonight now that the bulldog has bitten the dust. Whether they deserve the respite, or whether they've just dodged a bullet remains to be seen. It will be up to Minkus's capable second-in-command, Phil Cooper, to determine what terrorist cells our favorite film stars belong to. If any.

My focus today is not on these superstars, but on the dead man. Let us stop singing his praises. Let us stop eulogizing him as though he were infallible and a loveable teddy bear just because he no longer walks in our midst. Let us admit he was a canker to many, and a hero to some. But if, indeed, he met his maker before his time, then I want to know who did it. You should want to know, too. You should demand to know. Perhaps then we will have ourselves a genuine terrorist to persecute. Who did it? I don't know. Joel Minkus, the golden boy congressman — and soon to be senator if Ruth has anything to do with it — has not yet seen fit to make time for my questions. I hope he will reconsider soon. Time is our enemy. If anyone knows who Mean Minkus was targeting, we may have our best clue to our killer.

"You're not actually reading that garbage, are you?" Mom asked from behind me.

Nana peered over my shoulder. "What does that crazy man have to say today?"

I let out the breath I'd been holding. "At least Liss isn't attacking me again."

"Good," Mom said. "How anyone can subscribe to that man's rantings, I can't understand."

"Rantings," I said. "Good choice of word. This *Liss Is More* column might sell a lot of papers, but he sure seemed to be all over the place in terms of accusations. Today he's on a whole new rampage. 'Who was Minkus's next target?' " I frowned as I turned the page. "Maybe that's who the police should be investigating instead of me."

"He's a lunatic," Nana said as Mom poured her a cup of coffee.

"What does that say about me?" I asked rhetorically. "I read him every day now."

Mom patted me on the shoulder. "Well, of course you do," she said in that soothing voice she used to use when I woke up during a nightmare. "He pulled you into this situation."

I didn't want to argue that I was already part of this situation before Liss ever got a hold of it, but the phone rang. I'd turned it back on this morning, hoping the onslaught from the press had subsided.

Nana looked up. "Do you think that's your handsome hunk, Tommy?"

Mom and I exchanged a look. "No," I said, with more than a little disappointment. "Ollie Paras," I said into the receiver, forgetting this was my home phone. "I mean . . . Hello."

"Oh my God, Ollie, there are people out on our front lawn. With cameras!"

In my effort to process the woman's panicked words, I couldn't place her voice.

"Why does anyone think we had anything to do with Minkus? You know we didn't. Can't you tell them? Steve is ready to go out there with a baseball bat."

"Suzie," I said, relieved to know who I was talking to. "Please, don't let him do that, okay? It will just make it worse."

"I know," she said. "He knows it, too. But we can't even leave the house to get the newspaper on the driveway without a hundred people shoving microphones at us and asking a million questions."

"A hundred?"

"Well, at least a dozen. Hang on." I heard her counting. "Well, there are five on the lawn and two by the street."

"Have they been there since Monday?"

"No, just today. This morning. Why are they targeting us?"

I thought about that. Except for the camera crew and the White House staff, no one knew that Suzie and Steve had been part of Sunday night's dinner preparations until I'd mentioned it to Jack Brewster, and then to the two detectives when Craig interrogated me. I couldn't imagine who might have leaked that information to the press, but it was obvious someone had.

"I don't have an answer for you," I said, but my brain was trying to piece it together. "Did anyone come over to question you about Sunday's filming?"

"Yeah," Suzie said uncertainly. "Last night a detective stopped by and asked us a few questions, but he said it was just routine. Now this." I could practically picture her gesturing out her front window.

"Try to keep a low profile," I suggested.

"Do you have any idea what our schedule is like today?" Suzie asked, her hysteria returning. "We have two segments to film at the studio this afternoon. How can we get there if there are news vans blocking our driveway? What do they want from us?"

"Let's take it easy," I said, trying to work the same soothing magic on Suzie that my mom had been able to work on me. "First of all, they can't be on your private property."

"Hang on, let me peek out the window." I heard the soft shift of metallic blinds. "No, they seem to be mostly on the street. Some are under the tree at the parkway."

"Where do you live?"

She told me. I recognized the name as a posh Virginia suburb. "Okay," I said. "As long as they —"

Suzie screamed.

"What?" I asked into the receiver. "What? What happened?"

When she answered, her breath came in short gasps. "One of them jumped up at my front window and took my picture."

In the background I heard Steve swearing and threatening to grab a gun.

"Stop him," I said.

My mom touched my arm. "What's going on?"

I held up my palm to her. "Suzie," I said, concentrating. "Stop him. Call the police. They can make the media back off. Trust me on this one."

She dropped the receiver and I heard snippets of conversation as she pleaded with Steve to calm down. I turned to my mother. "The news folks are camped out at Suzie and Steve's house."

I'd already explained the SizzleMasters' role in the current White House drama, so my mom didn't need clarification. "Can they do that?"

I shook my head as Steve snatched up the phone on the other end. "Goddamn media!" he shouted.

I held the receiver away from my ear. Steve bellowed expletives, complaining about the lack of privacy they were suffering. "And now they go and scare my wife. Ollie, can't the Secret Service do something about this?"

This didn't seem like a good time to tell him that this didn't exactly fall within the Secret Service's jurisdiction. In the background, I heard Suzie ask, "What do we do?"

"That's a good question, Ollie," Steve said into the phone. "What *do* we do?"

"I'd suggest you wait them out —"

"You mean cancel our filming for today? That's just wrong and you know it. We shouldn't be prisoners in our own —"

"You're right," I said, interrupting him. "You shouldn't. But can you think of any way to keep your commitments and avoid being run down by the newshounds?"

He was silent for a long moment. "Do you think they'll give up by the end of the day?"

I doubted it. "Let me see if I can help," I said, thinking that this conversation was exactly the sort of thing Tom wanted me to avoid. "Give me your number." I had it on Caller ID, but giving Steve something rote to do might help calm him.

"Let me give you my cell and Suzie's, too."

I dutifully wrote down all the numbers he provided. "I'll get back to you as soon as I can."

"I think we ought to sit down with you and talk about all this," Steve said.

In the background I heard Suzie agree. "That's a great idea. When can she come over?"

Come over? No way. "I don't think that's a good idea," I said to Steve, effectively cutting off Suzie's train of thought. "Can you imagine what the press would do to us if I showed up at your house?"

"I still think we need to talk with you," he said gruffly. Then, away from the receiver he addressed Suzie: "We can't have her come here. Those vultures out there would skewer us."

Suzie's reply was inaudible.

"Let me call you back," I said. "We can talk after I get more information."

"Do you think they have our phones tapped?"

"Who?"

"The press. The Secret Service. The police. The NSA. Homeland Security." With each tick of his list Steve's voice rose until he reached fever pitch. "Do you think this is part of keeping us under surveillance? Do you know why they suspect us?"

"I don't believe anyone really does, Steve," I said. "I just think this is today's news . . ."

"They suspect us all right," he said cryptically. "But I'm not saying anything further on the phone."

When we hung up, I ran my hands through my hair.

"What's wrong?" Mom asked.

"I need to call Tom."

I wondered how this would sound to him. Less than a day after he'd warned me to stay out of the investigation, I was essentially dragged back into it. He had to realize this was no fault of mine. These were just friends who were asking for my help. But I couldn't do anything for them — nothing at all — without risking Tom's career.

Although I had no desire to keep secrets

from my mom and nana, I stepped out onto my balcony when Tom answered, shutting the sliding door behind me. The morning was brisk but the bright sunlight that had kept us cheered during our trip to Arlington yesterday was nowhere to be seen.

"How are you?" I asked him.

His voice was wary. "What's going on? You sound like there's a problem."

"No," I said, trying to inject a tone of "pshaw" in my voice. "No problems. I just was thinking about what we talked about and I figured I should bring you up to date."

He expelled a breath. "What happened?"

I talked fast, explaining about Suzie and Steve and how they wanted to meet with me. I expected him to get angry about this turn of events, but after a long, thoughtful pause he spoke. "Some interesting facts have come to light," he said slowly. Then, as though anticipating my question, he said, "I can't tell you what they are, but we may need to talk with you again soon."

"Like an interrogation?"

He didn't laugh. That made me squirm. "I'll tell you what. I'll see what I can do to get the media to back off Suzie and Steve. And if you want to talk with them, go ahead. We're not suggesting you can't maintain your friendships."

The words were pleasant enough, but the effect was ominous. "You're going to be watching me?"

"Not necessarily."

"You're going to be watching *them?*"

"I never said that."

I pursed my lips, frustrated. I wondered what these "new interesting facts" were that he wasn't sharing. "There's something else you should know."

"Uh-oh."

I hesitated. There was no easy way to say this, so I just blurted. "I ran into Ruth Minkus yesterday and she accused me of killing her husband."

Tom was quiet for so long I thought he'd hung up.

"You there?" I asked.

"My God, Ollie. I can't keep up with you." I heard scratchy noises, as though he were rubbing his face. I shivered and it wasn't just because it had started to drizzle. I stared up at the overcast sky.

"We went to Arlington," I said, trying to explain. "And she was just . . . there. It wasn't as though I sought her out."

"Why didn't you call me about this yesterday?"

Why hadn't I? Truth was I'd been nervous about letting him know I'd had a run-in

146

with the deceased's wife and son. "I called you today. Besides," I added, my own anger starting to return, "it's not as though I'm ingratiating myself into the investigation. For crying out loud, I had a conversation with Mrs. Minkus. There's no law against that, is there?"

I could practically see him shaking his head. "No, Ollie," he said with such resignation in his voice that I was sorry I'd raised mine. "There's no law against you talking with people you run into — or people you have a relationship with. I just . . ."

"You just . . . what?"

"I hope Craig is able to see things the same way I do."

"Does he have to know about any of this?"

"Suzie and Steve — yes. I'll want to suggest that you're present when we take a look at the DVD of that day's filming. For whatever good that will do. And if you do talk with them, he'll want to know if they said or did anything you consider unusual."

"So they are suspects!"

"I'm not saying that."

"Okay. Sorry," I said. But my mind was racing.

"I have a few other things I want you to take a look at."

"Like what?"

"It'll wait. I'll call you."

Effectively dismissed, I hung up, but I stood outside, leaning on the balcony's rail, even though it was wet and the chill seeped up through my forearms, making me shiver. When we'd first started our relationship, Tom and I both knew that our jobs — no, our careers — could cause strain. Emotional relationships were always fraught with peril, but his being a Secret Service agent, sworn to protect the president and his family above all else, made this one so much harder. I understood that there were things he couldn't tell me. I had no problem with that. I also understood the pressures he was under. Craig and I had been friends before the first time I'd inadvertently gotten involved in Secret Service matters. Since then he had cooled toward me, and avoided me when he could. I suppose he didn't believe I was worth his time, and I further supposed that Jack Brewster's antagonistic bent during my intake questioning had more to do with Craig's influence than with Jack's personal impressions.

The street below was quiet except for the occasional car slicing through puddles, causing a sad sound that made me want to retreat into the warmth of my apartment — to where my mom was probably making something for us to eat, and where Nana was devouring the newspaper in my absence, pretending that she wasn't hunting for mention of my role in this White House drama.

At least Tom had said he'd take care of Suzie and Steve. Still on the balcony, now ducking closer to the building to avoid the heavier rainfall, I dialed them back and let them know that the Secret Service had been alerted. "They better do something," Steve said with uncharacteristic roughness. "They got us into this mess."

I wanted to argue that it hadn't been the Secret Service's fault — but to what end?

"Where do you want to meet?" Steve asked as I was about to say good-bye.

"Excuse me?"

"We need to talk," he said. In the background, I heard Suzie reiterate his statement.

"I don't know if that's such a good idea."

Suzie must have been listening in, because she grabbed the phone and started in on me. "Please, Ollie. You know we only agreed to come film at the White House because you wanted us to. We did this as a favor to you."

That wasn't how I remembered it. "I thought your production team wanted to use this for ratings week."

"No," she said, chastising now. "We did this because we knew it was important to you."

It hadn't been important to me in the least. I'd done it as a favor to them. Correction: The White House had agreed to the favor. I'd been left out of this decision entirely. Although they were indeed friends of mine, I'd been against them being in the kitchen while we were preparing a dinner for actual White House guests. I would have preferred to stage a fake dinner and treat the staff to whatever delicacies we came up with. "Actually, Suzie," I began, but I was interrupted by a beep on the line. I took a look at the number. Tom. "I better let you go," I said in a hurry to hang up.

"Please," she said. "We really do need to talk."

"Later," I said. "I'll call you back."

"Please," she said again. "But we have to meet in person. Just in case others are listening in."

"I highly doubt anyone is tapping your line."

"I'm sure you're right," she said, sounding unconvinced. "But Steve and I will be more comfortable in person."

I heard another beep. I wanted to switch

over to talk with Tom. Now.

"Okay, fine. But I really need to get going."

"Hang on."

Steve took the phone. "We can't get into this over open lines."

"Got it," I said, my exasperation evident. "But I can't . . ." I took a look at my handset and realized Tom was no longer waiting for me to pick up. I bit my lip in anger and hoped he would leave a message.

"Let's meet later," Steve said.

Tom had said that there was no law keeping me from talking with friends. And right now there was no longer any need to get off the phone quickly. I sighed. "Sure. Where and when? I know my mom and nana will be excited to meet real television personalities."

After a beat of silence, he said, "Just you, Ollie. Okay? Maybe we can meet your family another time."

This was starting to feel a little bit strange. Steve persisted. "How about tonight? Do you think these camera crews will be gone by then?"

I heard Suzie in the background. "A police car just pulled up."

"What do they want?" Steve asked her.

"How should I know?"

"Are they coming for us?"

"Steve," I said, "you sound busy. How about I let you go?"

The balcony door opened behind me. "Are you okay out there?" Mom asked. She held the receiver of my apartment phone.

"I'm fine," I said.

"Tom's on the line." She held out the receiver and looked at me with hopeful eyes. "Maybe you should take this one."

Steve was pleading in my ear. "Ollie, no. Don't hang up."

"I really have to —"

"The police are making them leave!" I heard Suzie say.

"But are the police coming for us?" Steve's obvious tension made me wonder what he was so worried about.

My mom gave me one of those looks only moms can give and shook the phone at me. "He's waiting."

I tried again. "Steve, let me give you a call back in —"

"This is great," he said. "They're all taking off." He breathed heavily into the phone. "The cops are gone, too. Good. We'll be able to make it to the studio after all. Thanks so much, Ollie."

"I really didn't —"

"Let's make her dinner tonight," Suzie

said in the background. "Have her come to the studio."

"Yeah," Steve agreed. "The studio will be better than here." Sounding a bit distracted, he added, "Tonight, you're our guest. We'll have a chance to chat in real privacy."

"Okay, fine," I answered hastily, trying to pantomime my frustration to my mom. "You have my e-mail, right? Just send me the address and a time. I really have to go now."

"Sure thing, Ollie. And thanks again for all your help."

I said good-bye quickly and grabbed the apartment phone while snapping my cell shut. "Sorry," I mouthed.

My mom smiled and headed back in, leaving me on the cold balcony once again. "Tom?" I asked. "You still there? I was on another call with Suzie and Steve."

"That was quick. You sure didn't waste time getting in touch with them."

And just like that, his tone annoyed me. I faced the glass doors that looked into my living room. My mom and nana were watching me, turning away when I caught them. I scratched at my head and was surprised when my hand came away wet. I'd been out here in the damp morning longer than I thought.

"Like you said," I answered my tone sing-song, "there's no law stopping me from having conversations with my friends."

He made a noise — acknowledging the jab. "Are you going to be home later? Say, around eight thirty, nine tonight?"

I thought about Suzie and Steve's offer to make me dinner. I should be home by eight-ish. "I'll be here."

"Craig wants you to look at a few things." The dismissive tone was back. "I'll stop by then."

"You remember my mom and nana are still here?"

He blew out a breath. "I forgot."

I started to appreciate how much pressure he was under. "They'll give us privacy if we need it."

"Fair enough." He sounded all-too-eager to get me off the phone. "See you then."

When I reentered the apartment Nana shook her head. "You look like a drowned rat."

"Thanks."

Mom wore one of her worried looks. "What's up with Tom?"

"He's stopping by later."

At that they both brightened. I held up my hands. "Just official business," I said, and just like that, their cheer dissipated.

154

"Sorry."

"Oh, Ollie," Mom said. "We just want you to be happy."

"Then let's get out today," I said, longing for something — anything — to get my mind off this mess. "I'd like to take you to the National Mall." Turning, I cast a glance outside at the rain. "Of course, it's not a very good day for that, is it?"

"It's going to clear up by noon," Mom said.

"It said that in the newspaper?"

"Nope," she said with a grin. "I checked the forecast online."

I touched base with Cyan, then Bucky. Neither had heard anything more than I had, but my second-in-command was greatly agitated.

I searched for something calming to say. "It's just a matter of time before our staff is vindicated."

Through the phone's receiver I heard a rhythmic click-clack and I realized that Bucky was pacing across what sounded like a tile floor. At the same moment, I realized I'd been pacing as well. Weren't we a nervous bunch?

Click-clack, click-clack. "How can you stay so calm?" he asked.

I couldn't tell him that I wasn't calm. That every moment of every day was agony until the word came down that we'd be allowed back into the kitchen. I couldn't tell him that having my mom and nana here was both a blessing and a burden. If they weren't here, maybe there would be something I could do to hasten the process along.

I thought about my promise to Tom and reconsidered that. Maybe having my family close by right now was the best thing I could ask for. They kept me out of trouble.

"I'm calm because I believe in our team," I finally said.

"Do you? Or are you just saying that to make me feel better?"

"When have I ever said anything just to make you feel better?"

That got a laugh out of him, and I pounced on the break in the tension.

"Bucky, you know what a tight ship we run."

"But what if someone set us up? What if this is a conspiracy?" He sucked in an audible breath. "We all know what the press can do to us. Won't matter whether it's really our fault. People are just too happy to watch other people fail." There was validity in his words. "Every day people are uncovering dirt about each other. Even if none of it is true."

He had a point. How many times had I received forwarded e-mails bashing a political figure, only to find out that the so-called "breaking story" held no truth whatsoever? Occasionally these stories were rescinded, but after the damage was done. As I gripped the phone, I vowed never to forward another negative-spirited e-mail again.

I needed to convince Bucky that everything would be better soon. If I could make him believe that we'd come out on top, maybe through cosmic energy and all-is-right-with-the-world equality, it would become so.

"I can't stand all this waiting," he said. The rhythmic pacing started again.

"Neither can I, but there isn't a lot we can do right now. It's not like they're giving us access to the kitchen."

"Oh my God," he said, his voice panicked again. "Minkus's dossier."

"What about it?"

"You know we had it — we had all the guests' dietary dossiers on file before the dinner."

"So?"

"I —" He hesitated. "Remember that salad dressing we used?"

I started to get a crawling feeling in my

157

stomach. "The one you came up with the day before the dinner?"

I heard Bucky swallow. "I created that one at home. I thought it would be a good idea to put a little extra effort . . ." He began to hyperventilate.

"I'm not understanding the problem," I said. "Bucky. Talk to me. Was there something in the food that —"

"I have his dossier," he said. "Minkus's dossier. I sent the file to myself at home so I would have all his dietary needs on hand. Here."

"You kept a list of his dietary preferences," I said slowly, to clarify.

"Yes, but —"

"I don't see anything wrong with that. Unless he had an allergy and you didn't —"

"Don't you understand? The fact that I sent this information to *my home computer* will be suspect. They're going to ask me why."

I did understand. But I couldn't react to the alarm I felt. "And you have a perfectly valid answer." I took a deep breath and tried again. "We all take information home. I've done that myself."

"But have you ever had a guest die before?"

I knew better than to answer. Bucky's

voice had notched up a few octaves and he sounded on the brink of a breakdown.

He made an incoherent sound. "They're going to investigate and find this. They're going to put me in a room and interrogate me. What's going to happen? My career is ruined."

"Bucky." I said his name sharply. "Is it just Minkus's dietary restrictions, or do you have the whole file?"

Misery wrung out every word. "The whole file."

While we were never granted access to classified information, we occasionally were given guests' entire files, rather than just a list of their dietary needs. It came in handy to know, for instance, if a guest spent years in South America, or Russia, or Japan. Little tidbits helped us design creative and enjoyable menus.

The first thing that came to mind was that Bucky was right. Pretty soon someone would notice that Minkus's information had been sent from our kitchen to Bucky's home. The second thing that came to mind was that I wanted a look at that file. Although we worked hard to never make even the slightest mistake, I wanted a closer look at the information we'd been provided. Having it on Bucky's computer was too tempting to pass up. I was sure we hadn't missed anything, but it would feel very good to reassure ourselves.

"Tell you what, Bucky, sit tight. Make a copy of the file, okay?"

I heard him click-clacking across his floor. "Don't you think I'll get in trouble if I do that?"

"Why should you?" I asked. "You're a member of the White House kitchen staff. You have every right to information about the guests you plan to feed. Make a copy — or two — and I'll come by later. We'll go over it together."

"When can you be here?" he asked. "How soon?"

I opened my mouth to say that I'd be right there, but I caught sight of Mom and Nana sitting in front of the television, with their spring jackets folded neatly on their laps, ready to shut off the TV just as soon as I hung up the phone. I couldn't disappoint them. "I've got a few things I have to do."

"Huh?" His voice squeaked. "I need help on this."

Subscribing to his growing hysteria would only make things worse. "As do we all right now," I said calmly. "Now sit tight and I'll be over later."

Bucky grumbled but we agreed on a time

to meet. As I hung up I wondered if Tom would think this was "getting involved" in the case where I shouldn't. But I would argue that this dossier was given to me and to my staff. We had every right to examine it again now, especially if doing so would help prove our innocence. Though Tom might disagree, he would be wrong.

No, I decided. This foray with Bucky couldn't possibly come back to bite me.

CHAPTER 11

The afternoon did clear up, and when the sun came out, so did some unseasonable warmth. My mom tied her pale blue jacket around her waist and pulled out her sunglasses as we strolled along the National Mall. Nana kept her pastel pink–striped jacket on, but she'd unzipped it, not just because the day was warming up nicely, but because it gave her easier access to her fanny pack. She, too, wore sunglasses — the wraparound kind to protect her recently repaired cataracts. Trailing behind my mom by a couple of steps, she studied the pamphlet we'd picked up at one of the Smithsonian buildings.

"There's a lot we're missing," I said, as we walked west from the Capitol building. "Don't you want to see the National Air and Space Museum?"

My mom shook her head. "It sounds a lot like the Museum of Science and Industry at home," she said. "We can do that on a rainy day. Today I want to be outside and enjoy this beautiful scenery."

Nana, shuffling behind us, said, "I want to see the Washington Memorial."

"That's *Monument*," I said gently. "It's the Washington *Monument* and the *Lincoln* Memorial. I made that same mistake when I first got here," I said. "But a kind woman named Barbara set me straight."

My mom turned around. "Do you and Tom come out here very often?"

I took a look at the blossoming trees, the clear blue of the sky, and the crowds milling around out enjoying the gorgeous day. When was the last time he and I had spent a day together just enjoying the beauty that surrounded us in our nation's capital? I shook my head. "Not often enough." There was so much here to be thankful for — so much to appreciate, and yet he and I were constantly pulled apart by our conflicting schedules. The last few times I'd been out here, I'd been on my own.

"Is that a carousel?" Nana asked, pointing behind us.

"Yeah," I said, hoping she wouldn't want to go for a ride.

"I bet the little kids love that."

I thought about my own experiences with

that carousel — and witnessing a murder — as I made a noncommittal reply. "It's a long walk to see all the memorial exhibits. You sure you're up for it?"

We stopped a moment to stare out toward the Washington Monument. "Says here it's over 555 feet tall," Mom said, taking her turn with the pamphlet. "Guess how much it weighs?"

"Weighs?" Nana asked. "Why? You planning to pick it up?"

"Take a look," I said, pointing. "See that line? Where the color changes? They started building it in 1848 but ran out of money. It sat here for twenty-seven years before they started work on it again."

The three of us stared at the tall white obelisk. With the sun almost directly overhead, we all had to squint. Tall, spare, stark, and circled by snapping American flags, it was a breathtaking sight.

"Hello again, ladies."

We turned. My mom made a funny noise, halfway between a teenage squeak and a gasp of surprise. "Why, Mr. Kapostoulos," she said. "How nice to see you."

He smiled. "Please call me Kap. All my friends do."

Kapostoulos had sidled up to us — sidled up to my mom, I should say — and was

164

smiling a bit too much for a man whose best friend had died just three days before. I struggled to remember his first name — heck, I would have struggled to remember what "Kap" stood for. But Mom sure remembered.

"Nice to see you again," I lied.

He nodded acknowledgment. Wearing a navy blazer, khaki-colored pants, and a blue striped tie, he looked more like a cruise director than someone in mourning.

"Enjoying our beautiful sights?" he asked, but before we could answer, he continued. "Have you been to the Lincoln Memorial yet?"

"Not yet," Mom said. "Is it as pretty as this is?"

"Each of the sights near here has its own beauty," he said, with a meaningful gaze at my mom. "It's worth spending time getting to know them all."

I wanted to roll my eyes, but there was no one to appreciate my discomfort. Nana had stepped closer to him, and I could tell she was sizing him up. I was disheartened by the deepening smile lines on her face.

"We should get going," I said. "Lots to do, you know."

"Perhaps I could accompany you," Kap said, moving toward me. "It has been a while since I have had time to appreciate the magnificence of this area."

"I thought you lived here," I said.

"But I've been out of town for a long time."

I couldn't help the brusqueness in my tone. "I would think you'd be spending time with Ruth and Joel Minkus."

My mom shot me a look from behind Kap. It was meant to reproach, but I didn't care. Who was this guy? And why was he bothering us?

"Although Carl and I knew each other for many years, there is no love lost between me and Ruth." He held out his hands as though in supplication. "But Joel and I get along very well. In fact, he informed me about how Ruth treated you yesterday when you saw her at Arlington."

I started to scoot away, but Mom and Nana didn't move.

"I would like to offer my apologies," he said

"For what?"

"On Ruth's behalf. She's under considerable strain, and I'm sure she didn't mean —"

"First off, no apology necessary," I said. "Families in the midst of shock and grief aren't always responsible for what they say"

— I didn't let him interrupt — "and second, I think it's rather presumptuous of you to apologize on behalf of someone who you just admitted doesn't care for you very much."

He smiled. That bugged me.

"Now," I continued, "we have to be going."

"Ollie!" Mom said. She looked like a seventeen-year-old who was just informed of a ten thirty curfew.

"We have a lot to do," I said.

"But if Kap wants to come along with us, I think it would be nice," Mom said.

Nice?

As if given a great gift, Kap's smile grew. I wanted to ask my mother what was wrong with her all of a sudden, but the words died on my lips. Kap pointed to something in the distance, which immediately captured Mom's full attention. They started walking south, and I fell in behind them with Nana.

"What the heck just happened?" I asked.

She leaned in toward me. "Your mother's been going through a tough time."

"She has?" I stared down at her. "What kind of a tough time?"

Nana linked her arm through mine. "I'd call it a delayed midlife crisis, but that sounds too pat. She's been moved out of the counselor job she loved at the women's shelter into a position that's far below her skills. They're downsizing, or so they say. What's really happening is that they're pushing the older, well-paid workers out or into lesser jobs so that they get disgusted and quit. She used to be excited to go to work every day — to help people. Now she just sits at a desk and makes phone calls to raise money."

"They made her a telemarketer?"

Nana nodded.

"She never told me."

"Of course not." Nana slid a look at the two of them in front of us. "And on top of it all, she's been lonely, Ollie. Very lonely. I'm not the most exciting company, you know."

"Nana . . ."

"It's true. I'm still pretty active and I still volunteer at the hospital, but when your mom comes in from work I can see the dejection in her eyes. There's nothing for her to look forward to anymore."

"She has friends . . ." The image of Mom sitting in a dark room lit only by the flickering television flashed through my mind. "Doesn't she?"

"Most of them are married, and they do couple things." Nana shrugged, and then answered my unasked question. "Even though your mother has been on her own for a long time, things have changed for her now. It's as though when she lost her job she lost a part of herself."

I didn't know if I could talk around the hard lump that had suddenly lodged in my throat.

Ahead of us, my mom laughed. Kap laughed, too, their heads leaning toward each other.

There was something about him that didn't seem authentic, but I couldn't put my finger on what it was. The two of them laughed again and my mom smiled at Kap in a way that made her look ten years younger.

Nana whispered — close to my shoulder. "This trip out to see you, Ollie, was all your mother talked about for weeks. It gave her something important to look forward to."

I nodded, not knowing what else to say.

"In some ways, it's nice that you don't have to work while we're here."

I felt the now-familiar stab of disappointment. For fleeting moments, the horrible specter of Minkus's death disappeared. But then it all came rushing back with a sharpness that made me suck my breath. "I wanted so much to show you the White

House."

"Your mother wants so much to spend time with you. Maybe all this is working out for the best."

Nana's arm in mine felt small, yet it was a comfort. She patted me. "Sometimes we just need to wait and see. Time will tell and before you know it, you'll be back in the White House kitchen again, and everything will be back to normal."

I bit my lip. Weren't those the exact words I'd used to reassure Bucky just this morning?

"Thanks, Nana," I said.

My mom hummed as she made us a late lunch back at my apartment. I'd offered to do the cooking — after all, that was what I did for a living and I wasn't doing much of it these days — but she insisted. Said she wanted to take care of me while she still had the opportunity to do so. A pointed look from Nana warned me not to argue.

"So what did you and Mr. Kapostoulos talk about, Mom?"

He'd accompanied us to the Vietnam War Memorial and to the World War II Memorial, which Nana had particularly wanted to see. He spent most of his time chatting with my mom, leaving me and Nana to wonder about their conversation. At the World War II Memorial, after we'd walked around the expansive structure, he thanked us for sharing part of our day with him and he spoke briefly to my mom, alone.

"He prefers to be called Kap," Mom said.

"Right." I wondered if my smile looked as disingenuous as it felt. "So what *did* you talk about? Did he want to know all about your life history?"

"Not yet, not all of it," she said with a sly smile. "But he did tell me that he encouraged Ruth to call and apologize to you for her outburst at Arlington yesterday."

"He didn't."

"It seemed important to him." She glanced at her watch, then at her purse on the counter.

"That's all I need," I muttered. A thought occurred to me. "Did he ask for your phone number?"

"Ollie. I don't even have a phone number here. He knows I live in Chicago."

"You have a cell phone."

She turned away and went back to humming. Nana warned me with her look to stop asking questions. But I couldn't let it go. "Did you give it to him?"

Finally, Mom turned. Her hair was pulled back, and her face was flushed, but she was

171

smiling. She looked so pretty, so vivacious and so full of life. Kap had put that sparkle in her eyes just by paying her some attention. I sighed, knowing I should let it go. But I couldn't.

"Yes, I did," Mom said in a tone that dared me to object. She placed three bowls of tortilla soup on the table. They steamed with freshness and a hint of spice. I started in on mine and was immediately rewarded with a taste of home. "Do you have a problem with that?"

Nana kicked me under the table. I took another sip of soup and pretended not to hear.

Mom waited. Nana kicked me again.

"Nope," I lied. "Not at all."

"Good, because he and I are going out Friday."

I opened my mouth in protest, but a third swift kick to my shin shut me up. Bending my head, I concentrated again on my soup.

"That's wonderful, Corinne," Nana said. "Where is he taking you?"

"I don't know yet."

"Mom," I said, putting my spoon down, "we don't even know this man. How do you know it's safe to go out with him? He could be a masher."

"A masher!" She laughed. "I used to use

that line on you when you were a teenager."

"Mom, I'm serious. You know nothing about him."

"He was good friends with Carl Minkus," she said. "A very famous NSA agent."

"Yeah, and that famous agent is dead."

She shook her head, but kept smiling. "You sound like an overprotective parent."

"But you just met him."

"In fact," she added mischievously, "I think you'd make a great parent." She fixed me with a glare. "Exactly when do you plan to give me grandchildren? I'm not getting any younger, you know."

She always knew what buttons to push to circumvent an argument. I'd only finished about half my soup, but I stood up. "I'm sorry, this is great, but I'll have it later. I promised to stop by Bucky's house, and then I have dinner plans with Suzie and Steve." I carried my bowl to the side to cover with plastic wrap before placing it in the fridge. "And I need to call Tom."

Excusing myself, I blew out a breath. My mother knew we were on dangerous ground here. Marriage and babies were not something I cared to discuss. Not now at least. Maybe not ever. I didn't see myself toting around tots anytime soon. My chosen career was in a male-dominated field and while all the rhetoric claimed that women could have families and maintain careers, too, I knew that in this extremely competitive arena I needed to hold tight to every edge I could wrap my enthusiastic fingers around. I'd been top chef here for a relatively short time. And as soon as the next administration took over, I could be out of a job. Kids were not on my horizon. The topic wasn't open for discussion, and Mom knew it.

Her bringing it up when I pressed her about this Kap fellow was her attempt to strongarm me into silence. For now, it worked. But I'd figure out a way to talk with her about him. There was something about the guy I just didn't trust.

I thought about my upcoming visit with Bucky. He and I would have to discuss the situation. If the Easter Egg Roll were to be permanently canceled, the press would have a field day. There would be no way to recover from such a public-relations nightmare. I thought about calling our contact at the American Egg Board, Brandy. Effervescent and eager to help, she was just the sort of person who could get things rolling.

I started to look up her number, but stopped myself. Tom would probably consider that "meddling" in the situation. Anger rumbled up from deep in my throat. I was thwarted, no matter which way I turned.

I dialed Tom's cell but hit "end" when I heard my house phone ring. Geez! I hadn't gotten this many phone calls at home in the past year. I picked up the kitchen phone because it was closest. "Hello?"

A woman asked, "Is this . . . Olivia?" Familiar, but I couldn't quite place the voice.

"Yes."

"I . . . that is . . . this is Ruth Minkus."

Fortunately I was right next to a chair. I sat. "Hello," I said, and because I couldn't come up with anything better, "How are you?"

She sucked in a breath, but didn't answer. "My husband's 'friend,' Mr. Kapostoulos" — her emphasis on the word "friend" dripped with sarcasm — "suggested I call you."

My face must have conveyed my pure shock because both Mom and Nana stopped eating to stare at me. Mom pantomimed, "Who is it?"

"He suggested you call me?" I echoed into the receiver. Then pointing into it, I mouthed back, "Ruth Minkus."

They exchanged looks of horror and both started mouthing questions at me. I couldn't follow them and pay attention to Ruth at

175

the same time, so I averted my eyes. I chose to stare at the ceiling, hoping its blankness might aid my concentration. My brain couldn't absorb the fact that Ruth was calling me. And, based on the stammering on the other end, she didn't quite believe it either.

"I suppose I mean to apologize for my behavior yesterday."

I was quick to interrupt. "There's no reason to —"

"Kap said I offended you."

"Kap's wrong," I said, with more than a touch of vehemence. Movement from my right caused me to look over. My mom made a face and got up to work at the stove. Nana stayed put, watching me. I returned my gaze to the ceiling. "I was not at all offended. I understand completely. You're going through a lot of strain right now."

"I am," she said in a tiny voice. "It's been so much pressure. I've been working hard to help my son, Joel, in his bid for the senate seat and now this . . . I don't think I'm handling it very well."

I felt for her. She had just lost her husband and was being bullied into making unnecessary apologies. Embarrassed to have been pulled into this, I said, "I am very sorry for your loss."

"Thank you."

I was about to make another pleasant, innocuous comment — one that would allow me to segue into an excuse to get off the phone — when she said, "Joel thinks I was wrong to accuse you, too."

"As I said, Mrs. Minkus, there's no need —"

"Were you planning to come to Carl's wake tomorrow?"

"Ah . . . no, I wasn't."

She made a *tsk*ing noise. "That's because of my outburst, isn't it?"

"No," I said. "I didn't —" I was about to say that I'd never had *any* intention of attending her husband's wake, but realized how rude that might sound. Softening my response, I tried a different approach. "I know this has to be a very stressful time and I wouldn't want to compound that tension. I'm sure my presence at the wake would be distracting."

"Distracting? How?"

"Because . . ." I groped for a quick explanation. "My staff is still banned from the kitchen."

"Oh, I didn't know that," she said. "I confess I've been trying to avoid reading the papers. It's just too much, you know?"

I did know. "I want to express my sympa-

177

thy again, Mrs. Minkus."

"I would appreciate it if you would reconsider."

"Reconsider?"

"It would mean a lot to me if you would come tomorrow night," she said. "I feel just terrible about my behavior yesterday. In fact, I feel terrible about everything these days. I can't go around burning bridges just because my life has fallen apart."

I heard her voice crack. I didn't know what to say, but she continued. "I mean, I have to think about Joel. He needs me to be strong right now. And I made him ashamed yesterday. Would you please come to the wake? Even if the rest of your staff can't make it, it would go a long way to proving to Joel that I didn't mess things up." She sighed deeply. "I may not always agree with Kap, but this time I think he's right. Please come, Olivia." Her next breath seemed to shake, and I sensed she was close to tears. "I'd better go now." With that she hung up.

I stared at the receiver for a long time. What in the world had that been about? Kap had forced her hand, no doubt about it. But to what end? And why would Joel care whether his mother offended the executive White House chef? I was about to tell Mom about this bizarre conversation, but realized she had left the room.

Nana pointed to the guest bedroom, where I found my mom at the computer. "That was Ruth Minkus," I said.

She turned toward me, arranging her body to block the screen from my view. "What did she want?"

"To invite me to her husband's wake."

Mom twisted, quickly minimized the window, and then returned her attention to me. I'd seen a tiny bit of the page she'd been viewing. "Were you reading the *Liss Is More* column again?" I asked.

Nervous laugh as she stood. "Why would I read that trash?"

"Then what were you reading?" I felt like a parent who just caught her teenager visiting inappropriate sites.

"Just silly stuff," she said, trying to guide me out the door. "Nothing worth mentioning. Let's go see what Nana's up to."

"Mom —"

Her shoulders dropped. "I wasn't reading that crazy man, Liss," she said. "But I found out that his articles are reprinted on the Internet and people can write in and make comments on what he wrote."

"And?"

"There are some very odd people in the world," she said. "I mean, I thought Liss was out of his mind, but people go off on the strangest tangents and say very mean, very cruel things."

"Let me see," I said, moving toward the computer.

She blocked me.

I laughed. "Mom, you can't keep me from reading what's out there."

She suddenly looked so sad, my heart hurt.

"Did someone mention me?" I asked.

"Not exactly." She bit her lip. "It's just that people were asking about the Easter Egg Roll, and I knew how worried you were about that. I didn't want you to see all the questions."

"That's not all you didn't want me to see, is it?"

"Some people don't know what they're talking about."

I made it around her and maximized the browser window again. I sensed her resignation both from her deep sigh, and from the hand she placed on my shoulder as I scrolled through the comments.

There were, indeed, a lot of strange people in the world. I wondered if these were the same folks who, for kicks, sent out indecipherable spam in their spare time. I started at the top — the most recent commentary

— and worked my way through several screeds that had more to do with battling the writers' own demons than Carl Minkus's death. Seemed to me that the earliest posts stayed on topic and the more recent ones were lame attempts to discredit earlier posters.

"What about the Easter Egg Roll?" asked Theda R. from Virginia. "My kids have been looking forward to this all year! Can't someone just boil a few eggs so the kids won't be disappointed?"

From Sal J.: "What do we care if another bureaucrat is dead? He got what he deserved, if you ask me. Minkus was screwed up and whoever took him out deserves a medal."

Yikes.

"These people have too much time on their hands," I said, continuing to scroll. I stopped when I saw the next one. Blood rushed out to all my extremities, rendering me light-headed.

"That girl the president hired to cook for him — that Ollivia Parras — she's nothing but trouble since she took over the job. She can't cook worth a nikcl and she can always try seeing how she can get in the headlines. It's all her fault your poor kids don't get to roll their eggs this year. I say the president should fire her butt and fast!"

No matter that the writer of this little diatribe — R. I. — spelled so many things wrong, including my name. No matter that he, or she, was grammatically challenged. The message was clear.

"I can so cook," I said unnecessarily. But the accusation stung.

"You see, this is all garbage," Mom said. "I shouldn't even have been reading it."

I wanted to shake it off, but my eyes were scanning again. There were more postings questioning whether there was any way to keep the Egg Roll on schedule, a few that talked about Minkus and who might have wanted him dead, and a couple more that called for my immediate dismissal.

"Cheery stuff," I said, trying to swallow a hot bubble of disappointment.

"They don't know what they're talking about."

She was probably right, but the attacks were brutal. And they hurt.

I'd been on enough Internet pages like this to know that at the bottom there should be a form available to add your own commentary. But this time, no little box appeared. Instead, in red italics were the words: *Please allow several minutes for your comment to post.*

I spun. "You didn't."

Mom blushed, waving a hand at the screen. "I couldn't let them talk about you like that and not do anything."

I dropped my head into my hands, took a deep breath, and hit "refresh."

CHAPTER 12

Of course the page took forever to load. Of course. Sometimes my connection was blazingly fast, and times like this — when I really wanted information quickly — the computer became uncooperative and petulant, like I was still on dial-up.

While I waited for the Liss commentary to blink back into existence, I chanced a look at my mom. "Just tell me you didn't mention me by name."

She opened her mouth but no words came out.

Just as the website popped up to tell me that it was temporarily unavailable, my cell phone rang.

"Aargh!" I took a look at the display. Tom.

"Did you try to call me?" he asked when I picked up.

"I started to, but then Ruth Minkus called."

"She called you? Why? Did she start accusing you again?"

"No," I said wearily. I didn't feel like explaining. Over the past few days all I'd done was explain. What I wanted — what I *needed* — right now was to be back in the White House kitchen, working on the Egg Roll. We were already three days behind schedule. "She called to apologize," I said. "Long story."

He waited a beat. "So, what's up?"

Was it my imagination, or was there a lilt of impatience in his tone? "The White House Egg Roll," I began.

"We've been over that."

"No," I said carefully. "You said you expected they would cancel it. But they can't."

"They 'can't'?"

"You know what I mean." I grimaced at the pleading tone in my voice. "I think it's a mistake to cancel the Egg Roll."

"Oh you do?"

"Yes I do," I said, getting my back up. "Who can I talk to about it?"

"I'll look into it for you."

"No, Tom," I said, regaining a little composure. "You're responsible for my actions, remember?" Without waiting for him to answer, I pressed on. "That means that you have a conflict of interest. You believe keep-

185

ing me out of the kitchen will keep me out of trouble. Or," I added, with a smidge of sarcasm, "your perception of trouble. I think it makes more sense for me to talk with someone else about this. Do you have Craig's cell phone number handy?"

"You would go over my head?"

I wouldn't really, but I was desperate and I didn't want him to call my bluff. Even though we occasionally got angry with one another, we knew our limits. Calling Craig would push things and I truly didn't want to cause irreparable damage to our relationship. Even if this *was* turning into my career versus his career. "Maybe Craig isn't my best option. How about if I talk with Paul Vasquez?"

Seconds ticked by without my being able to read his mood. Why were so many of our conversations so antagonistic lately?

"That might be a good idea," he finally answered and I sensed conciliation in his words. "I do understand how important this is for you."

"I know you do, and I also know you're in a tough position."

We were both silent for a long moment.

"I'm probably less likely to get into trouble if I'm at work," I said.

He made a noise that might have been a

laugh. "You may be right." Shifting gears, he asked, "Anything else new?"

I debated telling him about Bucky having the Minkus file on his home computer, but decided to hold that back for now. No need to get Bucky into trouble unnecessarily. "I'm planning to go over every step of dinner preparations. I'll make notes of anything that might be helpful to you."

"Sounds like a plan."

"Thanks for helping out with Suzie and Steve earlier. They're having me over for dinner tonight to thank me for getting the news hounds off their front lawn."

"Nice. I do all the work, you get the reward."

"Want to come with?"

"Some other time." He made a sound — like he was sucking his bottom lip. "Until this investigation is complete, it's a good idea if you and I aren't seen out together."

That stung, too. Even more than the Internet postings had. "I guess you're right."

"Try not to talk about the case with your SizzleMaster friends, okay?"

"Pretty hard to do after reporters showed up on their front lawn."

He was silent again. "Just try to keep a low profile."

"I did just think of something."

"Uh-oh."

"I know we're under suspicion, and so are Suzie and Steve. But what about the other guests at dinner that night? I mean, Carl Minkus's second-in-command sure stands to gain now that his boss is dead. And what about Alicia Parker? Or her husband? They were there, too."

Tom's long, deep breath wasn't quite as annoyed-sounding as I'd expected it to be. "First off, people don't just go killing one another to get job promotions. At least not usually. Sure, you'll be able to quote some news story where that happened, but in the real world, most people just don't operate that way."

"What about —"

"Alicia Parker?" He laughed. "She's too big for even you to touch, Ollie. Alicia Parker is a cabinet member. I'm sure there are people looking into her background, but this is one hot wire you don't want to even get near. Trust me."

He was right about that. I'd only met Secretary Parker in passing once or twice, although I'd seen her interviewed on TV fairly often. She came across as strong-minded, honest, and brave. "Yeah," I agreed. "And anyway, she strikes me as the type who — if she wanted you dead — would just come straight up and shoot you. I don't see her sneaking poison into an eggplant entrée."

"Keep in mind, Ollie," Tom said, and the warning was back in his tone, "Minkus might have died of natural causes."

"Natural causes could also mean a food allergy," I said. "And if the medical examiner proves that, then I'm out of a job for sure."

"I'm sorry," he said, the gentleness in his tone catching me off-guard. "With this new directive from Craig, I haven't been very supportive recently, have I?"

"You have," I said, remembering that he picked up my family from the airport and stood by me while I was being interrogated. "I shouldn't be so difficult. You're under a lot of pressure."

"I am. And I hope you can understand that."

"I do," I said. And I did. Mostly.

My mom cornered me when I got off the phone to let me know that Mrs. Wentworth and Stanley had invited us out to dinner. I declined because of my meeting with Bucky and dinner plans with Suzie and Steve. Mom and Nana had, however, jumped at the chance to see more of the area, and I was glad. Knowing they were in good hands with my neighbors allowed me to feel a little less guilty leaving them.

I called Paul on the way. Although I was lucky enough to get to speak with him directly, he was running late for a meeting. When I pressed him about letting us back into the kitchen, he hedged. But that was better than saying no. Plus, they hadn't yet canceled the Egg Roll. I took that as a positive even as I got him to promise to get back to me. But when I hung up, I realized he hadn't said by when.

Bucky's Bethesda home surprised me. I'd never been inside, and except for the recent trip in the limousine when the Guzy brothers dropped him off, I'd never even known exactly where he lived. This was a cheerful little neighborhood, with lots of shiny cars outside tidy front lawns. Parallel parking on residential streets was never difficult for a native Chicagoan, and I tucked my little coupe into a tight spot between two SUVs.

Although this was an old neighborhood, every town house on this street and the next sparkled like new. I'd heard that this section had undergone major renovations in the past decade. I could see the allure of living here. The trees were mature, the homes well-tended.

Bucky met me at the door, wearing a wide

cotton apron tied over pale legs. It gave him the appearance of not wearing any pants, and I breathed a sigh of relief when he turned around to gesture me in and I saw his blue cutoff shorts. "It's warm in here, sorry," he said. "I'm working on a new quiche. Just drop your jacket anywhere."

Sniffing the savory air, I shut the front door and followed him through the pristine living room toward the kitchen. My stomach growled as I picked up the scent of baking cheese. "How long have you lived here?" I asked.

"Eleven — no, twelve years," he said, raising his voice so I could hear him. Whatever he was concocting in the kitchen must have needed his immediate attention, because I heard him clanking things in and out of the oven, even as I peeled off my jacket and draped it over the back of a purple couch. I ran my hand along its back pillow. Suede. Not at all what I would have imagined in Bucky's home. "You should have seen this place back then." He peeked his head around the corner. "Took a lot of work to get it to where it is now."

"It's gorgeous." I wanted to ask if he lived alone, but I held my tongue. Bucky and I had never been friends in the sense that we discussed personal lives, and my being here suddenly seemed like an intrusion.

The living room was painted ecru, with matching crown molding and bare maple floors that shone, but didn't squeak. Lights were on everywhere and I stopped on my way to the kitchen to admire some black-and-white photographs on the dining room wall. The shots had an Ansel Adams look to them, but the photographer's name was listed as "B. Fields."

"Did you do all the remodeling yourself?"

"With the hours we work at the White House? Are you kidding?" Back out of sight again, his voice was muffled. "I did do a lot, though. It's invigorating."

I joined him in the kitchen. What must have once been a tiny galley kitchen had been updated and expanded into a huge space that made me salivate. With gleaming pots hanging over a center island, not one, but two built-in stovetops, and two double ovens, this was the sort of kitchen I hoped to have in my own home some day. While my apartment's small space was serviceable for my personal needs, I knew that if I ever settled down somewhere permanent, my kitchen would look just like this.

"Wow," I said. "This is amazing."

"We like it."

Time to bite the bullet. "We?" I asked. "I

didn't know you were married. Are you?"

He gave a small smile. "Not yet."

"Kids?"

This time he fixed me with a glare, though not an unfriendly one. "Do I really seem like the type who would have kids?"

"Whatever you're making smells wonderful," I said to change the subject.

"Good. I know we're not going back to the White House anytime soon, and I don't want to get rusty."

"Bucky," I said sincerely, "I doubt that could ever happen."

He wiped his hands on a towel and removed his apron. "There. Everything's good for now." He set a timer. "Let's go into the living room and take a look at that dossier."

By the time the little clock dinged, we'd come up with almost nothing, dietary-wise, that we couldn't have recited from memory.

Bucky pulled out a gently browned spinach quiche.

"Looks great," I said, coming close to breathe in the aroma. "Smells wonderful, too."

"Want some?" he asked.

"I'd love to, but I have dinner plans."

His reaction was small: a slight drop of his shoulders, the quick twist of his mouth.

"But boy, it really does smell good," I amended. "Maybe just a small piece?"

"Sure," he said without reacting. But when he sliced a generous portion onto a piece of black and gold rimmed china and placed it in front of me, his eyes were bright with anticipation. "Let me know what you think."

"Fancy plate," I said.

"Why save the good stuff for special occasions?"

I forked a piece of the pie-shaped slice and pronounced it heavenly. If I hadn't had plans to meet with Suzie and Steve in the next hour, I would have asked for seconds — even after this generous first serving. The quiche was so good, in fact, it was all I could do not to request a sample to take home to share with Mom and Nana. "You'll have to give me this recipe," I said.

"Already on our books." He smiled, and it dawned on me what an unusual sight that was. "I plan to include it . . ." Stopping himself, the smile faded. "I should say, I *planned* to include it in the next set of samplings for Mrs. Campbell to taste."

I patted his hand. He flinched but didn't pull away.

"Well, that's just another reason why we need to work hard at getting back into the kitchen. I don't see anything in Minkus's dietary profile that could have had such disastrous consequences, do you?"

Bucky had started to clean up the area and I marveled, again, at how pristine the place was. At the White House, when we were in the midst of preparing a state dinner, or other big event, the kitchen got a little cluttered. Although we had help and we cleaned up as we worked — there really was no way around that — at home I was not quite so fastidious. Bucky, however, was.

"You know," I said, "we read over the rest of his dossier but we really didn't digest it."

He half turned. "What do you mean?"

"Here, for instance." I pointed. "Minkus was appointed to his position during the prior administration. He worked hard to make a name for himself as a terrorist fighter. But he also held a position as a counterintelligence liaison to China."

"So?"

"So isn't that a little weird? Kind of a strange combination, I think."

Bucky didn't seem as interested in my musings as he was in putting his quiche away. "Who appointed him to the liaison position?" he asked.

"Don't know. Obviously there's a lot in his file we wouldn't have access to. They

195

only provided us this top-line information. Stuff that anyone could probably find in an Internet search, if they knew what they were looking for."

"Hmph," Bucky said, bustling around the kitchen as I pored through the file.

I mused aloud. "And what about Phil Cooper?"

"That's the guy who reported to Minkus, right? Another security official."

I pointed again, but Bucky just worked around me. "Exactly. Cooper worked for Minkus for about two years. It doesn't say much here about him, except to mention that he's part of Minkus's staff."

"You're not thinking Cooper killed Minkus just to get his job?" Bucky scowled. "People don't usually do that. At least not in the real world."

Almost word for word, Bucky had just echoed Tom's sentiment.

"What about China?" I asked. "Didn't they just have that double-assassination in Beijing? The one that's been in all the head-lines."

Stopping mid-stride on the way to his stainless steel double refrigerator, Bucky cocked his head. "Yeah. Wasn't that the day after Minkus died?"

"Do you think it's related?"

"Like . . . some Chinese official sneaked poison into Minkus's food? Yeah. Sure."

"Think about it. According to rumors, the Chinese had insider spies in the United States. Maybe Minkus discovered who that spy was who was selling our secrets. Maybe a Chinese operative got to Minkus before dinner."

"An operative." Bucky snorted. "You sound so official. Like a character in a movie, figuring out a global conspiracy."

Put like that, it sounded ridiculous. I felt stupid for seeing patterns where there were none. For suspecting people like Phil Cooper when I had no reason to do so. I closed the file and placed both hands on top of it. "You're right," I finally said.

Wiping his hands after putting the food away, Bucky shrugged. "If someone did get to Minkus before dinner, then I guess we just have to be patient. Let the medical examiner figure out what killed him. God, I hope that's it. I'm not saying I'm glad he's dead, you understand. But now I care less about that, than about how it happened. I just hope they find out what — or who — killed him. Until then, no matter what we say or do, we'll always be known as the killer kitchen."

Oh God, I thought. The killer kitchen.

■ ■ ■ ■

Sufficiently full from my healthy helping of quiche, I nonetheless headed to the studio where Suzie and Steve filmed their *Sizzle-Masters* television shows. I hoped for two things: that whatever they served would be light, and that the newshounds who had been staking out their home had given up. After my day of interruptions, the last thing I needed was to deal with the media.

The directions they'd provided were perfect and I pulled up to the studio five minutes early. From the outside it looked like a typical industrial building, but once inside, I felt as though I'd just stepped into someone's home.

"Ollie, thank goodness," Suzie said, giving me a quick hug hello. Hugging her was like being enveloped by a favorite aunt, all soft and smooshy, and smelling like White Linen cologne.

"How are you doing?" I asked. "Were you able to lose the reporters?"

Suzie was the type who didn't understand the principle of "personal space." She held my hand as we meandered through a waiting area that felt more like a cozy living room: two softly glowing lamps, red walls, jewel-toned accents. "Thank you so much for helping us out," she said, her face close to mine. "I thought Steve was going to lose it."

"Lose what?" he boomed from behind a thick wall. The side door was open to the filming portion of the studio and I stepped in and then up onto the raised portion, blinking into the high illumination.

This room was peculiarly lit. While the stage area was hyper-bright, the audience section was dark. I could make out rows of seats, rising toward the back of the studio, guaranteeing everyone a good view. From the looks of it, there were six rows in two sections. Maybe a dozen seats per row. Things sure looked bigger on TV.

"We're keeping the lights off in the outer portion so that no one knows we're here," Suzie said as though I'd asked the question. She squeezed my hand. "I'm so glad you were able to come."

Her voice held a strange quality. Not relief. Not a shared understanding of what we were all going through.

"Is there something else going on I should know about?" I asked.

They exchanged a look. Suzie let go of my hand. "Like what?"

I gave an exaggerated shrug. "Nothing.

Anything. I'm just trying to make sure you haven't been bothered any more."

"No," Suzie said, leaving my side to tend to a pot on the stove. She kept her back to me. "Everything has been really quiet since we got here."

"So your filming went well?"

"Very," Suzie said.

Steve nodded. He stood in front of the central countertop, which faced the cameras. A large overhead camera pointed down, the better to show the folks at home precisely how items should be prepared. Before him was a heaping mound of grilled vegetables — peppers, onions, zucchini, mushrooms. I wondered how many people they were planning to serve.

The two of them worked at their stations with their backs to one another. Very straight, very tense backs. The pressure in the room was so thick I could swim in it.

"So why here?" I asked.

Steve lifted his head, but his eyes didn't focus. "Hmm?"

"Here? You mean at the studio?" Suzie spoke over her shoulder. "Oh, we just thought you'd like to see it."

"Come on, guys," I said to their backs. "Something doesn't smell right and I can tell you it isn't the grilled portabella."

Suzie said, "How about we eat first, discuss business later?"

"Business?"

"Suze," Steve said, finally turning to face her. "There is no business to discuss. Remember?"

Now my curiosity was piqued.

Suzie turned. Her smile showed too much teeth. "I thought we decided —"

"Yes." His smile was an almost perfect mimic of hers. "We decided to have a nice dinner and then give Ollie a copy of the DVD."

Surprised, I asked, "You have a copy?"

"Of course," Steve said. "We're co-producers."

As if that explained it to non-TV-savvy me. But that didn't matter. "Where is it? Can I see it?"

He flung a derisive look over his shoulder and said, in a too-casual voice, "Sure. That's the whole reason we wanted to have you for dinner tonight. But let's eat first."

We made our way to the table. "I'm very glad to hear about the DVD." I carried a basket of fresh-baked sesame rolls, which warmed my hands. "I had asked our chief usher about getting a copy, but he didn't know if we could."

They exchanged another look.

The dining area was beyond a half wall — sliced vertically — that made it seem as though we were in an entirely separate room. Open to the cameras yet again, this part of the stage was decorated with home-spun accessories, giving the area the feel of a middle-class American home.

Suzie gave me a funny look as she gestured me into a chair. "Why do they want a copy of the DVD?"

Steve speared a perfectly grilled ribeye and placed it on my plate. "Medium-rare okay with you?"

"Perfect." I turned to Suzie. "I was hoping to use the DVD to prove that nobody in the kitchen could have added anything to Minkus's plate before it went out. Your crew was still filming right up to the end, remember?"

She nodded, but stared down at her own steak. She looked ready to cry.

"What's wrong?" I asked.

She shook her head. "I should have served the soup first."

"I make the finest grilled vegetables in North America," Steve said, leaning over to spoon a helping onto my plate. "Say when."

But I was looking at Suzie. Her downcast expression was not soup-related. Of that I was certain.

I reached over to touch her hand. "Suze?"

Vaguely aware of a steamy scent wafting upward, I heard Steve say, "Should I keep going?"

I glanced at my plate, alarmed at the pile of vegetables he'd mounded there. "When — when!" I said, jerking my hands up. The quiche in my stomach shifted. "I'll never be able to eat all that."

"Sure you will," Steve said with over-the-top ebullience. "I'm telling you, you've never tasted better."

I twisted my head from side to side, to keep an eye on both of them. "What's really going on here?"

Suzie sniffed.

Steve sat. "Eat," he said. It was more an order than invitation.

I tried to manage my impatience by slicing off a small piece of ribeye. Steve had, in fact, grilled it to medium-rare perfection. Popping it in my mouth, I savored its tenderness. "This is wonderful."

"Don't forget your veggies."

I couldn't possibly forget — not with him constantly reminding me. I speared a green pepper. The vegetable's skin, shiny with marinade, was cross-sected with grill lines and topped with an ingredient I assumed was chopped garlic. Waves of heat tickled my lips as I took my first bite.

I froze, mid-chew.

It was all I could do to keep from violently spitting the pepper out onto my plate. It tasted like nail polish remover. Or at least what I imagined nail polish remover might taste like. My eyes widened — I didn't have any idea how to remove this vile thing from my mouth with Steve watching me. Waiting for me to proclaim his creation fabulous.

"Mmm," I said, grabbing desperately for the napkin on my lap. Damn. Cloth. I needed paper.

"What do you think, Ollie?" Steve asked, his eyes glittering. "Bet you've never tasted anything like it."

I stood.

All of a sudden, it hit me. What if Suzie and Steve *had* poisoned Minkus? Were they now trying to get rid of me? I raced out of the stage area, ducking into the washroom, where I yanked the wastebasket to my face and spit the offensive vegetable out.

Was my light-headedness because I'd jumped up so quickly — or was I about to die just as Minkus had? I gripped the countertop and looked into the mirror. The lights were still off, so I couldn't see much. My lips tingled. My tongue was numb.

Just like Minkus.

I had to get out of here.

"Ollie, what's wrong?" Suzie asked, following me into the room. Blocking my exit.

Suzie's careworn face had paled. Steve stood behind her, looking grim. Why? Because their plan had failed?

"Sick," I said, my tongue sluggish and swollen. "I better go."

Steve shook his head. "I'll drive you home."

"No!" I shouted. "My car is here. I'll be okay."

Now it was Suzie shaking her head. "I won't feel comfortable with you driving alone. Is there someone we can call? Maybe I'll drive with you and Steve can follow us."

She reached over and felt my forehead. "You're clammy."

No kidding.

"Come on," she said, taking my arm. "Let's sit for a few minutes."

I tugged away. "Gotta go."

"But what about the DVD?" Suzie asked. "You really wanted to see it."

Not at the expense of my life, I thought.

She pressed. "Come on back to the table. I'll get the DVD and then we'll figure out how to get you home safely."

Working my way to the door, I tried to still the thudding of my heart. Was its extra-speedy beat from that single bite of green pepper? Was I about to go into cardiac arrest?

Ready to run, I looked at Suzie and Steve. Really looked at them. These two had been my friends for several years. Why was I suspecting them of murder?

Because they'd been acting like weirdos leading up to dinner. That's why.

"My purse," I said, hurrying back to the table. I chanced a look at Suzie's and Steve's plates. Neither had taken the grilled vegetables.

My stomach churned and I put a hand over my mouth.

Suzie beat me to the table and picked up my purse but didn't hand it over. Steve told me to wait while he got the DVD.

Would he come back with a meat cleaver?

"I told my mom and nana that I was coming here tonight," I said.

Suzie looked distracted. "Will they be able to come get you?"

"No — they don't have a car." I held out my hand for my purse.

She stepped back, out of my reach. "I don't know if you're safe to drive." Worry wrinkled her forehead. "You seemed fine until you started eating."

"No . . . I've not been feeling well."

The platter of vegetables sat directly in front of Suzie's plate. She eyed them, then looked at me. "It's too bad," she said. "Steve was so excited to have you try this new marinade."

I'll bet.

Eyeing the veggies again, she leaned forward and picked up a piece of grilled portabella. If she tried to force-feed me, I was going to run for the door.

She surprised me by taking a big bite. "Oh my God," she said, around the mouthful. She looked around wildly, but didn't run away, as I had. Instead she grabbed the cloth napkin off the table and spit into it. "My God," she said again. "That's horrible."

"Found it!" Steve said, emerging from the back area. No meat cleaver. No gun. He held a DVD in a jewel case near his head. He waved it triumphantly.

"Steve," Suzie said, pointing at the vegetable platter. "What did you do to those?"

He looked from his wife, to me, to the platter, and then back again. "What's wrong with them?"

"They're disgusting. What's in that new recipe you used? This is the worst thing I've ever tasted. I swear, if I didn't know better, you were trying to poison us."

Suzie's hand flew to her mouth as she realized what she'd said. Then: "My tongue is numb."

Steve's smile dissolved. Anger and disbelief took over, as he leaned over the table to grab one of the grilled veggies. He threw two peppers into his mouth and began to chew vigorously. But not for long. Within seconds he was gagging.

Steve spit out the veggies, just as Suzie and I had. "What the hell?" he asked.

"Should we get to a hospital?" I asked. "All of us?"

Frantically wiping at his tongue with his napkin — a truly unappetizing sight if there ever was one — Steve shook his head. "I can't imagine . . ."

He slammed the DVD onto the table and ran out of the dining room back into the stage-kitchen. We followed.

Digging out an olive oil container, he smelled the top of it. "Seems fine," he said. Then, with a look of dawning realization, he pulled a plastic bowl from the refrigerator and removed the top. He stuck his face close to its contents. He then tipped a finger into the mix and touched it to his lips, grimacing at the taste. "Dear Lord," he said.

"What?" Suzie asked.

Overhead lights were still pouring brightness down onto the stage and the two of them looked like characters in a play — characters that had just been delivered very bad news.

Perspiring heavily, Steve shook his head. "This isn't garlic," he said. "This was supposed to be a tomato-garlic topping."

Suzie and I looked at each other in silence. Steve stared up with confusion on his face. "How could I have not noticed?" He touched the chopped-up substance.

My heart resumed its trip-hammer beating. "Maybe we should try to figure out what it is," I said, feeling like the only voice of reason in the room. The two of them were staring at the bowl, perplexed. "We may have to call the poison control hotline."

Still grimacing, Steve said, "This doesn't even smell like garlic."

"I get it," I said. "It's not garlic. How about we try to find out what it is?"

"How could I have made this kind of mistake?"

Since Steve's lament was rhetorical, I turned to Suzie. "Do you have a list of inventory? Stuff you've ordered? You have a lot of assistants here, right?"

She nodded, staring at Steve.

"I'm guessing one of them made this mistake. And since this is probably a food item, I'm sure we're all going to be okay."

She nodded again.

"Can I have your lists?"

Luckily, their computer was on and in minutes we had accessed their inventory, and meals planned for the next several days' shoots. "What's this?" I asked. "I thought you guys didn't do desserts on the show." The item I pointed to was a persimmon-and-lemon cookie.

Suzie looked over my shoulder. "Oh," she said. "We thought it might be fun to branch out, to start including desserts, too. We have a one-hour show coming up where we prepare everything from soup and salad to dessert. This was going to be one of our experiments."

The light was beginning to dawn. "This calls for persimmon pulp," I said. "Where would that be?"

She rummaged around the kitchen, then held up a finger and headed to the rear of the studio. Steve had been paying attention. "Oh geez," he said. "You think this is chopped persimmon?"

"Unripe persimmon," I corrected. "If you have an assistant who confused persimmon with garlic, I think you need a new assistant. It makes sense though. The bitter taste. The numb tongue."

Suzie returned. "According to our records we received a shipment of persimmon. But there's nothing here."

"Ollie," Steve said, "I can't tell you how embarrassed I am."

"At least we know we're okay," I said, thinking the fruit in the bowl had to be *very* unripe. Nothing else could taste that vile and still not kill you. Tannins in unripe persimmon made the fruit unpalatable. And that was being kind.

There was a stool next to the counter. Steve backed up onto it. "Oh my God," he said. "Can you imagine if this had happened in front of a studio audience?"

Unripe persimmon wasn't toxic in such a small dose. And though it had the potential to cause bezoars, nasty masses that can accumulate in the esophagus or intestines if consumed in large quantities, I doubted anyone would ever eat enough to allow that to happen.

I rolled my tongue around in my mouth, willing the taste away. "Do you have anything to drink?" I asked.

"Sure, of course," Suzie said, hurrying toward the refrigerator. "I could use something, too." Over her shoulder, she stuck out her tongue. "Ick."

"I'm so sorry," Steve said, for about the

fifth time. "I can't understand how this happened. I mean, the assistants know that I keep my garlic in that bowl. I always use the same bowl for garlic." He looked about to cry. "But this time it was supposed to be a tomato-garlic combination. How could they have made such a stupid mistake? And why didn't I notice it?"

"Let's just be glad it wasn't anything really bad for us," I said, relief making me ultra-chatty. "For a minute there I was wondering . . ."

I stopped myself. Did I really want to tell them that I'd felt threatened? That I'd been ready to dash out the door? Wouldn't that make it obvious that I suspected them in Minkus's murder?

"Ollie!" Suzie said. The look on her face was one of incredulity. "You didn't think we were trying to —"

"No. No, of course not," I lied.

"It's all my fault." Steve placed both elbows on the countertop and buried his face in his hands. "I made this mistake because I was preoccupied. What other mistakes am I liable to make?"

We both looked at him.

"This isn't going to go away," he said.

"What isn't?"

"We didn't have anything to do with

212

Minkus's death," he said, looking up. "I swear I didn't. Neither did Suzie."

"I didn't think —"

Suzie placed a hand on my arm. "Yes, but the Secret Service probably does think so."

"Why?"

"The NSA, Suze," Steve said. "I think the NSA will be the first on our tails." He lowered his head into his hands again. "But they won't be the last."

CHAPTER 13

The worry lines on both their faces told me they were terrified. "What are you talking about?" I asked.

Steve seemed to have aged ten years in the past five minutes. "Want to finish dinner?" He tried a small smile. "I promise I won't make you eat your vegetables."

It was a lame attempt at levity, but I think we all needed some sort of relief. "It's okay," I said. "I'm really not all that hungry. I'm sorry about wasting such a nice steak. Can I take it home?"

My request cheered them up. Professional chefs hate to ruin meals. Asking for the remaining steak told them I liked the dish, and that I trusted them.

"Of course!" Suzie said. "As soon as I pour you something to drink, I'll get the steak wrapped up for you."

The iced tea was sweet and I let it pool in my mouth to help rid myself of the persimmon aftertaste. Within minutes, the dining room table was clear. Suzie put down a fresh tablecloth and we all leaned forward over our glasses of iced tea to talk. At the center of the table was the DVD. What I wanted most of all were answers. The DVD might hold some. But I had a feeling that Suzie and Steve held more.

"Tell me why you think the NSA will be 'tailing' you."

They exchanged a look.

"Come on!" I said. "Just tell me. Spit it out."

Suzie fingered her neckline. "Are you still dating Tom?"

The question startled me into silence. "Uh . . ."

"Because, first, you have to promise you won't tell him."

Alarm bells rang in my head. And they weren't from eating unripe fruit. "I can't promise that."

They exchanged another look. "They probably already know anyway," Suzie said.

"But what if they don't? What if the files are lost right now? Or maybe they put all of Minkus's stuff in limbo. Then we'll just be opening up a can of worms."

Their argument zinged my curiosity into high gear.

Speaking very slowly, I asked them again, "Tell me what's going on." I stared at Steve — a warning not to beat around the bush any longer. "If you mistook chopped raw persimmon for garlic, there's got to be something weighing on your mind."

"A long time ago," he began, blinking sandbaggy eyes, "back in college, in fact, Carl and I were friends. Roommates freshman and sophomore year. He was a political science major. I was . . . well" — Steve gave a wry grin — "I was undecided for a long time."

I'd had no idea that Minkus and Steve had ever known one another. "Why didn't you say anything while we were preparing dinner Sunday?" I asked. "You obviously had a copy of our guest list. You should have mentioned something."

"Well . . ." Steve dragged the word out. "He and I didn't exactly part on the best terms."

I chanced a look at Suzie. From the encouraging expression she was plastering on her husband, I knew she'd heard this story before.

"Go on," I said.

"There was this girl . . ."

Uh-oh, I thought. *Isn't there always?* "And you both fell for her?"

Steve shook his head. "I wish it were something like that. No."

I waited.

"She was a nice girl. Mary. She was on full scholarship and she worked really hard to keep at the top of her class. Going to college meant everything to her. She lived on the floor above us."

I took a look at Suzie. She was squinting, like she knew this would be hard to hear.

Steve took a deep breath. "Mary was actively involved in student government, and was president of the honors fraternity."

"She sounds like a real go-getter."

Steve's mouth twisted. "She was my good friend."

"Was?"

"More iced tea?" Suzie asked.

At first I thought it was an odd time to interrupt, but when I noticed Steve having a hard time maintaining composure, I took a big drink and said, "Thanks, that would be great."

When we were all settled again, Steve squared his shoulders. "By the time we were juniors, Mary had become a powerhouse on campus. She was destined to do great things — we all knew it. And we all supported her. She was one of those people who had a thousand things on her plate, but who always could make time for you, if you needed a hand, or help with studying, or advice — whatever. Mary made you feel like you were the most important person in her life at that moment. We all adored her."

I was starting to have a queasy feeling. "And Carl Minkus?"

Steve spat an expletive. "Carl was a drunken idiot. He and I wasted a lot of our freshman year. By sophomore year, I got tired of the constant partying. It was time, you know?" He looked up at me.

I nodded.

"Carl's father had been the president of Zeta Eta Theta — the same fraternity Mary was now president of. And Carl was jealous. He was under pressure to bring his grades up." Steve gave an unhappy laugh. "There was no way he could even qualify for membership, let alone be an officer, but that didn't stop him."

This story seemed like something that couldn't have anything to do with dinner last Sunday, but I let him continue.

"The elder Minkus pulled some strings and — what do you know? — Carl was initiated into Zeta Eta Theta. He called me to brag. Like this was some kind of real achievement." Steve made a face. "Mary's hands were tied."

"He and Mary didn't get along?"

"Not at all. She was upset about having to initiate Carl. She fought it, hard, because she believed in preserving the integrity of the organization. But once he was a member, she didn't make waves. She was like that. She fought as hard as she could for what she believed in, but when the battle was over, she gave in graciously."

Now Steve was squinting. He cleared his throat. "That wasn't good enough for Carl. He wanted to be president, just like his old man. He had a lot of money, but Mary had brains and guts. She was the epitome of grace under pressure. He made her life difficult but she outclassed him in every way. And then he snapped."

"Over a fraternity presidency?"

Steve rolled his glass back and forth between his hands. "You have to understand. At the time, this was a very big deal. Every Zeta president since the chapter's inception had gone directly from college into a solid, lucrative position, thanks to elder 'brothers' in the business world. Mary had a spectacular future in front of her."

"But?"

"Carl kept me updated. With the benefit of hindsight, I think he was doling out just enough information to keep me off track.

He told me he had given up his craving for the Zeta presidency and that he had offered Mary an olive branch. He said he would stop badgering her if she'd meet him for coffee to talk about it. She agreed."

I waited.

"That was the night she disappeared."

I sucked in a breath so hard and so fast that it made me cough. "What?"

"We never saw her again."

"But . . ."

He held up a hand. "Carl said he waited for her for hours at a coffee shop. Lots of people there — lots of witnesses. The barista commented that he was surprised Carl didn't float out of there after all the coffee he drank that night."

I shook my head. This wasn't making sense. "You're trying to tell me —"

"I believe Carl had something to do with Mary's sudden disappearance."

"Are you saying she's dead?"

He closed his eyes for a long moment. "After a few days we heard from her. She left. Went back home. Said she was giving up school for personal reasons — and not to contact her again. But you had to have known Mary to realize this was the last thing she would do. Attending the university was everything to her. She would never have gone without a fight. Something happened that night. I know it. But knowing something and proving it are two different things." Steve's eyes welled up. "Kids began calling her a dropout." Another expletive, this one under his breath. "She was carrying a four-point-oh on a full-ride scholarship. No way would she just drop out.

"All sorts of rumors started — ranging from her being gang-raped to having had a nervous breakdown." He blinked, and swallowed. "I never did find out the real story, but I knew Carl was behind it."

Aware that anecdotal stories didn't prove a person's guilt or innocence, I was hard-pressed to offer any consolation. But if Steve's suspicions were right, it certainly made it seem as though Carl Minkus was a poor choice for the NSA. "I don't know what to say." I also didn't know exactly how this impacted Minkus's death investigation.

"Here's the thing, Ollie," Steve said, his voice shaking. "I pushed it. I went after him. I told him I knew he'd done something to Mary."

"What did he say?"

"What do you think? He told me I was nuts because I had a crush on her and that I couldn't face the fact that the campus sweetheart had up and left us. He told me that she told him she'd met a guy the week before and she was considering running off with him. A biker. Yeah." Another bitter laugh. "But the school believed him."

"What about her family?"

"I called them, once, about a month later." Steve swallowed and I could tell it hurt. "Mary killed herself. This bright, wonderful girl had taken her own life. I couldn't believe it. Her father was angry I'd called and told me never to bother them again." He shrugged. "What could I do? I was a kid. There was no way to make the administration listen to me. And even if they didn't believe Mary dropped out on her own, they weren't going to give me the answers I wanted. It was all Carl's fault. One time, I grabbed him and told him I swore I'd see this through until we discovered the truth."

"What happened?"

Steve's eyes were bright red. "Nothing. But Carl — maybe he wasn't school smart — was street smart. He didn't give up anything that might point to him. And after a while I just couldn't do it anymore. I gave up. Eventually I discovered the culinary arts. I started working hard in my major. I didn't forget about Mary, but I just stopped pushing."

I patted his hand.

"You don't understand," he said, jerking away. "I got a great job out of college." He stared at me and spoke slowly. "A great job."

"That's good."

"No," he said. "I got it through Carl's father. He made sure I landed well. He made sure I had everything I needed." He shook his head. "He bought me off."

Suzie looked ready to cry. "I'm sure it was just coincidence."

Steve slammed the table with a fist. "No. It wasn't."

I sat back, unsure where to go from here.

Steve wiped his eyes. "I stopped looking for answers. I failed."

"I'm so sorry," I said.

"There's more," Suzie said.

I glanced at her, then back to Steve, who picked it up again. "Everything went quiet for a long time. We all worked hard, all graduated. Carl moved into bigger and bigger positions of power, and eventually got to his position at the NSA." Steve wagged a finger at me. "I always made it a point to keep up with his career. Just in case. I figured Carl forgot about me. Well, at least until Suzie and I got the TV show. Then, all of a sudden, we're stars." He smiled. "Small stars, but, you know, kinda well known."

I nodded.

"Out of the blue, Carl calls me. About a month ago, I think. Wasn't it?"

Suzie was biting her lip. She nodded.

"He starts out like we're old friends, but pretty soon he's gloating, saying that he remembers what his dad did for me all those years back. He tells me that he never had anything to do with Mary leaving school or killing herself, but he always resented the fact that I believed he did. And that's when he tells me that our positions had been reversed."

"What?" I was totally confused.

"He says that now that he's in charge of NSA investigations, he's going to take a look into my file and see if I've ever been involved in any terrorist activities."

My mouth opened. I didn't know how to respond to that.

Suzie spoke up. "We didn't know who the guests were going to be before we scheduled the White House shoot. If we had, I can tell you that we wouldn't have picked that particular day."

"I've never been involved in any terrorist activities," Steve said. "But my father was a salesman who traveled extensively to the Middle East. Minkus found that interesting. He said he was going to see me hang."

"Literally," Suzie said.

Steve fixed her a look. "Even if he didn't find me guilty of terrorism — and I don't know how he could — he could kill my career." To me, he added, "I think that's what his ultimate goal was. To see me ruined."

"That's a terrible story," I said.

"And that's why we think the NSA might be looking at us now that Minkus is dead," Suzie said. "We had a motive."

Steve stared at the table. "I say: Good riddance to bad rubbish."

"Wow." I knew it would be a while before I could take it all in.

"Don't tell your boyfriend, okay?" Steve asked. "I mean, just in case Minkus was bluffing. Maybe he wasn't looking at me at all. Maybe he was just playing mind games. He was always good at that."

"I don't know what to say."

"Please, just keep this to yourself," Suzie said. "For now. The news says they're working really hard on determining the cause of death. As soon as they figure out it wasn't something he ate" — she tapped on the DVD case — "and they see we didn't do anything to poison his meal, we should be okay. I don't think it would be in anyone's best interests to bring up all this old history."

I licked my lips, realizing that the feeling had come back to my tongue.

Now only my brain felt numb.

CHAPTER 14

On my way home, I called Bucky and told him I'd gotten a copy of the DVD. He and I made plans to go over it the next day and he said he'd call Cyan to include her as well. While I was on the phone, Tom beeped in, and I hung up with Bucky to take the call.

"Hey," I said. "Busy night, but I'm finally heading back. What time were you planning to stop by?"

"Ah . . ." he said. "Looks like plans have changed."

"You're not coming over?"

"No."

"But you mentioned that Craig wanted me to have a look at something. What about that?"

"Craig changed his mind."

"Do you want to stop by anyway?"

He hesitated.

"Forget I suggested it," I said. "Never mind."

"I just think it's best if we aren't seen together too much. At least until this investigation is over."

"Yeah, you said that before." What I wanted to say was that coming over to my apartment was hardly "being seen" together.

"Well," he said awkwardly. "I guess I'll talk to you later."

"Yeah," I said. But my heart wasn't in it.

When I finally made it to my apartment, I was completely worn out from the day's craziness. Voices — more than just those of my mom and nana — and the scent of fresh bakery met me as I unlocked the front door.

"Ollie, is that you?" Mom called.

I tossed my jacket to the side and put my keys in the front bowl. "Sorry I'm so late."

"You hungry?"

I was. After the story Steve had told, we were all so drained that Suzie had forgotten to give me my leftover steak. "What smells so good?"

Mrs. Wentworth, Stanley, and Nana were sitting at my kitchen table, all drinking coffee. Stanley stood up. "Here, you sit down."

I waved him back and poked my nose into the refrigerator.

"I made pork chops," Mom said. "With that topping you like. Want some?"

Having my mom here made me feel the

228

comfort of being a little girl again. She seemed to enjoy bustling about, and as I took a bite of her homemade pork chops, I thought nothing had ever tasted so wonderful. I must have made a noise of pure pleasure, because they all stopped and looked at me.

"Rough day?" Nana asked.

Mouth full, I nodded.

"The news is saying that the president won't be able to make it to Carl Minkus's memorial service," Mrs. Wentworth said. "They're having the wake tomorrow."

Stanley didn't like the fact that the president wasn't planning to attend services for a man who had died under his roof. "Not right," he said. "Sure, I know he's got a country to run, but would it kill him to take a few minutes out to pay his respects?"

None of us answered him. I took another bite.

"Your mother says you were visiting with the SizzleMasters," Mrs. Wentworth said. "How did that go? Do they have any idea what might have gone wrong at dinner?"

Stanley gave her a stern look. "Now you're making it sound like you know for sure that whatever killed Minkus came out of the kitchen. For all we know, he did himself in. He was in the NSA. Maybe he took one of those suicide pills."

Mrs. Wentworth raised a skeptical eyebrow.

"All's I'm saying is that we can't go jumping to conclusions or nothing. We have to wait until somebody finds the answers. Like Ollie here." He turned to me and smiled.

I looked away, but found Mrs. Wentworth staring at me the same way. "I think it's up to you now."

For the second time that night, I nearly spit my food out. This time, instead, I held a hand up in front of my mouth and chewed quickly. "What are you talking about?"

My two neighbors wore twin "Are you a simpleton?" looks on their faces. Mrs. Wentworth patted my hand. "Just do what you've done before. Try to figure out who did it. Before long, you'll have the whole thing solved. And you'll make the headlines again."

"I appreciate your faith in me," I began, "but I think that's exactly what the Secret Service *doesn't* want me to do."

Mrs. Wentworth snorted. "They're just jealous."

The sudden warmth that suffused me had nothing to do with the temperature of the room. It was something much more. I was home, fed, comfortable, and surrounded by family and neighbors who cared about my well-being. And, on top of that, they were convinced I would be able to figure out what the medical examiner, Secret Service, NSA, and other professionals could not. I patted her hand in return. It was nice to feel appreciated.

"Thanks."

Unfortunately, the warm and fuzzy feelings were short-lived. When my newspaper arrived the next morning, I spread it out on the kitchen table, and sucked in sudden panic when I turned to the *Liss Is More* column. Reading the first line reminded me — with the subtlety of a gut-punch — that I'd forgotten to revisit Liss's Web version yesterday to see what comment my mom had left. With the flurry of activity, the plethora of interruptions, and so much on my mind, I'd simply forgotten.

"Oh my God," I said.

Today Liss Is More says: "Thanks, Mom!"

Faithful readers will be interested to know that it seems this lowly column has touched a high-pressure nerve. We caught a live one yesterday. One of our

"Anonymous" submitters posted the following (reprinted in its entirety from the Web):

Dear Mr. Liss,
Your column only exists to appeal to the lowest, most base of human interests. Why would you suggest that those working in the White House kitchen might have had anything to do with Carl Minkus's death? Don't you have better things to do? Olivia Paras runs that kitchen with energy, pride, and dignity. It's your column and the garbage you and your followers spew that's keeping her from being able to return to her job. Stop blaming her for canceling the Easter Egg Roll. It's your fault. You, and people like you, only want to sell newspapers, rather than find the truth.

Sincerely,
An Angry Reader

My, my. Angry Reader indeed. She asks (and I use the pronoun "she" with confidence) if I have nothing better to do. Well, today I want to say, "Thanks, Mom," because after reading your letter, I did find something very interesting to do. I took a closer look at our country's executive chef and discovered that Ms. Paras's mother and grandmother are currently in town visiting their famous progeny. You, faithful readers, will recall that Olivia Paras has already made a name for herself (can you say "notorious"?) while in our nation's employ. Earlier this week, I broached the idea that Ms. Paras may have gotten bored and played Russian roulette with dinner with no thought to its disastrous consequences, but I gave up that idea after White House press agents suggested I lay off. Fair enough. But yesterday's entreaty by Ms. Paras's mother (and can there be any doubt who wrote that?) now urges me to take a closer look.

Does Ms. Paras care to tell us why she spent so much time meeting in secret with Suzie and Steve — the SizzleMasters — last night? After all, they, too, are under suspicion. Stay tuned, faithful readers. In coming days *Liss Is More* may have more to share about SizzleMaster Steve's history with the dead agent Minkus.

Let's all take this time to look up the word *collusion* in our respective dictionaries, shall we?

"Oh my God," I said again. What had she done?

"What's wrong?" Mom asked, coming in

to the kitchen, still in her nightgown.

I expelled a hot breath and had about one second to decide my next move. "Nothing," I said. I shut the paper.

"You look like you've gotten some terrible news, honey." Moving toward the countertop, she started to pour herself a cup of coffee.

"Why don't you shower first," I suggested. "I made that a while ago and it's probably stale. I'll make fresh."

She gave the pot a curious look. "There's plenty in there."

"Yeah, but it's a little weak." I grimaced, lifting my half-filled mug. "You and I both like it stronger. I'll put some of the weaker stuff in the carafe for Nana."

Mom didn't seem entirely convinced that I gave so much thought to our morning coffee, but she shrugged. "All right. I won't be long. What are we doing today, anyway?"

"I have to make a few phone calls," I said. That was an understatement. All I wanted at this moment was for her to leave so I could start damage control. "But I have a few ideas. We'll talk about it after your shower."

Finally, she left the room.

Tom answered on the first ring. "So meddling runs in the family, eh?"

"Oh my God," I said, for the third time. "What am I going to do?"

"*You* are going to do nothing at all," he said. He gave a short laugh, which I thought was inappropriate, given the circumstances. "I guess it's like they say: The apple doesn't fall far from the tree."

"What do you mean by that?"

"The next time I chastise you for getting involved in situations you should stay out of, just remind me it's in your DNA." He laughed again. "Your poor mom. I know she was just trying to help. How is she taking today's new twist?"

Nana came into the room. She helped herself to a cup of coffee.

"She hasn't seen it yet."

"Are you going to show it to her?"

Nana settled down across from me. She squinted over the top of her mug.

"I don't think so."

Tom made a noise. "Do you think that's best?"

I had no idea what was best. I had no idea which way was up at the moment. I said so.

"Listen," Tom said, using his serious voice. "This Liss character is nothing more than a pain in the ass. Don't give him another thought, okay? You got that? People read his column for entertainment, not for news. By next week, they'll have forgotten all of this."

"Not if the Egg Roll is canceled." I was morose and felt like spreading it around. "Then nobody will ever forget. When was the last time they canceled an Egg Roll?" I asked. "I mean, except for weather, or world wars?"

"Ollie." Still the serious tone.

"Liss paints me as a lunatic chef who would risk her guests' safety for another shot in the limelight. Doesn't he understand how much I hate making the front page?" My voice had gone up. Turning my ear toward the hallway, I relaxed when I realized the shower was still running. Nana continued to stare at me, her eyebrows tight.

"Okay," Tom said, more soothingly than I had any right to expect. "Let's just take this slowly. I suggest you ignore Liss. He's the least of your worries right now."

I groaned.

"You called me for a reason," he prompted.

"I have a copy of the DVD from Suzie and Steve," I said. "They gave it to me."

Instead of being pleased, he got angry. "You couldn't get a copy from me, so you went out and got one on your own? Ollie, what did I ask you about staying out of this investigation?"

"That's why I'm telling you. They want me to go over it — heck, they want *you* to go over it — because they believe it will prove that no one in the kitchen could have done anything to Minkus's food."

"First of all . . ." I sensed a lecture coming on. "We aren't going to be able to tell anything from the recording. Give me a break. How would any of us watching know whether that was salt — or arsenic — someone is adding to a dish?"

"Don't you think the fact that we're all willing to make the DVD public is proof of innocence?"

"Hardly proof. No matter how much you, or the SizzleMasters, want to get involved, nothing you say or do will be of any help right now. This death has to be investigated step by step. All options will be kept open until we're able to eliminate —"

"Listen," I said, interrupting him. "There's a reason Suzie and Steve want you to see the DVD."

A heartbeat of silence, then, "A reason."

"I can't tell you what it is, but I —"

"Ollie."

"Trust me here, okay?"

I heard him give an exasperated sigh. "I asked you not to get involved."

I said nothing.

Tom broke the silence. "What did Suzie and Steve tell you?"

Although I wanted to honor Steve's request to keep the information about Mary and her history with Minkus to myself, Liss's column today intimated that it wouldn't be long before the whole world knew. "They told me something in confidence," I began. "They specifically asked me not to tell you about it."

"And you don't find *that* suspicious?"

"I would, except I know what they're keeping to themselves. Everyone has secrets, Tom."

Another exasperated sigh. "You just can't stay out of things, can you?"

"You told me to go about my business like normal. You told me it was fine to keep in touch with my friends. These are my friends," I said. My voice had gone up again, just as I heard the shower turn off. Nana still listened.

"These are my friends," I said again, more quietly. "And if I have to, I will tell you the story they told me. I don't believe they could have done anything to Carl Minkus, but I do believe there are other reasons they might come under scrutiny."

Sounds came through the receiver that made me believe Tom was scratching his face. "So what am I supposed to do?"

"For one, you can appreciate that I'm keeping you updated on all this, just like you asked me to," I said with a little snap. "I'm not getting involved, but as information comes to me I'm sharing it with you. I think that's fair."

He didn't comment.

"I'm going to take a look at this DVD," I said. "I'll have Bucky and Cyan take a look at it, too. If we see anything weird, I'll tell you immediately."

"Ollie," Tom said gently, "if anyone in that kitchen had intended to kill Carl Minkus, don't you think they would have made sure to do it off-camera?"

Frustration worked its way into my voice. "What am I supposed to do? Just sit on my hands until that medical examiner finally gets off his duff and tells the world it wasn't my fault? This is my career we're talking about."

"I know," he said. "And you know I can't share information with you. What I can tell you is that we're working around the clock to get this thing settled. The best advice I can give you right now is to find something to keep you busy. To take your mind off of the problems."

I blew a raspberry into the phone.

"I understand this isn't easy. Use this time off as a gift. You've got your mother and grandmother there keeping you company. I suggest you enjoy your time with them."

When we hung up, Nana's mouth twisted sideways. "Who hasn't seen what?" she asked.

Hoping my mom was still busy in the bathroom for a few more minutes, I opened the page to Liss's article and turned it to face Nana. I let her read a little bit before explaining, "Mom sent in a comment to his website yesterday. I don't think she realized what a Pandora's box she would open."

Nana put a finger on the paper to hold her spot. "What does Tom say about this?"

"He wants me to ignore it. Pretend it doesn't exist."

Nana kept reading.

I stood and began pacing the small kitchen, thinking about how Bucky's space was so much more the sort of kitchen I should have at home. Quick pang of jealousy. Why was it that when things were bad, suddenly *everything* seemed negative? Why did my tiny kitchen bother me today? It had never bothered me before. But I'd never been served up on a silver platter before, the way Liss was doing — with my mother's help. "How can I ignore that when he's clearly skewering me? I mean, this is personal!"

"What's personal?" Mom asked, as she came into the kitchen. Her hair was still wet, but she was dressed and made up.

Nana answered before I could. "That damn medical examiner."

She gave me a look that warned me not to contradict.

"Why?" Mom asked, making her way around the table to read over Nana's shoulder. "Did he say something more in the paper today?"

As unflappably as anything, Nana turned the page before Mom could see Liss's article. "No, there's nothing in here today about that. We were just talking about Ollie not getting back into the kitchen yet."

Mom gave me a funny look when she noticed the coffee hadn't changed. "I thought you were going to make fresh."

I apologized. "I wound up talking with Tom for quite a while. Sorry. I'll make some now."

She waved me away. "Don't worry about it."

Nana and I shared a conspiratorial look. She pushed herself up from the table, and tucked the newspaper under her arm. "I guess I'll get in the bathroom next."

Mom pointed. "I haven't read that yet."

Nana unfolded the paper, and dropped a few sections back onto the table. "Here's the weather, the fun stuff . . ." She rattled off a few more. "You're lucky I feel generous today," she said with a wink. "Usually if you snooze, you lose."

My mom rolled her eyes good-naturedly, and didn't seem to notice at all that Nana had tucked the front-page section back under her arm.

I did a few morning chores, checked my e-mail, then called Bucky and Cyan.

Mom and Nana were at the kitchen table looking ready to go, when I approached them with an idea. "How about you two come with me to Bucky's place?"

At their confused, expectant looks, I explained.

"First of all, I really wanted you to meet my team, and although this isn't the most optimal of circumstances, I think it could work."

"You've got a funny glimmer in your eye," Nana said.

I pointed to her. "That's because I want to put you both to work. Bucky, Cyan, and I are convinced that Paul Vasquez — he's our chief usher and in charge of just about everything at the White House — will eventually tell us that the Egg Roll is back on. I want to get started on boiling eggs."

"Should you do that?" Mom asked. "Until the medical examiner —"

"This isn't that *CSI* TV show. It may be months until we get a definitive answer." I shuddered at that thought. "I just have to do something. I mean, if the Egg Roll is canceled then we're stuck with a roomful of eggs. I get that. But what if they decide that the event will go on after all? What if they decide that on Sunday afternoon? Then what? We'll never get enough eggs boiled in that amount of time."

Nana said. "I'm up for it."

Mom nodded. "Me, too."

"Good. Bucky's expecting us there later this morning. If we work all afternoon, we can still quit in time to come back here and change before going to Minkus's wake tonight." The idea of going in there by myself was unpleasant at best. And if my family was with me, I figured I could make a polite and fairly quick exit after paying my respects. "You are both planning to come with me, aren't you?"

My mom's face went red. "Of course. I wouldn't want you going alone."

Nana laughed at her. "And you wouldn't want to miss the opportunity to pay your respects to — or should I say flirt with — Kap, would you?"

Darn. I'd forgotten about him.

"At a wake?" my mom asked with a touch of indignance. "I wouldn't do anything like that."

I could have kicked myself for forgetting about Kap. "I can go alone."

"No," Mom said, too quickly. "We wouldn't want you to have to face those Minkuses on your own, honey."

I swallowed my reply.

CHAPTER 15

Cyan pulled me to the side moments after we'd arrived at Bucky's. "Did you *see* this place?" she asked gesturing around the rooms with her eyes. "It's gorgeous. I don't know what I expected, but it sure wasn't this."

Bucky was still near the front door, hanging up coats, making small talk with my family.

"I know what you mean. I was here the other day for the first time — which is why I knew his place was perfect for our project. But" — I ran my hand along the living room sofa again — "purple suede?"

"Is he married?"

We were still talking in whispers. "I asked. He said, 'Not yet.' "

"Lots of work ahead of us today," Bucky said, clapping his hands together. He seemed unnaturally cheerful, and completely at ease with the four of us just hanging out at his house. "Let's get started."

Again, he was dressed in shorts, with an apron over. He ushered us all into the back of the house and his expansive kitchen. Mom and Nana exclaimed delight when they stepped into the bright, professionally appointed space. Cyan's mouth dropped and she turned in a slow circle, taking it all in. "Wow," she said. "If they ever decide to renovate the White House kitchen, I think you should design it."

Bucky glanced at me quickly — almost as though he was fearful that I would take Cyan's comment as a slam against me. "Yeah," I agreed. "Bucky, if they ever give us the money to redesign the kitchen, you're the man. I can't imagine anyone doing it better."

He gave a half smile, which was an odd sight. It didn't last long. He clapped his hands again. Bucky was ready to work, and in this domain, he was clearly the boss.

"I arranged for the eggs to be delivered here," he said.

Cyan had opened his super-sized refrigerator and turned to us with a pained look on her face. "This is nowhere near enough." she said. "Looks like maybe ten dozen or so."

My stomach dropped. Bucky had assured

me he could handle the egg acquisition, and I'd trusted him to do so, without any double-checking. Bucky shook his head. "The rest are downstairs," he said. "I'll show you."

Nana opted to stay on the main level, but the rest of us traipsed down the steps into the dungeon-like cellar. "Wow," Cyan said, her voice echoing off the stone walls. "It's cold down here."

At the head of our little troupe, Bucky turned. "Exactly," he said. "I keep it at about thirty-six degrees." He opened a heavy door and pointed to a thermometer inside. Flicking on the light, he kept talking, even as the rest of us gasped. "Here we are."

He wasn't kidding. There were eggs . . . everywhere.

"This is almost as big as our storage at the White House," Cyan said in awe. "You could start your own banquet business out of your house."

Bucky winced. I wondered if his fears about our losing our White House positions were working on him. He stepped forward and rested his hand on one of many stain- less steel carts filled, top to bottom, with fresh eggs.

"I talked with our friends at the American Egg Board," he said. "They're sympathetic to the situation and after a little coaxing, they agreed to let me hold on to these for transport." He turned to me. "But I had to promise that they'd get them back as soon as the Egg Roll was over."

"No problem," I said. "Bucky, you're a miracle worker."

Again, the half smile. "Have you talked with Paul recently?"

"I called him just before we left," I said. "No updates yet."

"So, we could be doing all this work for nothing?"

"We could."

Bucky nodded. "Well, you're the boss."

"And I think this is a great idea," Cyan said. "It sure beats staying home waiting for the phone to ring. At least we're doing something."

Upstairs, we settled ourselves into an assembly line of sorts. We estimated we had approximately six thousand eggs on site. "That's a great start," I said. "If we can get these done, then maybe in the next few days we'll be able to pick up the rest, and by the time Monday rolls around, we'll be all set."

Cyan and I were the runners. We went up and down Bucky's back stone steps, carrying large square crates of eggs. Mom and Nana made sure to gently place each and every one into giant pots of cold water, easing them in to prevent cracking.

Once the eggs were boiled, Bucky ran them under cold water, then dried and placed them back into their cradles. "Why do you bother to dry them off?" Nana asked. "I never do that. The heat makes the water evaporate."

He pointed into one of the crates. "If they're not dry, they tend to drip and then the eggs sit in little puddles of water." He shook his head. "I don't like that."

"But when we dye them, they'll just get wet again." Nana said.

"And I'll dry them again," he said patiently. The caustic, angry Bucky we knew from our White House kitchen was surprisingly gentle with my mom and nana. "You see, if we let them sit in the crates wet" — he wadded up a cloth and dipped it into one of the egg holders — "we would have to then go in one by one and dry these spaces out. If we don't, we'll wind up with little round water spots at the base of every colored egg." He wrinkled his nose. "Not nice."

While each new batch of eggs boiled, Nana, Mom, Cyan, and I took each and every dried egg by hand, and dipped them into vivid pinks, blues, greens, and yellows.

Eggs, eggs, and more eggs. I was going to dream about eggs tonight. After so many hours surrounded by steam, heat, dripping dye, and eggy smells, I started feeling just a little bit punchy.

"Hey Bucky," I said. "You did an *eggcellent* job of getting all this together."

He rolled his eyes. Cyan laughed.

Mom said, "Relax. It's just a *yolk*."

Nana held up a pink-dyed egg. She giggled. "Isn't this an *eggsquisite* color?"

This time we all groaned.

Bucky glanced up at the clock for about the third time in as many minutes. Cyan noticed, too. She and I exchanged a look.

He turned to us. "How many more eggs are left downstairs?"

Cyan stood. "I'll go check."

"No," he said quickly. "No, that's okay. I just was wondering."

Again he checked the wall clock.

"Are you *eggspecting* someone?" Cyan asked.

While the rest of us smiled at her attempt, Bucky frowned. He wiped his hands on his apron. "I think we should start wrapping up for today, don't you?" Without waiting for an answer, he poured out the boiling water, even though the eggs still had another minute to cook. "It's getting late and I know you wanted me to take a look at that DVD tonight. You made me a copy, right?"

"I thought . . ." I gestured to encompass myself and Cyan, "We were all planning to watch it together."

"I lost track of time," he said without apology. "Did you make an extra copy? Can you leave it with me? I'll get to it tonight."

"No, I didn't," I said, bewildered. "I didn't think we'd need any extras." Mom and Nana stood and started to clean up.

"No, no," Bucky said, stopping them. "I'll take care of it."

"You're acting a little weird all of a sudden," I said.

"Is it so strange to have another commitment?" he asked, the old crustiness back in place. "I told you I lost track of time and I'd rather not . . ."

Bumping sounds from the back of the house silenced us all. There was the unmistakable sound of a door opening, closing, and of footsteps coming up the back way. I turned to Bucky. He looked miserable.

A clear voice called out, "Buck?" Female voice. Slightly familiar. "Can you give me a hand?"

He'd gone red in the face. "Hang on," he called, then bolted for the back door.

We heard low conversation, all of us leaning closer to the door to hear better. They weren't having an argument, but Bucky's lower-timbered voice sounded terse. A moment later he came through the door carrying two eco-friendly shopping bags jammed with groceries, wearing a look of resigned indignation.

He stopped in the doorway and I got the impression that he intended to stay there, blocking our view. "Buck," the voice said, from behind him. "Can I get through?"

She was tall, with clear Irish skin, long red hair, and a smile as wide as the Potomac. Recognition kicked in a half-second later. "Brandy?" I said.

She placed the bags she carried on the nearest open countertop and came over to greet me. "How are you, Ollie?" With a glance around the kitchen, she said, "Looks like you've gotten a lot done today." Long-limbed and bright-eyed, she always wore an aura of confidence that allowed her to carry off such an unusual moniker.

Mom and Nana were looking at me, mildly perplexed. Cyan was wide-eyed. "Brandy," she said. "How are things going?"

I introduced my family, relying on my autopilot politeness to carry me through. When Cyan and I exchanged a glance a moment later, Brandy caught it. "Yeah," she said, tossing her head back in a laugh, "I'm the big secret." She held up her fingers to make air-quotation marks, then pointed at the back door. "Can you believe he was trying to convince me to tell you I was just making a delivery?" She laughed again. "Sorry, honey," she said, kissing him on the cheek. Even though he was obviously uncomfortable, he didn't seem entirely displeased by her display of affection.

Brandy had been our liaison to the Egg Board for as long as I'd been working at the White House. She was great. "How long have you two . . ." I gestured to encompass the house.

She glanced at Bucky, whose lips were tight. Then she winked at me. "Long time."

Inwardly, I groaned. I think I'd actually tried to set her up with another White House staffer some time ago.

Little had I known. About Brandy — about my colleague Bucky. To me, he'd always been a crochety older guy, brilliant in the kitchen, but difficult to deal with. Brandy was about five to seven years older than I was, and suddenly, next to her, Bucky seemed much younger. Talk about a paradigm shift.

"Hey," I said in delayed realization. "No wonder you were able to get all these eggs delivered here."

Brandy flung a grin at me. "It pays to have friends in helpful places."

"Eggsactly!" I said.

Mom and Nana were confused, but rolling with the punches. The same couldn't be said for Cyan. "You mean," she said, "all this time we've been working together, you two have been able to keep a secret relationship going?"

Bucky made a face, then turned his back to us. "Better than some people."

I felt my face redden. Brandy patted Bucky on the shoulder as she passed him to get to the fridge. "How is your handsome Secret Service boyfriend?" she asked.

I shook my head. "Minkus's death makes things a little rocky."

Brandy wrinkled her nose. "Yeah, I can imagine. Tough times. But Tom's a great guy. You'll be fine."

I nodded, not entirely sure I believed her — and at the same time amazed that she even knew that Tom and I were together.

Bucky had stopped cleaning up. "Seeing as how we're all here now, we might as well finish the job."

"Is anybody hungry? I can order in." Brandy asked. "I would offer to whip up something — heck, I've got plenty of groceries — but the fact that I've got not one, but three chefs here, is a little intimidating."

I was about to demur, but Bucky mentioned an ethnic carry-out place he liked. "If we have something delivered, we'll all be able to check out that DVD."

For about the fifth time that day, Bucky made my jaw drop.

Two hours later, we had gotten more eggs boiled, the kitchen cleaned, and the DVD started. Bucky maintained control of the remote and we fell into a rhythm of watching, then stopping, then discussing, all aspects of the dinner preparation.

Nana, on the purple couch next to my mom, had fallen asleep shortly after Bucky hit "Play" for the first time.

"This is all great," I said, when we'd finished dissecting our performances and had restarted the tape from the beginning, "but the camera people were more concerned about angles. Look." I pointed toward the screen, where Suzie was arranging salad greens on a plate. "Even though there are a bunch of cameras rolling, most of the angles are artsy, keeping focus on the plated food and our faces. All the busy preparation is going on in the background. There's no way to see if anyone dropped something into Minkus's food."

Bucky, looking thoughtful, pointed the remote at the television, but didn't press any buttons. Cyan stared at the screen as though waiting for it to tell her something. Brandy asked my mother if she'd like more iced tea.

"Maybe," Bucky said, "we should be looking at who's staying off-camera."

Together we accounted for everyone in the kitchen staff, including Suzie and Steve. Occasionally someone left the room — to get something from storage, or from the refrigerators, or for any number of reasons. With everyone in constant motion, there was no way to determine any unnecessary off-camera forays. Even after studying the outtakes.

"If there was anything in Minkus's food, I doubt it was in the salad," I said. "Everyone had that. Same with a few of the sides, and dessert. It had to be the entrée. Otherwise there would have been too much chance that he didn't get the right one."

As soon as the words left my mouth, I sat up.

"You don't think that maybe it was the salad — or the dessert — and it was meant for someone else?" Cyan asked.

The thought was too terrible to contemplate. Had someone targeted President Campbell and missed? I shook my head. "Let's not get crazy here. Let's just deal with what we know."

"We know squat," Bucky said.

Mom and Brandy got up and went into the kitchen. After another five minutes of futile food-prep-watching, I took a look at my watch and realized we were running much later than I'd expected. "I have to go to Minkus's wake tonight," I said, standing.

Cyan and Bucky both said, "What?" so quickly, it startled Nana awake.

I gave them the lowdown on Ruth Minkus's phone call.

"That's a little odd," Cyan said.

Mom was still out of the room, so I lowered my voice. "Not when you understand the back story." I told her about Kap and about his efforts to smooth things over between Ruth Minkus and me. "Probably just because he's attracted to my mom."

Nana had roused herself enough to add, "He sure doesn't try to hide it."

"So, you're actually going to the wake?" Cyan asked disbelievingly.

"I hate those things," Bucky said.

I gave him a look. "Like anyone enjoys them."

I had no desire to visit a funeral home

tonight, but I hardly felt able to refuse. Ruth had asked me to come. And though I barely knew the woman, I had to believe she would not have taken the time to call me if she hadn't felt compelled to. Who's to say how different people deal with grief? Maybe I represented closure for her.

After stopping back at my apartment to shower off the day's egg smell and to change into appropriate clothing, my family and I drove to the funeral home in a Maryland suburb.

"Don't they usually have services in the Capitol for big shots like Minkus?" Nana asked.

I smiled at her in my rearview mirror. "I think they save that honor for presidents," I said. "Besides, this place is probably near the Minkus home. I'm sure Ruth made the final decision on where her husband would be waked."

"Took them long enough," Nana said with a sniff.

"They had to wait for the autopsy," I said. My heart did that speed-beat thing it always did when I thought about how much my career hung on the medical examiner's findings. I knew things moved a lot more slowly than they did on television, but it had already been four days.

My mom was riding shotgun and was staring out at the scenery as we drove. "You okay?" I asked.

She had been twisting the rings on her fingers. "Fine, fine."

I waited.

"I was just thinking about your dad."

"Still miss him?" I asked.

"Every day."

CHAPTER 16

Ruth Minkus had chosen this funeral home with care. The parking lot was expansive, and the venue stately. I offered to drop Nana off under the huge canopy-covered entrance, but she snapped good-naturedly, "What, are you saying I'm too old to walk?"

I shook my head and parked in one of the last available spots, about a half block from the front door. We walked past dozens of dark government-issue sedans and shiny, expensive imports, my pumps making lonely taps on the sidewalk. Outside, people mingled. Men and women in business suits stood around in small groups. A few of them smoked, and all of them looked up to see who was arriving. Just as quickly, they returned to their conversations, dismissing us as unimportant. I was okay with that. People didn't often recognize me without my tunic and toque. Tonight, I was grateful for the measure of anonymity.

There had to be a hundred floral pieces in the chapel, all sadly bright and all giving off that peculiar scent that let you know you were at a funeral, even if you were blindfolded. The newspaper obituary had requested donations to charity in lieu of flowers, but apparently lots of mourners didn't get that memo. Either that, or this was yet another place where even politics didn't die. An impressive floral arrangement might not provide the family much solace, but it had the potential to say a lot about the generosity of the giver.

Well-dressed individuals waited in line to pay their respects to Ruth and Joel Minkus — there were at least fifty people in front of us. As we inched forward, I took the opportunity to read the cards on some of the floral sprays. Two huge red, white, and blue arrangements with gold ribbons flanked the casket. My mom raised her eyebrows, obviously impressed. "Those are probably from the White House," I said. Then, "Hey, look at this."

They leaned close. "It's from his health club." The three of us exchanged a look of amazement. "Geez, when a big shot dies, everybody sends flowers, huh?"

Over the course of the next ten minutes, we read all the other gift cards within our reach, but we hadn't moved more than a few feet.

"Maybe we can just sign the book and leave?" I suggested.

If my mom had been hoping to see Kap tonight, she clearly was dissuaded by the press of the crowd. "Maybe that would be best."

Nana was scanning the room, eyes sharp. "Where's the shrine?" she asked.

We both looked at her.

"You know — the poster board with pictures of Minkus. Milestones. Birth, marriage, vacations, his kid being born and growing up." She made a 360-degree turn, twisting, as she did, to peer around the gathered family and friends.

I pointed to a table on the room's far left where a silver-framed computer monitor stood. "No homemade poster," I said. "Nowadays people opt for a digital display."

She fixed me with a skeptical look. "You mean the family doesn't sit around and laugh and talk and cry as they make the posters and remember all the good times together?"

"Sure they do," I said. "But now, instead of messing up the original photographs with tape or glue, the funeral home scans them and presents them as a slide show."

"This I gotta see," she said. And she was off.

"Don't they have those in Chicago?" I asked Mom.

She shrugged. "Maybe the rich folks do."

I guided her out of line and sought out the line for the guest book. "With this crowd, Ruth Minkus wouldn't have even noticed us. I'm sorry to have pulled you and Nana out for this."

"Don't worry about it, honey. I'm just happy I raised a girl who does things right. I'm proud of you for coming here even though you didn't feel like it."

"Olivia Paras?"

I turned. A short gentleman extended his hand to me. Like all the other men here, he was wearing a suit, but unlike the other mourners, he wore a smile. "I'm very glad to make your acquaintance," he said. "I'm Phil Cooper. This is my wife, Francine."

I shook his hand and that of the knockout blonde woman next to him.

"I'm very sorry for all the trouble since Sunday's dinner," he said. "And, if I may say so without sounding crass, I truly enjoyed the meal you prepared for us." He gave a self-conscious shrug. "I was enjoying the entire evening up until . . . well . . ."

He turned toward the casket for emphasis.

He didn't need to do that. We all knew what he meant.

"Thank you," I said, not entirely certain that was the proper response.

Francine sidled up to her husband and tucked her hand through his arm. "It really was a wonderful meal," she said. "It was my first time visiting the White House — you know, as a guest. Can you believe it? I've lived here in D.C. my whole life, but I've only done the normal tours. I was so excited when Phil and I got invited." Her face was pink with animation and she smiled much more brilliantly than one should at a funeral home — no matter what the circumstances. "I had such a nice time. It's unbelievable."

"Thank you," I said again, this time wondering what, exactly, she meant by "unbelievable." Dinner at the White House or the fact that her husband's boss had dropped dead after the meal? Nodding acknowledgment, I searched for an excuse to step away. I was near enough to the end of the guest book line, so I stepped in, hoping it would move quickly and we could get out of there.

Phil stepped a little closer to me, speaking quietly. I had to strain to hear him over the din of conversation surrounding us. "Have you heard anything more about what happened that night?"

I shook my head, thinking it was an odd question for a security agent to be asking the executive chef. "Have you?"

"Not much," he said, glancing around. I got the impression he was making sure no one could overhear us. "What's happening with the Egg Roll Monday? And what about your staff? Any idea when you might be cleared?"

Since when did federal agents care about the kitchen staff? "We're still waiting for word."

The conversation was beginning to sound like something from a bad spy movie. It got worse when Cooper gestured with his eyes. "Look who's here."

I glanced over to the corner, near the back, where an elderly man hunched over his cane. "Who is he?"

"You don't recognize him?"

I looked again. "No."

Cooper came closer, so that he and I were now facing the same direction. His wife had disengaged herself from his arm and was now talking with my mom. "That's Howard Liss."

Instinctively I gasped, resisting the overwhelming urge to march over and tell him off. Not good form at a wake. "What's he doing here?"

"He likes to 'immerse himself' in his stories. At least that's his claim. Personally, I see him as a vulture, circling and hoping for some new tidbit to exploit." Cooper winked at me. "I just wanted to let you know because you seem to be on his radar lately."

"Thanks."

"Rumor has it he's targeting me next."

"Where did you hear that?"

Cooper didn't answer. "It was very nice to meet you, Ms. Paras. I wish you the best of luck."

He left as Nana returned.

When we finally made it to the front of the book line, I wrote my name and address and then turned away to allow the next person access. "Aren't you going to take a holy card?" Nana asked.

"No."

"Hmph," she said, as she reached in to snag one for herself. "I'll take it then."

"I think we can sneak out now," I said, speaking quietly. I told them both what Phil Cooper had told me. The three of us stole peeks at Howard Liss.

"He looks like a bad person," Mom said. "I can tell these things."

I thought he looked rather benign. I don't

know what I expected, but it wasn't a slim, white-haired, distinguished fellow leaning on a carved cane. His photo in the newspaper must be at least a decade old, I decided. Instead of a hard-hitting reporter who may or may not twist the facts to suit his journalistic fancy, this guy looked like a college professor. Somebody who taught economics, maybe. Or philosophy. And definitely nearing retirement.

"Let's get out of here before he sees us," I said.

We had just made it to the chapel doorway when we stopped short.

"Corinne!" Kap said with a bit too much pleasure for my tastes.

My mother said, "Kap!" with about the same expression.

"I'm so happy you were able to make it," he said. Turning to me, he squinted. "How was Ruth to you tonight? Did she seem better?"

"Ah," I said, hedging. "We didn't get a chance to talk with Ruth one-on-one." I gestured vaguely in the direction of the casket and the crowd of people surrounding it. It dawned on me that I hadn't even gotten a glimpse of the deceased. "The line is so long . . ."

"We can't have that," he said. Taking my

mother by the arm, he smiled down at me. "It's so hard for Ruth to talk to everyone she intended to. She would be very upset if you left."

"I don't want to bother —"

"No bother at all." He leaned down to speak close to my ear. "As a matter of fact, Ruth wants to ask you something."

The skepticism must have shown on my face, because he was quick to add, "I don't know what it is. She seems to be pushing for answers when there are none."

"I hope there are answers soon," I said, my impatience with being trapped at this funeral parlor with no clear means of escape showing through. "I don't blame her a bit. As soon as they vindicate the kitchen, I'll be able to get back to work."

Kap's reaction surprised me. "They haven't allowed you back yet?"

This was in the news almost daily. I wanted to ask the man if he lived in a cave, but politeness won out. "No. Not until the medical examiner clears us."

Howard Liss had sidled up to us and had heard most of our conversation. "Hello," he said. "You're Olivia Paras, aren't you? I'm —"

"I know who you are."

He didn't extend his hand. Thank goodness, because I would have refused to shake it. He tilted his head with a sly smile. "I see you've been reading my column."

"Yes," I said. "And I suppose I have you to thank for all my time off."

"That's one way to look at it." His eyes lasered in on mine, like Arnold Schwarzenegger's in the first *Terminator* movie. "You haven't gotten word that you're allowed back in the kitchen yet?"

"No," I said, keeping my voice light. "But if we were to be allowed back in, I'm sure you'd be the first to know."

His mouth twitched. Like he was enjoying this.

Which meant it was time for me to leave. "If you'll excuse us," I began.

"And you must be Olivia's mother," Liss asked, ignoring me and turning to my mom. "A pleasure."

I touched her arm. "Mom. Let's go."

Kap insinuated himself between them. "Why are you here, anyway?" he asked Liss.

They were about the same age. Both tall and white-haired. But where Liss had a cane, and the milky-white complexion of a man who spent his sunshine in front of a glowing computer screen, Kap was olive-complected, fit, and muscular. He looked like a poster boy for Viagra commercials.

Liss pulled himself up to full height, which was about an inch shorter than Kap's. "I was going to ask Ms. Paras the exact same thing." Again, the laser eyes. "I don't understand," he said, then a corner of his mouth curled up. "What is your connection to the deceased?" he asked. "Other than the fact that you fed him his final meal?"

Tiny Nana, with her big heart — and suddenly loud voice — thrust her holy card into Liss's hand. "You know what this means? You are at a wake, mister. If you can't behave properly, I think maybe you should go home."

People around us began to take notice.

Liss smiled down at the card in his hand. He pointed to Minkus's death date on the back of the picture of Saint George. "See this?" he asked. Without waiting for us to answer, he said, "This isn't right. Carl Minkus wasn't destined to die on *this* date." He shook his head. "And if you had anything to do with it, Ms. Paras, the world needs to know that."

My mom muttered, "You're despicable."

"Maybe so," he said. "But it's people like you who read my column." He smiled. "And when you respond so predictably, you keep me comfortably employed."

Much to my dismay, Ruth Minkus spotted us talking with Liss. She immediately made her way over to us, Joel at her side.

I desperately wanted to run.

"Olivia," she said, as she drew closer. "How kind of you to come."

If she recognized Liss, she didn't show it. She didn't even acknowledge Kap.

I took Ruth Minkus's hand. "I'm sorry."

Biting her lip, she looked away. Liss's eyes narrowed and his gaze bounced among us all. I released Mrs. Minkus's hand, expressed my condolences to Joel, then turned my body to exclude Liss from the group. Mom and Nana came in around me, and Kap followed, effectively closing Liss off from our conversation. "I don't want to keep you from your guests," I said to Ruth.

She glanced toward Kap, fixing him with a cool stare. "Would you mind? I need a moment alone with Olivia."

My mind screamed, *"No!"* I wished we had never come to this thing, no matter how much Ruth had entreated. "We really should be going."

Ruth turned to Joel, who seemed torn. "Go mingle," she said, giving his arm a little shove. "Your father would want you to talk to everyone here. To thank them."

Reluctant to leave his mother, he tried to argue.

"I'm fine right now," she said. "And this is important. Go on."

Joel left.

I wasn't keen on leaving my mother in Kap's clutches, but she was a savvy, grown woman. There wasn't much I could — or should — do to stop her. Plus, Nana was with her. I wondered for a moment if this was how parents felt when their children started dating: worried, protective, unwilling to let go. I blew out a breath and followed Ruth to the far left of the room. We were near the digital display where the slideshow of Carl Minkus photos played. The current shot was one of him in uniform.

Ruth's eyes clenched shut and she looked away.

This side of the room had at least as many — if not more — floral arrangements than the other side had. I tried not to breathe in the sickeningly sweet scent as I read the gift cards in an effort to give Ruth a chance to compose herself. After a moment, she spoke. "I really have to get back to greet everyone who came here." Her eyes widened and she again looked ready to cry. "But I needed to ask you something."

"Of course."

In the space of the seconds it took for her to speak again, I wondered what was hardwired into our brains that prompted us to forgive transgressions and promise co-operation to those who grieved. Ruth Minkus had been horribly rude to me not two days earlier. And yet, here I was.

"I read Mr. Liss's column," she began. "And I know you're friends with Suzie and Steve."

I waited.

She blinked a few times. "There was something about Steve my husband didn't care for."

I still waited.

"Do you . . . that is, would you have any idea what the bad blood is between them?"

Time for my best defense — deflection. "What makes you believe there was bad blood between them?"

Her eyes were glazed as though reflecting on old memories. Whatever she found there made her mouth tighten. "Carl wouldn't tell me. And I knew better than to press." Blinking again, she stared at the front of the room, where her husband lay in repose. I knew she couldn't see him through the throng, but her breaths became short and shallow. Looking away, she suppressed a shudder. "If I would have known the Sizzle-Masters were in the kitchen that day . . ."

"You don't really believe that they could

have had anything to do with your husband's death?"

Ruth Minkus's face flushed and I could see how much of a toll this conversation was having on her. Her entire body trembled. "Did they say anything to you? Did they do anything suspicious the day of the dinner?" She put both hands on my forearm. "Please, if you can think of anything that can help me make this go away, please do."

My logical brain wanted to tell her that nothing would make this sorrow go away except time, but I knew that victims, and families of victims, sometimes needed closure in order to begin the grieving process. With the suddenness of Minkus's death, Ruth needed anything she could to help her hold on. That's what she was searching for. I couldn't blame her.

"I'll do what I can. But right now, you probably have to get back."

She nodded. "Thank you for coming, Olivia. May I call you Ollie?"

"Sure," I said. Unable to resist my natural impulse, I again took her hand. "If there's anything I can do, please let me know."

We hadn't gotten a half block away from the funeral home when Nana piped up from the back seat. "Odd," she said.

I glanced at her through the rearview mirror to see her staring out the side window, with a look of concentration. Like she was trying to work something out in her head.

My mom twisted in her seat. "What's odd?"

"The photos on that digital whatchamawhoozis."

Relieved to be away from the place, and finding her choice of words humorous, I smiled. "What was wrong with them?"

Nana shook her head. "Not 'wrong' exactly." She made a face. "Just incomplete, somehow."

I hadn't spent much time checking out the digital display, and had only caught that one quick glimpse of Minkus in uniform.

"I mean," Nana continued, "when I go to these wakes, I always see pictures from the person's childhood — and college pictures — and wedding pictures." She resumed looking out the window. "The only pictures here were recent ones. Or political ones. I mean, I think there were three different shots of him with presidents."

"Maybe that's what Carl Minkus would have wanted," Mom said.

I nodded. "I'm sure it is. He was climbing the ladder, no two ways about it."

"By making enemies along the way."

I glanced again at Nana in the backseat. She was thinking about Joe McCarthy, I could tell.

"Who was that big military guy with all the medals on his uniform?" she asked.

There had to have been a dozen well-decorated military types in attendance. "Which one?"

She described him well enough for me to recognize. "General Brighton. He's another big hot shot," I said. "Why?"

"He was talking with your boyfriend."

"What?" I asked. "Tom was there?"

A half-second later I realized I'd jumped to an erroneous conclusion. Nana tapped Mom on the shoulder. "No," Nana said to me. "He was talking with Kap. For quite a while."

"Washington is a small place," I said, trying to process that "boyfriend" comment as it related to my mother. "Almost everyone knows everyone else."

"Something about their conversation," Nana said.

"You eavesdropped?"

"Don't I wish! I couldn't get close enough to really hear everything they were saying."

I was reminded of Tom's comment about the apple not falling far from the tree.

"But you heard something?"

"They both used words like China and classified," she said, clearly proud of herself.

She must have caught the look on my face, because she added, "I *did* hear them say that. They were about the only words I could make out, but they were clear as day. Of course, they also said Minkus's name. Several times." She held up a finger. "The thing is — I could tell from their body language that whatever it was, it was really important."

When we got home I decided to leave a voicemail for Paul Vasquez, and I was surprised when he personally picked up his phone.

"Good to hear from you, Ollie. How are you holding up?"

We talked for a while before I hit him with my big request. "Is there any way at all we can get back into the kitchen?"

I heard him take a breath, as though preparing to let me down, so I interrupted.

"This may sound stupid, Paul, but at the Minkus wake tonight nobody really seemed to pay me any mind. I think the big theory suggesting the kitchen staff had anything to do with Minkus's death has just about died down."

"You attended Carl Minkus's wake?"

There was uneasiness in Paul's voice. "I didn't realize you knew him."

"I didn't," I explained hastily. "I met Ruth Minkus for the first time just a few days ago at Arlington, and she insisted I attend."

He was silent for a moment. "If it were anyone else, I wouldn't believe it. Odd things seem to happen around you, Ollie."

"I know," I said. "I'm trying to change that."

He was silent for a heartbeat. "What about Suzie and Steve?"

I knew what he wasn't saying: that even if it hadn't been any of our staff members, we were — that is, I was — still responsible for every plate that left the kitchen. If Suzie and Steve were guilty of poisoning Minkus, my head wouldn't just roll. It would bounce down the stairs.

"I don't think they had anything to do with it."

"Oh, Ollie," he said with resignation. "I wish I could make the decision this minute to bring you and your team back, but my hands are tied. I'm sorry."

"Do you know if there has been any progress at all?" I asked, wanting to prolong the call. It was my only tie to the White House right now, and it seemed a lifeline. The longer we talked, I reasoned, the better the chance that an aide would rush in and tell Paul the ban had been lifted. "Are we expecting any news soon?"

Another resigned sigh. "You know I would tell you if I could."

"Yeah," I said.

"I'm working to get you back here," he said with the first glimmer of cheer I'd heard all night. "But I hope you're not planning to stir anything up."

I thought about my promise to Tom. "Don't worry. I'm behaving myself."

But I wondered if Tom realized how much that was killing me.

CHAPTER 17

Back at my apartment, over milk and coffee cake, I called everyone to order. "Listen," I said, "remember when those kids bullied me when I was little?"

Mom and Nana nodded.

"And remember how you told me that by giving in to my fears, I was allowing them power over me?"

Again, they nodded.

"Well, isn't that what Liss is doing?" I asked.

Mom nodded. "That's exactly right."

"Let's promise ourselves not to read his articles anymore," I said. "Let's refuse to let him have power over us."

"I like that attitude, Ollie," Mom said.

Nana yawned. "Me, too. As of right now — no more Liss."

In the morning, when Mom asked, "Anything new in the headlines?" her tone was light, but her eyes asked if I'd cheated and peeked at what Liss had to say.

"More unrest in China," I said, not rising to the bait. "Can you believe this?" I pointed. "The Chinese government is now claiming that the United States is responsible for the double-assassination."

Her interest was piqued. She leaned over my shoulder as Nana came in, freshly showered and dressed to go out. We both looked up. "Where are you going?" I asked.

"I have a very good feeling about today," she said, patting her fanny pack. "I want to be ready."

"Good," I said. "Maybe I can take you to see more of Washington."

"Wow," Mom said, scanning the article. "According to this, the two men who were killed had been wanted for questioning by the United States. The Chinese government is now saying it was the Americans who assassinated them instead."

"That doesn't sound right."

"Read it yourself."

I did. The story was written by a U.S. correspondent clearly attempting to distance himself from any factual inaccuracies. He repeatedly talked about his sources and suggested, more than once, that presented facts should not be taken as true until proven.

But, he also discussed the wild claims of the Chinese government and what it might mean to the United States if their allegations were true.

"So," I said, slowly, trying to distill the information down to its key points. "They're saying that they sent spies here and once we discovered them, we went over there to kill them? That seems so wrong." I shook my head. "That can't be the whole story."

Mom and Nana looked at me.

"Think about it. If they have two spies who have given them information on the United States — and God help us if they got anything important — why would there be any need to kill them? The two men were back in China, for some time. I'm sure they had been debriefed. What possible motive would the United States have to kill them at that point?"

"You know as well as I do that our government does plenty of things in secret," Mom said.

"True," I acknowledged. "But this seems pretty far-fetched. Now, if those Chinese spies gave their government bad information" — I shrugged — "There might be repercussions from above. But they shouldn't blame us for it. The United States gets enough bad-mouthing as it is."

"Other countries are just jealous," Nana said.

We both smiled at her.

"You two seem pretty chipper this morning," she continued. "I take it that means neither of you read that *Liss Is More* filth."

"You would be right," I said.

A knock at my front door. Being on the thirteenth floor in a building that required a buzz-up limited the possibilities of who it could be.

"I'll get it," I said, and wasn't surprised to see Mrs. Wentworth.

She held today's newspaper aloft, her arthritic right hand clamped around its edge, her other hand gripping her cane. "How come you're still here?"

I was about to ask what she meant when she pulled her cane up and used it to move me out of the way. "Looks like your friend Liss scooped everybody this time."

Before I could stop her, she'd tottered into the kitchen. "Good morning, ladies," she said. Then, catching sight of the newspaper on the table, she turned to me with a glare of impatience. "How come you didn't tell me you already saw it?"

"What are you talking about?" I asked. "Liss? No way we're reading him anymore. The lies he prints —"

She made an impatient face. "The guy is good." Waving away my protestations to the contrary, she said, "Yes, yes, I know what he's been saying lately. And I know he's been taking pokes at you. But if you don't look at his conjecture — if you just look at his facts — he's been pretty damned accurate so far."

"Accurate?" I started to protest. "I don't think so."

"Well, you better hope he is this time." She splayed the newspaper out before us. Standing back, she smiled at us expectantly. "Nice to be the bearer of good news for once," she said.

Curiosity got the better of me, as it usually does, and I leaned forward. I scanned quickly, looking for what might have spurred Mrs. Wentworth to come knocking at my door. And then I found it:

And You Read It Here First

We join the White House in saying, "Welcome back!"

Liss Is More has learned that the White House kitchen staff has been officially cleared of suspicion in Carl Minkus's unexpected death. Word is that the staff will be notified shortly and will be expected to return to work immediately. *Liss Is More* also has it on good authority that the president and First Lady have had their fill of food prepared by well-intentioned but ill-trained Secret Service personnel. I know my good friend Executive Chef Olivia Paras will be delighted by this new turn of events, both for herself and for her staff.

Side note to Ollie: See? You can stop blaming me for the cloud of suspicion that hung over your head. I just report the facts. I don't invent them.

" 'My good friend'?" I asked, fuming. "How does he come up with this stuff?"

Mrs. Wentworth tapped the words. "It sells papers, kiddo."

"Yeah, well, maybe I'll cancel my delivery." As angry as I was at Liss in general, I was mostly furious at his assertion that my staff and I had been welcomed back to the White House. "Accurate? I don't think so. If he were accurate, wouldn't I have heard from our chief usher by now?"

At that moment, a phone rang. The sound was faint and the tune wasn't the one I used for my cell phone, but I instinctively turned toward the little device and picked it up. "Not me," I said.

My mom got a split-second quizzical look on her face, then jumped up. "That's mine," she said, clearly surprised. "I don't get many phone calls, so I didn't . . ."

We missed the rest of her words as she turned into the bedroom. We heard soft scuffling sounds, then the tune ended and my mom said, "Hello."

Two seconds later, she shut the bedroom door.

"A gentleman caller?" Mrs. Wentworth asked.

Nana snorted. "And I think I know exactly who that gentleman caller is."

"Kap," I said. I had forgotten about their "date" today.

"Now don't get all worked up, honey," Nana said, patting my arm like I was a four-year-old. "Your mom is allowed a little bit of fun while she's out here."

Her words hit their mark. I had wanted to make this trip the best Mom and Nana had experienced. I'd wanted to make them love Washington, D.C., as much as I did — by showing them the White House from the inside. By letting them walk the halls — not like tourists, but like insiders. Instead, the vacation had been sliced to ribbons by Minkus's untimely death, and my obsession with getting back into the kitchen.

I had to face facts: The only real highlight this entire trip for my mom was her flirtation with Kap. In less than a week, Mom and Nana would be back in Chicago and Kap would still be here. Why was I behaving like an overprotective mother, trying to thwart my mom's happiness? If she wanted to spend time with a man her age, a man who was clearly interested in her, then why shouldn't she?

I argued both sides in my mind even as Nana and Mrs. Wentworth carried on a separate conversation. I had just about convinced myself that Kap's phone call was a good thing for my mom's ego when she emerged from the bedroom, her face flushed.

"Mom," she said to Nana in a voice that held slight urgency, "you won't mind if I take some time this afternoon, will you?" Almost as an afterthought, she turned to me. "You don't mind either, right?"

Nana spoke before I could. " 'Course not, Corinne." She slapped the back of her hand against my forearm. "Right, Ollie?"

Mrs. Wentworth asked the question. "Kap taking you out?"

In that instance, I felt a resurgence of fear. All the arguing I'd done with myself went out the window. There was something not right about Kap. I sensed he was not all he appeared to be, and if there was one thing I knew, it was to trust my gut. I couldn't let my mother go out with him. Not alone. It was all too convenient that he'd popped into our lives just at this time. What was he really after?

"Yes," Mom said. "He and I are going to dinner. But we plan to tour more of the National Mall first."

"I thought we were all going to do that today," I said, petulance creeping into my voice. "I thought we were all going to go together."

Mom smiled. "I know how busy you are, Ollie . . ."

"Why isn't he at the funeral?" I asked. "Shouldn't he be with the family today?"

"I asked him that, actually."

"And?"

"He said that Ruth and Joel preferred to keep the interment private. Family only."

A teensy bit of spite from me. "I thought he was as close as family."

Mom gave me a chastising glare.

"Hey," I said. "Why don't we go with you? Nana and I." I turned. "And you, too, Mrs. Wentworth, if you want."

Mom's eyes widened.

"I'm not up for that today," Nana said.

"In fact, I think it might be just a little too cool outside for these old bones. Thanks anyway, honey."

Mrs. Wentworth pierced me with a shrewd look that, in one second both berated me and mocked my attempt. "Sorry, dear. Stanley's coming by later. We have plans."

The idea of my tagging along with Mom and Kap by myself was unappealing, to say the least.

The phone rang — my house phone this time — preventing me from making that suggestion. "Hang on," I said, reaching for the receiver. "Before you give him an answer —"

"I'm going with him, Ollie." Mom said. "I already told him he can pick me up at two."

A thousand thoughts flew through my brain as I picked up the phone without checking Caller ID. "Hello?"

"Ollie, it's Paul."

Like a rerun of Monday morning, our chief usher was calling me at home — what could have happened now?

"Yes?" I said dumbly.

"I take it you've seen the Liss article?"

"Just a minute ago."

Paul sounded angry and resigned at the same time. "I don't know who leaked the story to him. It's a pretty sad day when our

289

staff learns that they're back to work through the newspaper rather than through official channels."

My mom's plight momentarily forgotten, I caught hold of what he was saying. "We're back? We can come back?"

"Right away. The sooner the better."

Relief washed over me, rinsing away the crustiness of fear. "Thank you so much, Paul."

"Don't thank me," he said. "The president and First Lady moved mountains to get the medical examiner to rush his decision. It's because they want to get to the bottom of this mess, of course."

I sensed he wasn't finished talking.

"But it's not just that. There's another tidbit Liss got right in the story," he went on. "The first couple is plenty tired of Secret Service food. How soon can you get here?"

There wasn't a lot of choice, really. I couldn't stay home — not when I was needed back at the White House. As much as I didn't want my mom heading out for parts unknown with the mysterious Kap, there was little I could do to stop her. In the end, I left Mom and Nana with a spare set of keys and strict instructions to call me if anything came up or if they had any trouble whatsoever.

"What sort of trouble do you expect, Ollie?" Mom asked with a little too much glee.

"None," I said. "Of course. But, you know, just in case."

Nana looked up at me, a twinkle in her deep-set eyes. "So, no wild parties while you're gone?"

A half hour later found me ready to board the Metro for my first trip back to the White House since Minkus's death. My head was everywhere but where it should have been — aware of my surroundings.

I entered the mostly empty train car and didn't pay any attention to the man who followed me in until he sat in the seat next to me. He wore an old-fashioned brown felt hat pulled low, and his overcoat was turned up at the collar. Except for his leather-gloved hand atop a cane, there was nothing distinctive about him. He smelled of too much aftershave.

In one instant, I berated myself for letting my guard down, but I'd been in situations more touchy than this one, so I didn't hesitate. "Excuse me," I said, and got up to change seats.

"Olivia," he said.

About to take an aisle seat kitty-corner

behind him, I turned. "What?"

"Come back. Sit down. We have to talk."

He lifted the brim of his hat just enough.

I was about to exclaim, "Liss?" but he placed a finger across his lips. *"Shh,"* he said, then tapped the seat next to him. "Sit down. Quickly. We don't have much time."

"What are you, some sort of conspiracy theorist?" I asked, not caring at all that I spoke loudly enough to be heard by other passengers. "Oh wait." I snapped my fingers. "That's exactly what you are!"

I turned my back and headed to an aisle seat even farther away.

He turned and glared at me. Though I could only see his eyes and nose out of the top of his collar, I could feel the heat blaze. I wished I had a paperback or something to read. Instead I turned my head to the window. Unfortunately, we were underground and there really wasn't much of a view, so I kept eye contact with my reflection, drawing from it a little sense of empowerment.

Liss scuffled to his feet and made his way over to the seat in front of me. There were a handful of other passengers in the car and they started to take notice. Not that I cared.

"I was right about you getting back into

the White House today, wasn't I?" he asked.

I didn't bother to answer. I stared at the window.

"I have sources," he said.

"Let me guess. Is his name Deep Throat?"

I felt his gaze rake me up and down. "Isn't that a little before your time?"

"Facts," I said, biting the word out, "and history are important to me. And should be to all of us."

I was feeling pretty good about holding my own against this despicable man. He had already hurt me — and my mother — with his vicious column. I had nothing to lose here. I almost wished he would keep at it, so I could knock him to his knees.

He lowered his voice and leaned closer. "What if I told you I have facts that would rock the country's very core?"

"I'd say you wouldn't know a fact if it bit you on the —" Stopping myself in the nick of time, I cleared my throat. "I'd say you were bluffing."

He raised a white eyebrow. "So you are a temperamental chef, after all."

Placing my hand on the back of his chair to boost myself, I stood to change seats, yet again.

"Please wait," he said, placing his hand over mine. "I apologize."

I yanked my hand out from under his. "You will never be able to apologize enough."

When I sat four seats forward, across from an elderly woman who gave me a worried glance before staring at the floor, I expected him to follow. He didn't.

He stayed in his seat for the entire ride to MacPherson Square. As the train pulled into the station, I stood to disembark.

Just as the train slowed, Liss stood up. He made his way over. Seconds before the doors were to open, he leaned close to my ear.

"There was trouble in the security office," he whispered. "It has to do with China. Minkus was about to investigate Phil Cooper, his second-in —"

I turned to him, and spoke in a clear voice. "I know exactly who Phil Cooper is. After everything you've written, so does the entire population of Washington, D.C."

Shock registered in his eyes and he looked from side to side, like a spy from a 1940s movie. "Not so loud —"

"Don't tell me what to do," I said. "And why are you bothering me with this anyway? I don't have time to listen to your crazy conspiracies. If you believe you have some burning scoop, why not publish it in your column? Why accost me on my way to work?"

By now the entire train was paying attention.

He whispered, "Because I think you can get me information on Phil Cooper and his anti-American activities." His teeth were clenched, his body was rigid, but his eyes didn't leave mine. "From your Secret Service boyfriend."

How did he know about Tom? Speechless, my mouth moved, but nothing came out.

He took the opportunity to lean in again. "You want me to go public with your romantic dalliances? I'm sure that headline will sit very well with MacKenzie's boss."

The car's doors opened. "Climb into that little hole of yours and dream up more of your nasty lies," I said. "It's what you're good at."

I stepped out and didn't look back.

CHAPTER 18

My anger at Liss didn't dissolve, but my mood lightened the moment I stepped into the White House kitchen. It was clean. One of our crews had evidently put everything back in its place after the investigators finished. And the smell was exactly right. Dash of yeast, a sprinkle of coffee, and hint of cleaning solution. Although the scents were faint — we'd been banished for four days — they were strong enough to make my heart race with possibility. I closed my eyes for just a moment to breathe it in. "Oh," I said quietly. "It's good to be home."

"It is, isn't it?"

At Cyan's voice, my eyes opened. "As much as I've been enjoying my family, I really missed coming to work."

She tied an apron around her waist and lifted her chin to say hello as Bucky entered the room. "I have so many friends who complain about going to work," she said. "Some of them really hate their jobs. I almost feel guilty because I love this place so much."

"We're blessed," I said.

"Yeah, but for how long?" Bucky wondered.

Cyan and I had the same reaction to Bucky's question. We both stared at him with puzzled expressions.

"This isn't over," he said. "I heard what that medical examiner said this morning."

"I didn't know he was on TV today."

Bucky's downturned mouth let me know that whatever Dr. Michael Isham had had to say wasn't particularly good news. "Yeah. After Paul called, I flipped on the news. The medical examiner's office isn't clearing us of anything yet. He said that results are still pending."

"Then why are we here?"

He shrugged with exaggerated motion. "They can't have the Easter Egg Roll without us, I guess. They can trust us to hard-boil a few thousand eggs for the kids to play with. But I wager they won't allow us to work on the food for the event." He held up a finger in emphasis. "I *guarantee* they'll come up with a reason why we won't be serving food on Monday."

"We always serve food at the event. That's part of the draw," I said. "I'm sure now that we're here, everything will start getting back to normal."

Bucky shook his head, scowling. As he turned away, Cyan's expression asked me where the pleasant fellow from yesterday had gone.

Paul greeted us from the doorway. "Welcome back."

We spent the next few minutes exchanging greetings and comments about being glad to be at work again. I mentioned to Paul the need for the kitchen to bring on a couple of SBA chefs and expressed my preference to have Rafe, and our recent recruit, Agda, as part of the team. With our workload, we would need a few more temporary chefs, too.

"Ah," he said. "Other than the three of you, and Marcel and his staff, we're not bringing 'unknowns' into the kitchen until the entire Minkus investigation is complete."

My mouth opened in disbelief. While we could handle the day-to-day meals with ease, we could not — by any stretch of the imagination — handle Monday's anticipated crowd by ourselves. "How are we going to feed all the partygoers at the Egg Roll?" I asked. "Rafe and Agda have worked here before. They're not exactly unknown. And even with them we'll be severely short-handed."

Paul waved away my concerns. "I understand. Let me explain. There has been a change in plans."

Bucky gave me a look that said "I told you so."

Paul took a deep breath. "After much discussion, the president and First Lady have decided that it would be in the best interests of all if we limited Monday's events. We will hold the Egg Roll as scheduled, but no White House party afterward."

If a person could look smug and unhappy at the same time, it was Bucky.

"But . . ." I didn't know what else to say. "Why?"

"Coming on the heels of Carl Minkus's death, the aspect of a formal party that evening might be construed as unseemly. In bad taste. But no one would disagree with keeping the Egg Roll for the benefit of the children."

Bucky's warning made me believe there was more to it than keeping up appearances. For his part, Bucky had turned his back while Cyan and I waited for Paul to finish.

"You have to understand that the president and First Lady believe in all of you.

They wanted you back here as quickly as possible. This" — he held his hands aloft — "is a testament to their belief. Don't underestimate it."

We nodded, but were silent. Paul patted me on the shoulder on his way out. "Things will start to get better soon. I'm sure of it."

He left, and we set to work on dinner, eventually settling back into our comfortable rhythms. When I signed onto the kitchen computer, I found a note from the First Lady:

Welcome back, Ollie — to you and to your staff. My husband and I are very much relieved to know you're back in charge. Thank you for your patience during these trying times.

I shared the note with Cyan and Bucky who, respectively, were cheered and unfazed. Tonight's dinner, capitalizing on the fresh veggies from my garden on the third floor, boasted a little Italian flair. We were serving a spring greens salad, bruschetta, and pasta primavera with chicken, asparagus, cherry tomatoes, and baby squash. Marcel, I knew, was planning the big finish of warm Brie with walnuts and maple syrup, garnished with fresh berries.

After we got the bruschetta topping started, I turned to Bucky. "I haven't spoken with the Secret Service yet about picking up the eggs."

He raised his head in acknowledgment but didn't respond.

"I'll talk to them as soon as we're settled here. But I'm sure they're going to want specifics. Do you have a good time I can ask them to be there? Will Brandy be home?"

Bucky's head snapped up. He made an imperative, unintelligible noise — halfway between a gasp and a *"Shh!"*

"What?" I asked, not understanding.

He gestured the two of us closer, his eyes wide with anger. "Do *not* say another word," he said, his voice menacing. He looked about the kitchen but there was no one else around. Keeping to a whisper, he said, "You will not refer to her in any way that might bring notice to our . . . our . . ."

"Relationship?" I prompted.

His glare darkened. "It does not exist."

"Uh . . ." Cyan ran her fingers over her lips. "What?"

Again the unintelligible noise. "The relationship you refer to is private. It does not exist" — he jammed a finger onto the countertop — "here. You will not refer to it, or to her, in that regard. We refuse to make ourselves a spectacle."

Perhaps reading the expressions on our faces, he quickly added, "We want to keep things private."

"Sure," I said, but his words hit me in a way I hadn't anticipated. As I went back to preparations — cleaning the asparagus and baby greens — Liss's not-so-subtle threat to make my relationship with Tom public sent a shooting pain of fear up the back of my throat.

"What's wrong, Ollie?" Cyan asked. "You're pale."

To tell the truth, I felt pale. A sadness I couldn't reach sickened me. And I knew this queasy dread wouldn't go away until I could make things right. The question was, how? I took a deep breath. "I need some air," I said. "Give me a minute."

Even as I strode out of the kitchen, I was pulling my cell phone out of my pocket. I made my way outside into one of the courts that flanked the North Portico. "Tom," I said when he answered.

"What's wrong?"

The fact that he could tell so quickly that something was wrong was not lost on me. He and I had gotten to that point where we could often anticipate what the other would say. Comfort. We'd had that. For a while, at least.

I wanted to talk. But I knew this wasn't a conversation for the phone. "Something's come up."

"Are you all right?"

"Yes, yes." Gosh, I was not handling this very well. "Everyone is fine. But Liss — Howard Liss."

"You're back in the White House, aren't you? I heard you got the all-clear today. I wanted to call, but I'm in training today."

"Oh, you're busy?"

"We're on a break right now. Your timing is phenomenal."

"At least something is."

"Talk to me, but make it quick. We're being called back in for the next session."

There was no way to put this in a thirty-second conversation. "Just do me a favor and call me when you get out, okay? Call me first before you do anything. Will you do that?"

"What's going on?"

"Nothing." I cringed. That was a lie. "It will keep until you call me." I hoped that was the truth.

"Ollie, you're making me nervous."

"Don't worry. I'll tell you later. But it'll be okay." I felt a swift stab in my heart. "I have it all figured out."

He gave a short laugh. "I don't know if that's good news or bad news. But I do have to go. I'll call you later."

"As soon as you get out, right?"

"That very moment."

I rolled my shoulders but didn't feel any better. That queasy sensation was still there. I stared up at the sky from between the court's side walls. Overcast today. I shivered. It was cold outside, but I just noticed it now. My sorrowful mood did not have its genesis in Liss's threat. Liss had only exacerbated an awareness that was already there. I knew what I needed to do. But I wondered if I had the strength to do it.

The sky above held no answers, so I made my way inside to the kitchen's warmth, where life always felt safest.

Marguerite Schumacher, the White House social secretary, met me in the hallway. "I was just coming to talk with you." Pert and dark, she had limitless energy, and a tenacity that I admired. "Have you heard about the plans?"

I told her I had. "I'm just disappointed that they're canceling the post-party. Everyone always looks forward to that."

She wrinkled her nose. "I have to tell you,

at first I thought canceling the party portion was a bad idea. But after talking with Mrs. Campbell, I understand where she's coming from."

"Having a party just a week after Minkus's death wouldn't look good?"

"That," Marguerite agreed, "and . . ."

"What else? What are they not telling us?"

She placed a finger on her lips. "Don't share this with anyone else."

I felt my heart skip a beat. "What is it?"

For the third time today, the person I was talking with looked both directions before speaking. Anyone else might have started to develop a complex. But I understood. That's part of the world I chose to live in.

Something else clicked in that moment. That realization that I was always in the middle of things. That's who I *was*.

"You remember our last big holiday?" Marguerite asked.

"How could I forget?" The days leading up to the official White House holiday open house had been eventful, to say the least.

"Mrs. Campbell doesn't want to take any chances this time. She wants the children to have their event, but, in her words, doesn't want 'to tempt fate' by entertaining all the adults later that evening."

" 'Tempt fate,' " I repeated.

Marguerite nodded. "At least until the Minkus investigation is completed."

"So she believes Minkus *was* murdered?"

"I really can't say."

I watched her reaction. "You don't know, or you don't want to tell me?"

She gave a Mona Lisa smile. "I really can't say." Then, deflecting my question, she brought me up to date on the expected guests, and explained that there would be additional security — more than usual — on the grounds that day.

"But they never considered canceling the entire event?"

Marguerite gave me a weary look. "You're damned if you do and you're damned if you don't. Canceling the kids' events would be such a disappointment. There are families who look forward to this all year. Some come from across the country just for the chance to participate. Mrs. Campbell doesn't want to let them down."

"What about the clowns and the book readings and the magic shows?"

"Of course. We'll still have all of that."

"But there will be added security."

"A *lot* of added security."

"And the guests aren't going to notice?"

She grinned. "In an effort to keep people from feeling uncomfortable, the extra Secret

Service agents will be in costume."

I raised an eyebrow. "Not bunnies?"

She laughed. "Some of them. Others will just be dressed like regular partygoers and will mingle in the crowd."

"Good plan," I said. "Thanks for the update, I'll let my team know."

A glance at my watch reminded me that my mom and Kap were probably on their date right now. I considered calling my mom's cell just to check in, but nobody likes a buttinsky, and that was exactly what I would be. I thought about calling my apartment. Maybe Nana would be able to give me an update on the situation.

I made sure to refrigerate tonight's bruschetta topping before making the call. Just as I pulled my cell phone out again, Bucky grabbed my arm, then let go almost immediately, as if surprised by his own action. "They want me upstairs."

"Who does?"

"The Secret Service." He swallowed. "They say they have a few more questions for me. Oh my God, they think I did it, don't they?"

My number one assistant, I was discovering, went from zero to sixty in the space of a heartbeat. I'd never known anyone who flipped from emotionless to panicked with such speed.

"Bucky," I said, with intense calm, "if they thought you did it, would they have allowed you back into the kitchen?" I extended my arm out toward our work stations and all the items we had in progress. "Would they allow you to cook for the president of the United States of America if they suspected you of murder?"

Bucky held his hands to his head. "We haven't served the food, have we? No. They just brought us here for more questioning."

"Why are you so afraid?"

My question seemed to stun him. "Why aren't you?" he asked, stepping back. "This Minkus situation gives them the right to poke their noses into our private lives."

"Yes, but —"

"What will happen if they find out that I'm living with . . ." He widened his eyes as if to say "You know who." Rubbing his hands over his face, he groaned. "I could lose my job. I could lose . . ."

He didn't have to finish the sentence. Personally, I thought his fear was over the top. I didn't believe for a moment that his relationship with a member of the Egg Board would cause any conflict of interest whatsoever. If it did, then what would be said about my relationship with Tom?

That thought dried my mouth. Thoughts of our talk later today sent pillars of fear driving down into my stomach. There was nothing I could say to Bucky to reassure him. And I wished there was because maybe then I could reassure myself.

But before I could even attempt, one of the Guzy brothers came into the kitchen. "Buckminster Reed?"

Bucky lifted his head.

"Come with me."

Cyan and I tried to smile as Bucky left — an effort to make this sudden summons seem like no big deal — but he wasn't buying it. His lips tight, he gave us a long, meaningful stare before following Guzy boy out of the room.

"He'll be okay." Hearing myself say the words actually made me feel a little bit better as though by virtue of will I could make everything okay. Weren't we back in the White House? That was a step in the right direction, for sure.

Cyan said, "Yeah," but her tone was unconvinced.

In addition to preparing dinner, we worked ahead. It had been so long since we'd been in the kitchen that there was a lot of catching up to do. Cyan and I barely spoke as we cleaned out old food that had gone bad and began chopping, cleaning, and slicing items we knew we would need going forward.

Just as we finished, Bucky returned. His pale face was covered with a sheen of perspiration. "What happened?" I asked.

His eyes were glassy. "The dossier," he said.

Minkus's. "What did they say?"

"They're considering suspension."

"That's not right," I said, untying my apron. "Let me talk with them."

Bucky's hands came up. "Don't."

"What have I got to lose?" I asked, anger making me reckless. "They're probably going to call me up there next and tell me I'm suspended, too."

Cyan wasn't understanding. "What dossier? Why will either of you be suspended?"

I explained about Bucky sending Minkus's dossier to his home computer. "Bucky made me a copy. So we're in the same boat." I cast a glance at the doorway. "Probably just a matter of minutes before I'm summoned, too."

"I didn't tell them that you have it," he said.

Taken aback, I could only ask, "You didn't? Why not?"

Bucky boosted himself onto the stool we

kept near the kitchen computer. He leaned his elbows on his knees and lowered his chin into his hands. "Why get us both into trouble?"

Never in a million years would I have expected this show of unity from Bucky. I patted him on the shoulder. "Thanks."

He nodded absently. "We have to worry about the eggs," he said. "If they suspend me, they sure as hell aren't going to want to use the eggs I have stored at my house."

That had the potential to become a problem. "Unless we work through Brandy," I said quietly. "She might be able to use other channels to bring them here."

I expected him to react — to scold me again about bringing up her name — but he just blinked. "Yeah."

"When will you know?" Cyan asked. "I mean . . . whether they're suspending you or not."

He shook his head. "No idea."

"I'm still going to talk to them." I folded my apron and placed it on the counter. "You know this is all for show — to make it look like they're running the most thorough investigation they can. If it were up to Mrs. Campbell . . ." I stopped myself before finishing the sentence.

"What were you going to say?" Cyan asked.

Bucky glanced at me with the most curious expression. Half-cynical, half-hopeful. This man was a walking contradiction.

"Just that I believe the investigators aren't seeing the forest for the trees."

"Huh?"

"Never mind," I said. "I'll be right back."

I caught Paul in his office. "Ollie," he said, not smiling. "I think I know why you're here."

"They can't suspend Bucky."

He shook his head. "My hands are tied."

"We all take paperwork home. It happens all the time."

"But guests don't usually die," he said, then added, "Thank God for that."

"You mean to tell me that if Minkus hadn't died, and yet the Secret Service had found out Bucky forwarded that document to himself, they wouldn't raise an eyebrow?"

Paul made a so-so motion with his head. "That's impossible to tell, but I have to believe they're cracking down especially hard in this case. There's no textbook on what to do when a White House visitor dies — or is killed — while at dinner with the president."

"What can I do to vouch for Bucky?"

Another so-so motion; this time Paul's eyes looked sad. "I don't think that will do much good at this point."

"My support wouldn't count for anything, would it?"

Paul looked away. "It's not that."

"Sure it is." I heard the bitterness in my voice and then I couldn't stop myself. "Doesn't anyone care about what might have really happened here? Why is everyone so suspicious of us? And why bring us back if the Secret Service isn't going to trust us? If they're so leery about us being here, how can they be so sure we won't try to poison someone else?"

My voice had gotten louder and even I realized I was approaching panic. Not very professional. I toned down immediately.

"Sorry," I said. "I guess I just don't understand any of this."

"As I mentioned," Paul said, "you — and your staff — are back because the First Lady requested it. When the word comes down from that high up, the Secret Service has no choice in the matter."

The thought that had occurred to me earlier sprang back into my brain. "Thanks, Paul," I said.

"Is there anything else you need?"

"No," I said. "Not unless you can prove

313

that Carl Minkus died of natural causes."

He opened his hands. "I'm sorry there's not much I can do."

I forgot about calling home to check with Nana until I was back in the kitchen. I would have pulled out my phone, but I caught sight of Bucky removing his apron with a look of abject defeat on his face.

"They didn't . . ." I said.

He didn't make eye contact. "One of those twin agents — Guzy — came by to tell me. Said I could finish out the day, but I figured why bother?"

When he finally looked up at me, his eyes were glassed over and held such weight that I could barely stand to look at him.

"Don't go yet," I said. "Please."

"Why?"

"I have an idea."

He started to shake his head — to argue — but I stopped him.

"Just a couple more hours, okay? Just trust me."

The words fell out of my mouth and with them, I realized I was almost promising him I'd fix the situation. But could I? Did I have the support I needed to pull this off?

"Come on, Buckaroo," Cyan said, with a lightness so forced I felt her pain. She pointed to the clock with a floury finger.

"It's only a couple more hours and we could sure use the help."

"Don't know what good I'll be here," Bucky said, but he tied his apron back on.

"Let's just worry about planning next week's menu," I said.

"Being suspended and all, I probably won't even be working here next week. They didn't even say how long I'd be off. Maybe indefinitely."

His tone was gruff, as might be expected, but yet again Bucky's vulnerability caught me by surprise. He'd always been my loudest critic and biggest annoyance. To say I'd been tempted to serve him notice — more than once — was an understatement, but recently I'd begun to see him in a different light. What had happened to cause him to be so contrary all the time? What made him so difficult? I was just grateful to know that apparently Brandy had been able to pierce his armor. At least he had some sunshine in his life.

I had an idea. A good idea, I thought. But it had the chance of coming back to bite me, too.

"Okay," I said. "We have no major events next week after the Egg Roll, so we can probably bring out a few of the family's favorites while tossing in a couple of new items. Any suggestions?"

We discussed the menu at length and I was encouraged to note Bucky getting into it — crabbing at me when I disagreed with him. Bucky's complaints actually made me feel good. Almost like we were getting back to normal.

When we had the week's worth of meals planned, I headed to the computer to put it into our standard format before submitting it to the First Lady. Behind me, I heard Bucky sigh.

"So, that's it, huh? I guess I should get going."

"Did you refill our tasting spoons?" Cyan asked him. "We sent the ones that had been sitting here over to the dishwashers, but they haven't brought us any clean ones back. Would you mind checking on that before you leave?"

Bucky rolled his eyes, but complied.

As soon as he was out of the room, Cyan sidled up next to me. "He doesn't want to leave."

"If I have anything to do with it, he won't."

She peered over my shoulder, then whispered, aghast, "You aren't."

Not looking at her, I shrugged, returned to the e-mail I'd been writing. "We all do our part," I said. A couple of keystrokes later, the message was sent. "Now, let's keep our fingers crossed."

At least I was doing something. My spirits buoyed, I took a deep breath and reveled in the joy of moving forward. But that feeling was short-lived.

"Olivia Paras." Peter Everett Sargeant III's pronouncement was not an inquiry. More like a command.

I turned, dismayed by the unexpected arrival of our sensitivity director. "Yes," I said. "What can I do for you?"

He stared at me through hooded eyes. "We need to talk."

"I am up to date on all the schedule changes, Peter," I said. "And since we are no longer serving dinner on Monday, we no longer are dealing with 'sensitivity' issues with regard to meal planning. The Egg Roll menu was approved a long time ago. If whatever it is you need to discuss can wait until next week, I would prefer we do so."

He tilted his head in his inquisitive yet condescending way, but I caught the underlying glee in his eyes. "I wish it were that simple," he said with a smile. "But I'm afraid this matter is much more grave than that."

I couldn't imagine anything more serious than canceling a White House event, but I took the bait. "Fine. Let's step —"

Wrinkling his nose, he turned to Cyan. "You will excuse us."

She looked to me. I nodded. "Sure," she said. "I'll be downstairs."

He watched her leave. "Why do you keep her on staff?" he asked. "For one thing —"

"I don't believe you came here to discuss my staff," I said, interrupting. "So if you don't mind, let's get to the heart of the matter, shall we?"

As it always did when I dealt with Sargeant, my posture became more rigid, my speech pattern more formal. There was nothing casual about this man. Perhaps subconsciously, in an effort to facilitate more efficient communication, I parroted his terse, prim demeanor.

He began: "You are incorrect in your assumption."

I startled, and it bugged me that he noticed.

His smile grew broader. "This is most certainly about one of your staff members. I am here to discuss the immediate dismissal of Buckminster Reed."

Whatever I'd expected, it wasn't this. Gathering my wits, I searched for a comeback. "Bucky doesn't report to you. He isn't even within your chain of command."

"Which is why," he said with exaggerated patience, "I am coming to you first. It is unfortunately true that I have no authority where Mr. Reed's continued employment is concerned. But I heard what he did, and I find that wholly unacceptable." The smile never wavered. "As should you."

"Bucky did nothing wrong."

Sargeant raised both eyebrows. "You can't possibly *sanction* the willy-nilly distribution of confidential documents?"

I took a breath, but before I could respond, he continued.

"I hope this doesn't mean that a closer look into your habits would turn up evidence of such irresponsible behavior."

"Studying a dietary dossier at home does not constitute irresponsible behavior."

"Perhaps not." His mouth twitched. "But you are seen as a 'golden girl' by this administration, and hence, none of your transgressions are ever seriously investigated. I would very much like to see that changed."

I was still processing that little mention of "golden girl" when he spun on his heel and turned away.

Stopping at the doorway, he examined the ceiling for a moment, before directing his attention to me. "Eventually President

319

Campbell will finish out his term. And then the spell you have on him — and the First Lady — will come to a crushing end." He wrinkled his nose, speaking in a conspiratorial whisper. "I look forward to that day."

Cyan found me still staring at the empty doorway when she returned a few minutes later. "Is Mr. Cheerful gone?"

I bit the insides of my cheeks.

"What happened?" she asked.

I couldn't find it in me to explain. "He's a piece of work, that one," I finally said, shaking my head. "We need to watch our backs."

Bucky returned with several stainless steel bowls of tasting spoons, which he put in prime spots around the kitchen. He stood for a moment with his arms akimbo, surveying the scene. "You two are going to have a lot of work by yourselves."

"I know," I said. "I am not looking forward to that at all. What are we going to do without you here?"

Bucky gave me a look that told me he appreciated my words, even as he maintained the scowl. "Maybe I should make room in the refrigerators for all those eggs."

"That's great idea," I said. "While you do that, I'll —"

I was silenced by the unmistakable sound of a new message on the computer.

Cyan, standing closer to Bucky, obviously didn't hear it. "You'll what?"

"Give me a minute," I said, turning my back.

They headed to the refrigerators while I opened my inbox. The note was brief and to the point.

Thank you for the information, Ollie. That is, indeed, sad news. It is my hope that Mr. Reed will be cleared soon to continue in our kitchen.

My heart sank. I don't know why I hoped for more from Mrs. Campbell — or why I expected an immediate turn of events — but I had. I supposed I should be happy to know that the First Lady had received my message so quickly. The menu I'd sent included a quick summary of what was happening with Bucky, and a polite entreaty asking Mrs. Campbell to intercede on his behalf. I had clearly overstepped my boundaries, but when one of my employees was in trouble, what else was I to do?

"You two should be able to handle it from here," Bucky said when he and Cyan returned. "I'm going to take off."

This time there were no tasks left to assign — and no way to logically argue for him to stay. I no longer held out hope that Mrs. Campbell would stay his suspension. We were out of options. "Keep in touch," I said.

"One of us will," he said. "About the eggs."

He untied his apron, and I could almost see the weight on his shoulders as he shrugged into his jacket and fixed a baseball cap on his head.

Impulsively, I said, "I'm going to do whatever I can to get this fixed."

One corner of his mouth turned up. "I know you will."

And then he was gone.

"We'll never get through a whole week without help," Cyan said after a long minute. "They're not letting us hire any SBA chefs and now without Bucky . . ."

I had been thinking the same thing. Best-laid plans. When I had arranged for my mom and nana to come visit, I'd done so with the belief that with a contingent of help and our full staff, we would be in fine position to get everything done on time. But there was no way to get through an entire week with just the two of us, unless we were both willing to spend every waking hour here.

I sighed. Mom and Nana would be on

their own for the next three days, at least. Maybe longer. This was not how I'd planned their visit.

I reached for my cell phone and dialed my apartment. Glancing at the clock, I tried to gauge how long it would be before I headed home. "Hi Nana," I said. "Can I talk with Mom?"

"She's not back yet."

I looked at the clock again, as though it might have lied to me a moment earlier. "She went out hours ago."

"They must be having a nice time."

"But it'll be dark soon."

Nana laughed. "You sound like your mother did on your first date."

"But that's different. This is Washington, D.C. She doesn't know her way around yet."

"I'm sure Kap does."

That's exactly what I was afraid of. "Has she called?"

"Did you call us on your first date?"

"Nana," I said, my tone serious, "aren't you worried?"

"No. And you shouldn't be either. Your mother's a big girl."

"When do you expect her back?"

"When the sun comes up."

"Nana!"

She laughed. I made an exasperated noise.

"Do me a favor — call me when you hear from her, okay?"

"I might be hard to get ahold of," she said merrily. "Your neighbor's teaching me a new card game, so I'm going over there now. Good thing you called when you did. Five more minutes and I'd have been gone."

When I hung up, I stared at my little cell phone.

"What's wrong?" Cyan asked.

It took me a minute to put it into words. "When I left my family to pursue a career, I guess I figured they would always just stay the way they were." I looked up. Cyan shook her head, not understanding. "I mean, I knew I was changing, but I never expected them to do anything, or be anything different than my mother and my grandmother. But they are. They've grown — they've changed."

"And that's a bad thing?"

"No," I said. "It's a good thing. I'm just not adjusted to it yet. It's my problem. Not theirs. I think I've been holding on to my memories of them — kinda like holding on to a bit of childhood. But now I'm realizing that's gone."

"I understand," she said. And by the look in her eyes I knew she did. "Just remember to appreciate every moment you have them with you."

I called Tom on my way to the Metro station, just a little bit perturbed that he hadn't called me back like he'd promised.

"Ollie!" he said with such relief that my anger immediately dissolved.

"What's wrong?"

"I was called in to a special meeting immediately after the seminar. And then after that, Craig needed to talk with me."

The heaviness in his voice made me ask: "About?"

"Can't say. I was going to call you in about ten minutes. But now that you called me, let's talk. What's on your mind that's so important?"

I swallowed, but didn't break stride. "Can we get together?"

"Tonight?"

I didn't like the mild peevishness to his tone, nor did I look forward to what I knew would be a difficult conversation, but I persisted. "I think that would be a good idea."

"Sounds ominous. What do we need to talk about?"

"I haven't gotten to MacPherson yet," I said, avoiding the question. Thinking quickly, I tried to come up with a place that would afford us a little privacy. "If you're nearby, we can meet at that martini bar you've always wanted to try."

"You want to go to a martini bar? What about Froggie's?"

I didn't want to tell him that I wanted to protect Froggie's. That we'd had a lot of good memories there. I didn't know exactly what I planned to say, but I did know that a conversation like this was best held elsewhere. "The martini bar is closer. I can be there in a few minutes."

He made an odd noise. "I guess I have no choice."

I didn't order a martini. I opted for coffee instead. Tom looked over the tiny leatherbound menu and asked the waitress for a Sam Adams.

"I thought you were looking forward to trying something new," I said.

We were seated at a tall table in the dark bar's front window. He leaned forward on his arms. "So . . . why are we here, Ollie?"

All day I had been rehearsing options. How I would open, how I would progress, what I might expect Tom to say. How I would answer. But all my preparation went out the nearby window. I turned to watch a couple across the street. Arm in arm, they laughed. Little puffs of air curled in front of them as they turned the corner and strolled away.

Tom touched my arm. "Ollie?"

It didn't help to look at him. Actually, it made it worse.

"This is hard," I said.

"What is?"

Was that fear in his eyes, or just the reflection of a passing car's headlights? I took a breath.

"Ollie, don't do this." He reached out and grabbed my hand. "I know you're upset about my comments recently. I know you think I don't understand you —"

"You don't."

He squeezed. "But I do."

I tugged my hand back. "I want you to tell Craig that he can stop threatening you."

He leaned back, looking hurt. "I'm not afraid of Craig."

"I'm afraid of what he can do to you. And to your career."

Tom waved his hand as though brushing away a fly. "I can handle him."

"You're not going to have to."

The hurt look came back.

My stomach flip-flopped, and my heart raced with panic. My words came out fast, almost as though I was afraid that if I took my time, I wouldn't have the courage to say them. "I want you to tell Craig that we've broken up." I swallowed. "I want you to tell him we're not a couple anymore."

He was shaking his head. "This is all wrong," he said, staring out the window. "We can't let Craig — or even this investigation — dictate how we live our lives." He made eye contact again. "We have to be true to ourselves."

I nodded. "That's the other part of it."

He looked confused.

"I can't be the person you want me to be."

He said nothing.

I folded my hands on the table then dropped them to my lap before continuing. "I can't let this go."

"You can't let us go?"

"No," I said sadly. "I can't let all these kitchen accusations continue without doing anything. Without defending myself."

"But, Ollie. You're not authorized —"

"I know I'm not," I snapped. "And I never intended to throw myself into the middle of the investigation, but I can't just stare in from the sidelines, either. Every move I make, I worry: Will this be construed as getting involved? Am I putting Tom's career at risk? Will Tom get mad at me because I talked with Ruth Minkus? Because I met with Suzie and Steve? Because I studied Minkus's dossier? It's making me crazy."

"Where did you get Minkus's dossier?"

Now I waved him off.

The coffee grew cold and the beer warm as I told Tom exactly how I had been feeling since he made me promise not to poke my nose into the investigation. "I never intend to get involved in these things. You know that. But I can't keep second-guessing myself. I can't keep worrying that I'm stepping out of bounds somehow." I met his gaze. "I have to be who I am, Tom. I have to be true to myself. And our circumstances are such that I can't be myself — not really — if you're part of my life."

He pursed his lips, not meeting my eyes. Finally, when he did, he said, "That's it then?"

"Is there anything you want to say? Anything else you want to talk about?"

His expression grew tight. "No. I think you made yourself clear." With that, he pulled out his wallet, tossed cash on the table, and stood up. "Do you want me to walk you to the Metro station?" he asked with no emotion whatsoever. "It's late."

I had expected questions, even hoped for him to argue me out of it. But instead, my now-former boyfriend stood next to the tall table, waiting for me to alight from my chair. "That's okay," I said. "I'll be fine."

He pinched the bridge of his nose with his fingers. "Let me rephrase that. I will walk you to the Metro unless you tell me I can't."

"Thank you," I said. When in doubt, always be polite, my mom advised. A sad thought flashed through my mind. Mom was on a first date — and I was on a last. "I appreciate it."

We walked in silence the entire way. Tom didn't accompany me down into the station, and at the top of the stairs, I was prepared for an awkward good-bye. But when I turned to him, he had already started away. "Tom," I called to his back.

He waved a hand, and half turned in acknowledgment. But he kept walking.

CHAPTER 19

I stared out the window of the Metro train, seeing nothing. My conversation with Tom replayed itself in my mind, like a wretched scene from a sad movie. I analyzed every movement, every nuance. Not that there was much to decode. Once I'd told him what was on my mind, Tom had made it clear he couldn't get away from me fast enough. Had I done the right thing? Was I inadvertently punishing him for not supporting me? Was I being selfish with my need for the freedom to poke my nose where I wanted to poke it?

My heart seemed to beat more slowly than it ever had, every lub-dub a crushing ache. The relationship might have ended, but that didn't mean my feelings for Tom had. I still cared deeply for him, and probably always would. I wondered again if I'd made the right decision. But Tom had been asking me to be someone I wasn't. He wanted a girlfriend who would follow the rules of life that made sense to him, but were anathema to me.

In his life, he was right — just as I was in mine. No fault to be assigned. But no happy ending, either. I looked out into the darkness.

I sighed again. Just because this was the right thing to do didn't make it easy.

"You're back," Nana said when I came through the door. Her face was bright with excitement, but I couldn't find it in me to smile back.

"Where's Mom?" I asked.

"She had a wonderful time," Nana went on, unmindful of my mood. "They only got back about a half hour ago."

Instinctively I looked at my watch, but the time didn't register. Still, I knew it was late. "Just a half hour ago?" I asked, still standing in my little foyer. My mind was slow to process her words. "But it's after midnight."

Nana grinned.

"Whatever," I said. My conversation with Tom was still fresh in my mind, and still stung. I wanted to crawl into my bed and sleep away my disappointment. I desperately wanted to be alone.

"Ollie," Mom said, coming in from the kitchen. She, too, looked at her watch. "I thought you'd be home by now."

Looking away, I said. "Lots of catch-up work."

Nana continued to beam at her daughter, but my mom was staring at me. "Is there something wrong?"

Making a face that said, "Nah," I lied, shaking my head. "Just a long day. That, and the fact that they've suspended Bucky."

They chorused their disapproval and started to ask me questions, but I really couldn't handle explaining everything right then. Cranky, tired, and feeling as though my hands were tied, I realized it was better to let someone else talk for a while. "How did Kap behave?" I asked.

"Behave?" There was levity in Mom's voice, but I could sense her displeasure at my choice of words. "Perfectly, of course. We went to a lovely restaurant for dinner." When she told me about the upscale seafood restaurant, I interrupted.

"You have that chain in Chicago. I've seen at least one of them downtown. And in Schaumburg. Probably Oak Brook, too."

Mom's smile faltered only slightly. "You may be right, but this was a new experience for me."

"It's a decent restaurant," I said against rising anger I knew I should contain, but couldn't. "But why not take you somewhere unique to D.C.?"

She blinked. "The restaurant didn't matter. What mattered was the company."

"The company of a man who was on a date with you instead of at his best friend's funeral?"

"Olivia!" Mom snapped.

"I'm sorry," I said. Although I meant it, I was not able to stand there and talk a moment longer. I didn't blame her. I blamed myself. But that didn't mean I had control over my emotions right now. I wanted to find a familiar hole and hide, letting the rest of the world go on without me. Every thread of my soul panged with disappointment. All I wanted was to be alone.

The looks Mom and Nana gave me were less of anger and more of concern. "I'm sorry," I said again.

"Something *is* wrong, isn't it?" Mom asked.

One thing about people who have known you since birth: You can rely on them to be your strongest allies when times get really tough, even if they don't fully understand. I knew they would cut me the slack I needed tonight. And despite my desire for solitude, I was glad they were there. "There's a lot wrong," I said finally. "But right now I better go to bed before I make things worse." I tried to smile, but I wasn't fooling anyone. "I'm going to put an end to this horrible day, and start fresh tomorrow."

Nana and Mom exchanged glances.

"That's probably best," Mom said.

I lay awake for a long time, staring up into the darkness until my eyes adjusted and everything in the room seemed clear again. *If only life were like that,* I thought. Look at something long enough, and see it for what it really is.

Mom and Nana sat in the kitchen, talking. I couldn't make out their words, but the soft murmurings — which I knew were full of concerns about me — reminded me of nights in my bed when I was a little girl at home and the comforting sound of their quiet conversation lulled me to sleep. Oh that I could return to those days, just for an instant . . . Just for tonight.

Sleep continued to dance in the darkness, just out of reach. As I stared at the ceiling and reshuffled my last conversation with Tom, I watched the dull luminescence of the clock. Its digital numbers inched upward with painful precision.

Tomorrow would be a better day, I promised myself. Until I realized it was already tomorrow.

CHAPTER 20

Despite my pronouncement never to read *Liss Is More* again, the man's appearance on the Metro yesterday spooked me enough to check if he had made good on his promise to "out" my relationship with Tom. Just wait until he found out we were no longer a couple. I'd scooped him on one story at least. But there was no joy in it.

I scanned the page quickly. Today's column made no mention of me, and none of Tom, thank goodness. Today, Liss seemed focused on Carl Minkus's next targets. He wrote extensively about Alicia Parker and Phil Cooper and why Minkus might have had reason to suspect them of consorting with terrorists in their free time.

Happy that he hadn't targeted me again, and convinced that Liss was certifiable, I shoved the newspaper away, and decided that this was a very positive omen. A very good way to start the day.

I made coffee, started breakfast, and resolved to beat away any negative thoughts — if not for myself, then for my family. I owed them that much. My behavior yesterday after Mom's date was inexcusable.

Homemade waffles, topped with bananas, strawberries, and blueberries would make a good start, I decided. The mixed scents floated above my head, and I knew — with a kitchen as small as mine — it wouldn't be long before the delicious aromas woke up my sleeping family.

A few minutes later Mom wandered into the kitchen. "What's the occasion?" Still in her bathrobe, she blinked at the kitchen clock. "You're up early."

"I have to be at work in about an hour," I said. "But I wanted time to visit before I left."

She looked at me quizzically. "Need any help?"

"No," I said. "Sit. Let me take care of you this time."

She sat, and turned the newspaper around to read. "Anything I should be aware of in here?"

"We're flying under the radar today," I said in a cheery tone. "So far, so good."

I poured her a cup of coffee and set out the half-and-half. "So . . ." I said.

She dragged her attention away from the newspaper. "So?"

I was at the counter, half facing her. Taking a breath, I messed with some of the waffle fixings and said, "I was out of line yesterday."

She nodded, but didn't say anything for a long moment. Then: "Yes, you were."

"I am sorry. Truly sorry."

"I know," she said, turning back to the news. "And you should be."

I sprinkled powdered sugar over a strawberry-topped waffle and placed it in front of her. "Did you want blueberries? Bananas?"

"No. This is just perfect."

Strawberries were always Mom's favorite. At least some things hadn't changed. "Whipped cream?"

She laughed. "You trying to fatten me up?"

"No, just trying to apologize."

"Sit."

I grabbed my own fruit-topped waffle and joined her at the table.

"Ollie," she said, gently, "I had a wonderful day out yesterday."

"I'm glad to hear that. Really, I am," I said. "I don't know what —"

She shushed me with a look. "You and I

both know that when this vacation comes to an end, Nana and I will be headed back to our trivial lives in Chicago."

"Trivial?" I shook my head. "You do so much —"

"*Shh,*" she said with force. "My life is good, for me. But it's . . . little. I'm not surrounded by the most important people in the world like you are. You see and hear and do things most of us only dream of."

"That doesn't make what you do *un*important."

"True, but what you don't seem to understand is that while I'm here, I get to share a little bit of your life. And Kap . . ." Her eyes went all dreamy for a moment. "He's part of that. He's interesting — different." She laughed. "And sexy."

I felt my face redden.

She laughed again and playfully tapped my hand. "All I want is to have fun," she said. "I don't get a lot of fun back home."

I nodded. Regret at my attitude from the day before soured my stomach. I looked down at the uneaten waffle and changed my mind about it. "I really am sorry," I said again.

"And you're forgiven," she said. "I do understand, you know. I remember when Nana went out on a couple dates."

"Nana dated?"

As if summoned, my grandmother appeared in the doorway. "Damn right I did," she said, sniffing the air and eyeing my plate. "Maybe someday I'll tell you about all the ones that got away."

"Ones?" I asked. "Plural?"

Nana lowered herself into the chair opposite mine. "You going to eat that, or you going to stare at it all morning?"

I pushed the heaping plate across the table. "For you."

She dug in as I stood up. With a hand on my mother's shoulder, I reached down to kiss her cheek. "Thanks, Mom."

Much to my relief, Howard Liss was not on the morning Metro train. Not that I'd expected him to be up and about this early. Most people weren't.

That's why it was such a surprise to get a voicemail beep when the train came aboveground at Arlington Cemetery. My phone had been off overnight but I'd turned it back on before leaving the apartment. That meant that whoever called had done so in the past few minutes. Maybe it was Mom or Nana.

The train slowed, then stopped to load new passengers at Arlington. As a lone person boarded the car in front of the one I was in, I took the opportunity to access my message: "Olivia," came the breathless voice. "This is Howard Liss. You must call me as soon as you get this. I'm sure your phone has a redial feature, but don't use that one. Use my private line." He provided the number, but I didn't even consider writing it down. At the same time, the Metro started moving again. "This is of the utmost importance." I heard him take a breath, before repeating: "*Utmost.* I know you think you should not contact me. But if I don't hear from you by mid-morning, I will move forward to make public that relationship we discussed. I know you —"

And just like that, I lost the signal.

I swore.

The two other riders in my car looked up.

I lifted a hand in apology. "Sorry."

One returned to his newspaper. The other leaned against the window and closed his eyes.

Just what I needed. More Howard Liss. Why on earth was he contacting me, anyway? What good could I possibly do him? "That relationship we discussed . . ." The creep. He was lucky I couldn't get a signal. Otherwise I would have called him back immediately just to burst his little bubble.

The train ride to MacPherson Square took an interminably long time. I'm usually the kind of person who stews about something before issuing a retaliatory response. Tom used to call me a little volcano. By the time I made it to the street level and pulled out my phone, I'd built up such a head of steam that I could barely contain myself. Somebody had to zip this guy's mouth shut, and I felt like just the person to do it.

I punched the redial button. He answered on the first ring. "Howard Liss."

"This is Olivia Paras," I said briskly. I had rehearsed a whole slew of powerful opening lines, but what came out was: "How dare you threaten me?"

He made a gurgling noise. "Oh, yes. Hello."

I pressed the phone tight against my ear. "All you can say is 'Hello'? After leaving me a threatening message, you can only say, 'Hello'?"

He dropped his voice. "You weren't supposed to call on this number."

"Oh, yes," I said loudly as I strode south toward the White House. "That, too. What do you think I am, some simpleton? Just because I was involved in a couple of" — I lost my intensity for a moment, thinking about my involvement in other situations —

"incidents at the White House, doesn't mean that I care to participate in your crazy schemes. And I don't —"

"Please," he said, interrupting me. "Can you call me back on that other number?"

What the heck was wrong with this guy? Convinced he was even more touched in the head than I'd originally assumed, I was tempted to hang up. But I couldn't. No matter the state of his mind, this fellow held the power to mess up my life. And Tom's career. Before I hung up, I knew I had to impart one very important piece of information.

Using the same name for Tom that Liss had when he accosted me on the train, I said, "You need to know that 'MacKenzie' and I are no longer involved."

Dead silence.

"Liss?" My footsteps made soft scratches on the sidewalk as I kept up a quick pace. "Are you there?"

A click and then my phone went dead. I muttered an angry expletive as I dialed my voicemail account and listened to his message again. This time I memorized his "preferred" phone number and dialed it as soon as I terminated the call.

"Olivia?" he asked when he answered. "Thank goodness."

"What is wrong with you?" I asked. "I have no intention of turning this into a chatty phone conversation. So just listen. The 'relationship' you threatened to make public is no longer an issue."

Dead silence, again.

If this unscrupulous, unprincipled blabbermouth hung up on me a second time, I swore I would march down to the newspaper office to confront him personally. He surprised me by whispering, "Hang on one second."

Moments later, the quiet background on his side of the connection was replaced by the sound of traffic and wind. "You there?" he asked.

"Not for long." I wasn't exaggerating. I'd made the trek from the station to the White House gate in record time. Anger does that for me.

A crowd lined up along the White House fence startled me for a moment, and I slowed my pace. But then I remembered what day it was. Egg Roll tickets would be handed out today and hundreds of people were already lined up — some of them having camped out overnight just for the chance to be part of Monday's festivities. Bundled up against the morning chill, they sat in small groups — in lawn chairs, or huddled in sleeping bags on the cold sidewalk.

"Listen," Liss said.

"No, *you* listen. Did you not hear what I just said about my relationship with Tom?" I clenched my eyes shut. I'd been careful not to use his first name in this conversation. Too personal. But I'd gotten so worked up with all the interruptions that I'd lost that small measure of control. I coughed and clarified. "I am no longer involved with Mr. MacKenzie."

"That's too bad," he said. "I'm sorry."

This man was definitely crackers. "The heck you are," I said. "If it weren't for you threatening to make it public —"

"That's not what I want to talk with you about."

I was within thirty feet of the gates. I kept my voice low to prevent eager ticket-seekers from overhearing my conversation. But most looked too sleepy to care. "In case you didn't understand me the other day, I have no desire to talk with you. About anything. And now that you no longer have Mr. Mac-Kenzie to hold over my head, our conversations are finished."

"But don't you want to know who killed Minkus?"

I stopped walking. "Like you have that

345

information. Give me a break. If you knew, you'd tell the world."

"Knowing something and proving it are two completely different things. You've learned that, haven't you, Olivia?" Now that he was standing outside his office building — an assumption I made based on the ambient noises and his intense desire for privacy — his voice took on a condescending air. "Wouldn't it help you — and help your assistant Bucky — if the real guilty party were brought to light?"

"When I find out," I said, "and I say 'when,' not 'if,' it will be through proper channels, not through some delusional journalist's mad ravings."

He made a noise that sounded like, *"Tsk."*

"Have a good day," I said, for lack of a better send-off.

"Wait."

"I don't have time for this."

"Well then maybe your mother does."

My hand tightened on the phone. "Don't you ever —"

"She really likes that Zenobios Kapostoulos, doesn't she?" he asked. "But I believe you know him better as Kap."

I was stricken silent until I remembered that we'd all been in the same small group at the Minkus wake. "You are mistaken," I said. "Yet again." I resumed walking to the gate.

"Am I?" His voice resumed its playful arrogance. I hated it. "Then I assume your mother didn't tell you about her dinner date last night."

"How the hell — ?" I stopped myself, took a deep breath, then continued. "Don't you have anything better to do than to poke into my family's life?"

"Your mother's friend Kap is involved with Minkus's death."

"What?" I asked. "How?"

"Oh, so now I have your attention." I heard him lick his lips. He must have covered the mouthpiece, because suddenly the background noises grew quiet and hollow. "I don't know precisely. Yet."

My mind raced as I tried to piece things together. "Kap wasn't at the dinner Sunday. He couldn't have done it."

"You sure about that?"

"I'm sure he wasn't at the dinner."

He chuckled. "That's not what I meant and you know it. How sure are you that he didn't do it?"

I wasn't. "Then why don't you tell me how he did?"

"I can't. But what I can tell you is that Kap isn't working alone. And I don't even

347

believe that's his real name."

I glanced at my watch. I needed to be in the kitchen posthaste. Not standing out in the chilly morning, listening to outlandish scenarios. This moment held a peculiar sense of déjà vu.

I started toward the gate again. "I gotta go."

"Wait," he said, so quickly and forcefully that I stutter-stepped. "Phil Cooper."

"What about him?"

He heaved a huge sigh. "I didn't want to get into this right away, but I'll tell you."

"Then hurry up."

"I have reason to believe that Phil Cooper committed the actual murder."

"You just said Kap did it."

It sounded like he licked his lips again. He'd be chapped before he knew it. Good.

"I said Kap was involved. Listen, please. The two of them are meeting today." He started talking very quickly. "I have a source."

"Why tell me?"

"Because another one of my sources trusts you. And through you — through your mother, to be precise — I can gain access to Kap."

This was getting totally out of hand. I would not allow him to involve my mother.

"I'm done," I said loudly. I excused myself to make my way through the line of waiting people, then slipped my employee ID through the card reader at the gate. "Goodbye."

"Kap and Cooper have ties to the Chinese government. They took Minkus out." His words were tinctured with an air of desperation. "I have a source that can prove this. I know I'm right. And you'll be reading about it in my column soon. Why not help me? You like all that attention, don't you?"

I passed the guard in the front gatehouse, who had been watching my animated movements with a look of concern. Giving him a little wave, I said into the phone: "No, I don't. And to be perfectly frank, I'm convinced that Liss is *not* more."

Before he could say another word, I hung up.

"Sorry," I said, stripping off my jacket and donning an apron. "I meant to get here sooner."

Cyan waved me away with a mixing spoon. "You're hardly late. I just got here myself."

"What are you working on?"

She brought me up to speed on breakfast preparations. She had gotten almost everything done already — so her protestation that she'd only just arrived really didn't ring true. I gave silent thanks for having such a reliable staff to depend on, then felt the immediate crush of disappointment when I remembered Bucky's situation.

"Howard Liss called me this morning," I said as I pulled an asparagus and artichoke frittata out from under the broiler. I eased it onto a serving plate and looked up just in time to see Jackson walk in.

The head waiter smiled. "Ready to go?"

"Just about." Cyan sprinkled a little cinnamon onto the president's French toast. He and his wife had completely different breakfast favorites. While he preferred basic fare such as scrambled eggs, hash browns, and French toast, his wife had a more adventurous palate. Today's veggie frittata wasn't exactly exotic, but it had been considered "unusual" the first time we served it to her. Now it was one of her favorites.

With all the recent upheavals, I thought that it would be nice to treat them to their particular comfort foods this week. I garnished the plates with fruit and edible flowers. "There you go."

Jackson took off, plates in hand, and Cyan and I cleaned up. "Howard Liss called you?" she asked. "Why?"

I tried to summarize his ramblings as best I could, but in the end all I could say was, "The man has crazy ideas. I'm ashamed to say I stayed on the phone with him as long as I did. I should have hung up immediately."

"You're just too polite, Ollie."

"And it gets me into trouble."

Cyan laughed. "Tom wouldn't argue with that."

My breath caught.

Her voice lowered. "What happened?"

I shook my head and started to pull out recipes for the next day's meals, but she stopped me with a firm hand on my arm. "Talk to me."

"We have a hundred things to do before Easter dinner tomorrow, and before the Egg Roll on Monday."

"And we're ridiculously short-staffed until Bucky comes back," she agreed. "But we can still afford a couple of minutes to talk. Tell me what's going on."

"It's over," I said simply. "I ended it."

Cyan had chosen violet contact lenses today. Her purple gaze unnerved me, so I kept talking. "Tom's job was on the line because of me. Craig Sanderson believes that pitting boyfriend against girlfriend is an effective deterrent to poking my nose into official business."

"Sounds like it was more effective in driving a wedge between you."

I gave an unhappy laugh. "It's been a hell of a week."

Cyan bit her lip, and I could tell she didn't know what to say.

I patted her on the shoulder. "We'll get through this."

"You and Tom?"

"No. Our kitchen." I settled myself on the stool in front of the computer screen. I needed to e-mail Brandy. "First things first. We have to arrange for getting all those eggs here. Even though we got a lot done already, we still have more to do."

"Speaking of tons to do, we have two extra guests for lunch today."

I clicked an open document. "It's not on the schedule."

"Paul called down here before you got in. I didn't get a chance to update the file yet."

"I'll do it." Hunching over the keyboard, I asked her for specifics. She dug a scribbled note out of her apron pocket and I turned to wait. "Phil Cooper and . . ." She shook her head. "I'm going to massacre this name. Zee . . . Zeno . . ."

"Zenobios Kapostoulos?" I stood up.

"How in the world did you know that?"

Cyan stared at me.

Speechless, I replayed the tape of my conversation with Liss in my head as I paced the small area. He had been right — again. "They're meeting with the president?" I asked. "Here? Today?"

Cyan nodded.

Liss hadn't mentioned the president, but he had known about the two men meeting. What else was Liss right about? That Kap had been instrumental in Minkus's death? The same guy who had taken my mother out on a date? My knees wobbled, and I eased myself back onto the stool.

Cyan, obviously shaken by my sharp reaction, kept asking, "What?" but I didn't answer. She brought her face close to mine. "You're scaring me, Ollie."

I tried to put everything together, but I was coming up woefully short.

"We have Cooper's information in our files," Cyan said. I could tell she was trying to understand me, and when she couldn't she tried throwing more information, hoping for a hit. "Paul says he'll have this Zeno guy's stuff sent down ASAP."

"Good," I said. "I can get a look at his dossier."

"Who is this guy?"

"Kap," I said. "The guy who's dating my

mother."

"He's coming here?"

Time was ticking and the longer we sat around talking, the worse things would get. Rather than answer her, I said, "We need help."

She waited, frustrated dimples framing her mouth.

"I'll tell you everything," I said. "But first we have to get those eggs delivered here, and we need another set of hands in the kitchen."

"But Paul won't let us —"

"Call Paul. See if he'll bring Henry back. Just for a couple days."

Cyan grinned. "Ollie, you're a genius! I'm sure Paul will agree to that."

"Just remember, tomorrow is Easter. Henry may not be able to make it."

Her cheer dimmed only slightly. "Well, there's only one way to find out."

CHAPTER 21

Lunch preparation at the White House should not be fraught with worry. But here I was, dropping utensils, spilling raspberry sauce, forgetting where I left the container of almonds, and having to re-confirm the oven temperature three times before I trusted I'd set it correctly.

We received Kap's dossier. His occupation was listed as "consultant" and he was apparently self-employed. I wondered exactly what sort of consulting he did that brought him to the White House today.

It wasn't just the fact that Liss had predicted this meeting that threw me off my game. And it wasn't because of Kap's alleged involvement in Minkus's death — although I had to admit that was a big one for me to get my head around. I was upset, worried, and uncharacteristically frantic because we were serving a meal in the White House to Phil Cooper. Not only had he been one of the individuals present at Sunday's disastrous dinner — according to Liss, he was one of the prime suspects. Like him or not, and I certainly didn't, Liss had an uncanny knack for being able to find things out.

I could not let anything go wrong — not with the food — this time. But what if Cooper had bigger game in his sights? But I couldn't go sounding the alarm to the Secret Service based on vague, unsubstantiated innuendo from a questionable journalist.

Cyan and I worked in almost total silence. In between lunch preparations, she and I also did our best to work ahead for tomorrow's Easter dinner. But when I dropped yet another one of our tasting spoons, she gave out a strangled cry. "You're making *me* nervous now."

"What did Paul say about Henry?" I asked.

She stopped long enough to look at me. "That's the fourth time you've asked me." She glanced at the clock. "In the past two hours."

I rubbed my forehead with the back of my hand. "I just can't seem to concentrate."

"You're going to have to, especially if Henry can't make it. Paul said he would call him personally. He'll let us know when he gets an answer."

"Of course," I said, realizing I *had* heard this information already. "But I can't stop thinking about how this luncheon meeting could go bad." I swept my hand out, encompassing the room. "We have to make certain that nothing happens to the president's food between the time we prepare it and the time it's served."

"How do you intend to do that?"

I shook my head. I didn't know. "Where are they serving?"

Cyan gave me a look that made it clear I'd asked that question before, too.

"Oh, yeah," I said, remembering. "The President's Dining Room." I stared down at the greens before me, looked up at the door, then studied the clock. "That will make it difficult."

"Make what difficult?"

"What if we accompanied our creations?" I was thinking out loud here, but the more I talked, the better the idea began to sound. "We can tell the wait staff that we need to prepare this tableside —"

She looked shocked. "But we don't."

"Who's going to argue with us?"

"The President's Dining Room is in the West Wing!" she said, although she clearly knew I was aware of that fact. "Are you nuts?"

"No, listen." I held up both hands, excited now. "The butlers will serve — just like normal. But we would be right outside the dining room, plating the courses just before they go in."

"That's crazy," Cyan said. "What do you think you can possibly accomplish?"

"We'll be able to ensure that the president's food is safe. That's paramount. There will be no chance for anyone else to have access to the food before it's served."

"You don't trust our wait staff?"

"I do," I said. "But call me paranoid. Something went wrong on Sunday, and we still don't know what it was. All I know is that I'll feel better if the chain of custody isn't compromised. The only way I can be certain of that is to be there myself."

" 'Chain of custody'? You're starting to sound like a TV cop show." She shook her head, but I noticed the glimmer of possibility in her eyes. "We'll have to clear this with Jackson."

"Not only that," I said, my mind in hyperdrive, "we can maybe even get a sense of what's going on in there. I mean, why are they meeting with the president anyway?"

"Ollie!" Cyan's expression was one of utter disbelief. "You know that's none of our business. Besides," she added, her tone softening, "they'd never let us close enough to actually overhear anything. Not in the West Wing."

"You're right," I said. "But maybe we can find out what Kap is doing here."

She gave me a skeptical look. "Is that what this is all about? You're playing detective because of him cozying up to your mom?"

"No," I said. And I meant it. "I don't know what the guy's story is, but I can't help feeling that we need to be there. Liss swears that Kap and Cooper were responsible for Minkus's death. If he's right, then our president will be dining this afternoon with two assassins."

I didn't understand Cyan's sudden sympathetic expression. "Ollie," she said. "I know you're taking this Minkus death personally. I understand that. I feel it, too. But there's really not a thing either of us can do. It's completely out of our hands."

She had a point. The heightened tension I'd felt from making elaborate plans fell suddenly away. I picked up the greens I'd been working with. "You're right."

"Plus we have so much work to do . . . ."

"What's this?" came a booming voice from the doorway. "Are we standing around chatting or are we working?"

"Henry!" I dropped the greens and wiped my hands on my apron to give him a big hug. "You came!"

"I left home the minute I received Paul's call." He reached out to hug Cyan, too. "How could I resist? He said you needed me."

A lump lodged in my throat. It was so good to see Henry — so good to have him here. His face was ruddier and more wrinkled than I remembered, but he had slimmed down, and — did I imagine this? — had developed significant muscularity. "You look great," I said. "What have you been doing?"

"I added a secret ingredient to my diet," he said with a wink. "Powerful stuff."

Cyan teased: "You should consider sharing your secret ingredient with the world. You'd make millions."

"No sharing," he said, wagging a finger, his smile bigger than I'd seen it in all the time we worked together. "Nope, nope, nope."

"Secret ingredient, huh?" I put my hands on my hips. "Okay, Henry, 'fess up. What's her name?"

"Now what makes you think that a woman is responsible for my . . . renaissance?" His

360

eyes twinkled.

We waited.

"Her name is Mercedes. And now, you two astute detectives, tell me what needs to be done."

We brought him up to speed on all menu decisions and discovered that Paul had already briefed him on the Bucky situation. "We are most certainly under the gun," he said. "But this kitchen has been in dire straits before. We shall prevail, as we always have." Finished with his proclamation, he turned to me. "Ms. Executive Chef, I am at your command."

With Henry on our team, we flew through tasks, the three of us so comfortable and confident with one another that we required minimal discussion to get things done. Even better than having two extra hands and an extra brain in the kitchen, Henry boosted our morale by his very presence.

Lunch was due to be plated in about thirty minutes and I still hadn't completely given up the idea of finagling a way into the West Wing to ensure President Campbell's food made it to him safely.

Swinging past the computer, I noticed I had a new e-mail. "Excellent!" I said aloud as I read it.

"What's up?" Cyan asked.

I turned. "Brandy says she'll be able to help us with . . ."

I stopped.

At the opposite end of the counter, carving cherry tomatoes into tiny flower-shaped garnishes, Henry looked up. Cyan tried to prompt me. "With what? The eggs?"

"I've got it!" I said.

They shared another quick glance. "Great. Got what?"

"Brandy managed to get all the eggs transported back to a staging warehouse," I said, talking quickly. "This is perfect."

Cyan nodded, clearly dubious.

"I need to arrange to have the Secret Service pick up all the eggs. Which means I have to coordinate with Craig Sanderson. How about if I head over to the West Wing when the butlers come for the president's lunch? I'll be able to make sure that the meal gets there safely and while I'm there, I'll try to snag a few minutes of Craig's time."

"Lame," Cyan said.

"Maybe, but I don't trust Cooper or Kap. I have to do this."

"I know you do."

Henry had been watching us, his eyebrows raised. As I started to explain, he held up a hand. "Maybe it's best if I don't know."

More often than not, President Campbell held casual luncheon meetings in the White House Mess, which was the navy-run kitchen and dining room in the basement of the West Wing. The fact that he had requested today's lunch brought in from the residence kitchen, and the fact that he was choosing to dine in the President's Dining Room, told me that whatever this meeting was about, it was important enough to warrant privacy.

Jackson kept his eyes forward, not saying much for most of our passage across the residence. The lack of conversation was okay by me. I was salivating. But that was more from curiosity than from the delicious aromas drifting upward from the cart the butler pushed.

He and I took a roundabout path to the basement of the West Wing and when we finally arrived at the elevator that would take us to the main floor, Jackson gestured with his chin. "Secret Service office is that way."

"I know."

He waited a beat. "You aren't here just to talk with Sanderson, are you?" He flicked a glance down toward the covered plates and accompaniments. "You're making sure this food stays safe."

I nodded.

"If I didn't know you as well as I do, Ollie, I'd take offense."

"Jackson, I don't think for a minute . . ."

He held up a hand, but was interrupted when the elevator opened. We got in, Jackson backing the cart in so he could exit gracefully at the first floor. When the door closed again, he said, "I know you're not thinking about me doing something bad to the food." He pointed. "Brand-new salt, brand-new pepper. Freshly sterilized flatware. Everything here is clean."

Each diner was always provided his own set of everything, including condiments — to prevent the inexcusable "boarding-house reach." I nodded. "I'm sure it is."

His nostrils flared. "You're wondering about Cooper."

Astonished by his astuteness, I nodded again.

The elevator opened and we made our way out, the cart's contents clanking softly as we traversed the carpeted floor. "I guarantee you I am not going to turn my back on this cart for one moment." He nodded solemnly as we walked.

"Thanks, Jackson. You're the best."

We'd both lowered our voices. In this wing of the White House, I was always awestruck. This was the epicenter, the heart of the free world — at least, in my unabashedly patriotic way, that's the way I saw it. I knew from firsthand experience how much time and effort went into every decision here. While I certainly wasn't privy to classified information, I knew the people who were. I saw the toll the weight of responsibility took on each and every member of the administration. These were good people, making the best decisions they could, every single day.

We stopped our trek just outside the President's Dining Room. To my left was the Roosevelt Room, and straight ahead, through a small angled corridor, the Oval Office. Even after working here for so long, being in this part of the White House made my skin tingle.

With so many people navigating the hallway, Jackson wheeled the cart into the empty Roosevelt Room. Across the hall from the President's Dining Room, and with access to the Oval Office, the windowless space housed a long table that comfortably sat sixteen. President Nixon had named the room to honor both Theodore and Franklin Delano Roosevelt. Sitting Republicans traditionally displayed Teddy Roosevelt's *Rough Rider* painting over the mantle, and sitting Democrats traditionally displayed Franklin Delano Roosevelt's portrait.

President Campbell, who expressed great admiration for both men, opted to feature both paintings in the room and instructed the staff to alternate the artworks' positions so that they equally shared the position of prestige.

"Good thing you're here," Jackson said. "I can use the help." There were butlers he could have called, but we had an unspoken agreement: The fewer people involved, the better we could keep our suspicions under wraps. Although I knew this was probably overkill, neither one of us wanted to leave anything to chance. "I'll be right back," he said.

While he disappeared into the dining room across the hall, I waited near the Roosevelt Room's doorway, the serving cart directly behind me. I knew Jackson was preparing the dining table for the meal. Seconds later, he emerged, dodging several staffers in the hall as they walked past. "We may serve."

Usually, at dinner, the butlers handled no more than one plate at a time. In fact, at the most formal affairs, all guests are served at the same moment by individual butlers. It's quite a sight. Since today's luncheon was informal, however, Jackson carried in one plate of baby greens with raspberry vinaigrette dressing for the president, then came back for the other two plates.

I maintained my presence near the doorway, the cart safely stowed behind me. Now that I was in the heart of the West Wing, I tuned in to passing conversations. I caught a few vague references to headline topics, but nothing about Minkus. Until Jackson returned.

"I will check back with them in a moment. They will be ready for the entrée shortly," he said. "Right now, it's quiet. I don't think they plan to do any serious talking with their mouths full of your famous salad."

I shrugged, feigning nonchalance.

"What were you hoping to overhear?"

"Me?" I asked. "Nothing at all."

"Yeah, like I believe that," he said with a smirk, then lapsed into the folksy speech that he probably reserved for times when he was relaxing with friends. "Don't you be trying to pull one over on old Jack."

"Okay," I said. "The other guy . . . not Cooper . . . goes by the name Kap." Jackson must have detected the disdain in my voice because his eyebrows raised. I frowned. "He took my mother out on a date."

The look on Jackson's face would have been enough to make me laugh if the situation hadn't been so serious. "Well, that's about the last thing I expected to hear."

"Not only that, he's a good friend of the Minkus family. I have to believe there's a connection now that he's chumming up with Cooper."

Jackson glanced at the dining room door. "You wait here," he said.

As he continued to serve, he provided me with a play-by-play of the conversation going on in the dining room. "Just discussing the assassinations in China," he said. But then he shook his head. "Cooper, I understand why he's here. But not that other gentleman. I wonder what his story is."

I thought about Liss's allegations. I wondered if Kap could have poisoned Minkus before dinner — I thought about how much Ruth Minkus despised the man. Did she have a sense about him? I would probably never know.

Jackson came in, his eyes bright. "You want the scoop?" he asked. He scanned the room and lowered his voice. "President Campbell took a call while I was in there. From the medical examiner."

I swallowed. Waited.

He whispered, "And he shared this information with the other two men."

"Well?" My throat was so dry I could barely ask, "What did he say?"

Jackson's brow furrowed. "You aren't going to like it."

Visions of heads rolling — mine, Bucky's, Cyan's — made my legs weak. "Just tell me."

"They figured out what killed Minkus."

I held my breath.

"It was a toxin."

Oh my God, I thought. *It couldn't be.* "Like . . . botulism?" I asked.

Jackson shook his head. "Don't know. President Campbell wrote it down while he was on the phone, but I couldn't get a look. Soon as he got off the phone, he showed the note to the other two. They didn't say it when I was in the room, but they did say 'toxin' a couple of times."

I prayed it wasn't botulism. It couldn't be. I took great care in my kitchen to keep food safe. That was part of my responsibility. It just couldn't be. It couldn't be.

"I have to find out," I said.

Jackson looked as upset as I was. "Don't know how you can."

"They aren't going to announce it?"

"No, ma'am. All three agreed to share this on a 'need to know' basis until . . . something — don't know what — can be verified. They're keeping mum. Heck, the president won't even say it in front of me and you know we're usually invisible." Jackson's face was creased with worry. "I probably shouldn't have told you that much."

"Don't worry, it won't go anywhere." I closed my eyes for a long moment. "That means the kitchen is under suspicion again, doesn't it?"

"I can't answer that, Ollie," he said. "But I can tell you that they aren't sharing this information with the media yet, so . . ." He held a finger to his lips. "Okay?"

My brain was on hyper-drive. "If it was botulism . . ."

Jackson grimaced. "For your sake, hope it isn't."

I nodded. I supposed I'd find out soon enough. I hated waiting. In this case, however, I had no choice. He left me again.

Moments later, Jackson came back into the Roosevelt Room.

Followed by Cooper.

My shock at the agent's unexpected appearance rendered me speechless.

"Hello," he said pleasantly. "It's nice to

see you again, Ms. Paras."

I murmured a polite reply, not understanding this turn of events. Jackson intervened. "Mr. Cooper needs this room to make a private phone call," he said with just the proper eloquence to usher me out. He followed me into the hall with the now-empty food cart.

Already dialing, Cooper offered absent-minded thanks.

As soon as we were in the corridor, Jackson pointed to the dining room. "Come on, let's get in there."

"In?" I asked. "Where?"

He brought a finger to his lips. In hushed tones, he urged me forward. "President Campbell was called away by his secretary. It's your chance, Ollie. Take it now or . . ."

He didn't get to finish his sentence.

I stepped into the President's Dining Room, Jackson behind me. He began clearing the plates around the room's sole occupant, Kap, who was leaning on the table, his head propped up with one hand.

"Good afternoon, Mr. Kapostoulos," I said.

He looked up immediately. "Ollie," he said, standing and closing his portfolio as he did so. "It's good to see you again."

Making small talk while I helped clear the

tabletop, I forced a smile. "You, too. I happened to be over here, with Jackson" — I gestured out the door — "and I took the opportunity to stop by and say hello."

"I'm glad you did." But he didn't look glad at all.

In record time the table was clear except for coffee cups, a few ancillary items, and three leather portfolios. All closed. Darn it.

"How is your mother?" he asked.

"Great," I said. "She really enjoyed dinner the other night."

"I'm glad."

Calling on moxie I didn't know I possessed, I said, "Small world. I'm surprised to run into you here at the White House."

"Yes, I imagine you are." He glanced down at the table, as though eager to get back to work. "And it was nice to see you again."

I took the hint. I was being dismissed.

"I don't want to bother you any longer, but . . ." Acting on whim, I blustered forth. "If you wanted to stop by the kitchen before you leave, I would love to show you around."

Kap looked up from his papers, regarding me with a bit of wariness now. "That's very kind of you. I may take you up on it."

Was he as eager to find out more about me as I was about him? I hoped so. That would give me an opportunity to figure out exactly what this man was after.

Jackson was finished in here. And so was I.

As we left Kap sitting there, I worked up my most welcome smile. "I really hope you stop by."

With this new toxin information running through my frenzied brain, I almost forgot my Secret Service mission. No longer encumbered by the wheeled cart, I took the stairs just outside the Cabinet Room down to the lower level.

I was glad to find Craig in his office. As much as I didn't want to talk with him directly, I knew I had to. I waited in the anteroom for his assistant to announce me, and was shown in at once.

"Do you have a minute?" I asked.

Craig would be so much more handsome if he smiled once in a while. He had been writing longhand when I walked in, and he was slow to pull his attention from the paper before him. Slower still, was the drawl in his question. "What can I do for you, Ms. Paras?"

I pasted on a cheerful face. "Two things."

His eyebrows arched and he placed his pen on the blotter, carefully arranging it exactly parallel to the blotter's edge. "You may proceed."

"First, I need to arrange to have the eggs delivered to the kitchen. Our Egg Board liaison has our supply ready. I just need the Secret Service to coordinate with her."

He nodded, pulled out a fresh sheet of paper, and wrote on it. "Specifics?"

I provided Brandy's name, phone, e-mail, and the location of the eggs. He recorded it all.

"Consider it done," he said. "And second?"

This was the hard part. "It's about Agent MacKenzie."

His expression utterly neutral, he blinked slowly, waiting for me to continue.

"You need to be aware that Agent MacKenzie and I . . ." I faltered. Biting my lip, I tried again. "There is no need for you to . . ."

Again, the slow blinking. "Ms. Paras, exactly what are you trying to communicate about one of my agents? Are you reporting improper behavior on his part?"

"No!" If it were anyone but Craig, I might think he was trying to make a joke. But this guy was all serious, all the time. My voice naturally rose, but I struggled to lower it, cognizant of others in the anteroom. I stepped closer and spoke quietly. "Tom and I broke up, okay?" When there was no reaction on his part, I clarified. "We are no longer in a relationship. You got your wish."

His brow creased. "And you are telling me this, why?"

He knew exactly why, but I took another step closer to his desk. "You can no longer hold Agent MacKenzie responsible for my behavior," I said. And then I said the words that hurt most of all. "He is no longer part of my life."

I didn't wait for Craig to respond. I turned and hurried out the door and didn't stop walking until I was safely back in the haven of the kitchen.

"You okay?" Cyan asked.

I nodded. "Mission accomplished."

She and Henry wore expressions that said they didn't believe me, but we had so much work ahead that neither of them pressed me for more.

CHAPTER 22

"Here comes trouble," Cyan whispered.

In the midst of chopping chives, I looked up.

"And this is the kitchen staff," Sargeant said, sweeping his arm forward to encompass all of us. "Although I confess I'm stymied as to why you wished to visit this part of the residence. Are you, perhaps, an aspiring chef?"

Standing a head taller than Sargeant, Kap halted in the doorway before entering. He ignored Sargeant's question and addressed me. "I hope I'm not interrupting you, Ollie."

"No, not at all." I wiped my hands on my apron and stepped forward.

Nonplussed, Sargeant attempted to regain control of the conversation. He glared at me. "I wasn't aware you and Mr. Kapostoulos were acquainted."

I opened my mouth to form a vague reply

when Kap said, "Ms. Paras and I have friends in common." Kap looked at me. "Good friends, wouldn't you say?"

Well, wasn't that a little presumptuous. "Yes," I said, more to annoy Sargeant than agree with Kap, "very good friends."

Sargeant sniffed. "I have a list of questions for you, Ms. Paras. They came from the president himself. We are very concerned with sensitive food issues that relate to religious observances and belief systems. In fact, when Mr. Kapostoulos expressed his desire to visit the kitchen, the president suggested I accompany him. He believes that this way I can kill two birds with one stone, as it were."

The hairs on the back of my neck stood up, but Sargeant poking his nose into the kitchen was nothing new. Doing so in the presence of Kap, however, made it odd. "Of course," I said. "Let's get started."

I watched Henry and Kap size each other up. They were about the same height, about the same age. Henry resembled a kindly uncle, while Kap could have graced a senior edition of *GQ*. Henry offered to show Kap around, but our visitor declined and politely suggested Sargeant carry on.

At that, Sargeant opened a portfolio and clicked his pen. Kap's dark eyes visibly hardened, almost as though the irises had swallowed up the pupils. He fixed his laser gaze firmly on our sensitivity director.

Sargeant asked, "What sort of delicacies do you generally prepare for the president and his guests?"

"There are many," I said. "That's a difficult question. Is there something specific you want to know about?"

"No. No." Sargeant smiled, but I could tell it was just for show. "I just need to clear up these loose ends." He consulted his notebook. "For instance . . . have you ever served truffles?" He looked up at me.

"Yes."

He wrote that down. I got the feeling he was gauging my truthfulness. But why would I lie? "Foie gras?"

"The president doesn't like it. So, no."

"Caviar."

"Yes."

"Puffer fish."

"No," I said, aghast.

He watched me as I answered. "You have never served puffer fish?"

"Of course not. It's too dangerous."

With a prim smirk, he nodded and wrote that down.

A moment later, he continued with the questions, finishing off a list of about ten items, most of which we had served at one time or another. But never puffer fish. It wasn't worth the risk. The skin and organs contained deadly toxins.

I looked up at both of them.

"What is it?" Kap asked.

I lied, "Nothing."

"You're sure?"

"I . . . I have a lot to do for tomorrow. I just thought of something I forgot."

Sargeant wrinkled his nose as he shut his notebook. "I suppose that will be enough for now. I'm no longer needed here." He waited, as though hoping we'd correct him. We didn't.

"It was a pleasure to meet you, Mr. Kapostoulos," Sargeant said with a little bow. He ignored the rest of us and left the room without looking back.

Kap turned to us. "Who hired *that* . . . gentleman?"

Cyan laughed. "We haven't been able to figure that one out yet."

Kap smiled at her and at Henry. "Would you mind if I borrowed your boss for a few minutes?"

My heart gave a little thump of disappointment. I didn't know what he might want to talk about, but it was probably about my mom, and not something I wanted to hear. I steeled myself and followed him out. He led me into the Center Hall. "I don't want to worry you, Ollie," he began.

"I'm not worried," I said. "My mother is a smart, strong lady."

"She is," he agreed. "And her daughter takes after her."

Blatant flattery always made my teeth hurt. I clenched them. "What was it you wanted to talk about?"

"I would appreciate it if you didn't mention my visit here."

That seemed like a peculiar request. "Your visit to the kitchen?"

"My visit to the White House."

"Who would I tell?"

"Your family?" He shot me with that laser gaze again. "Howard Liss?"

"What?" I laughed my disbelief. "Why do you think I would have anything to do with that repulsive —"

"He hasn't contacted you?"

The question shut me up. "How did you know that?" I asked. "What kind of consultant are you, anyway?"

"Let's keep my visit to the White House between us, okay?"

I didn't understand. "But other people have seen you here." I held up my fingers, one at a time. "Henry, Cyan, Jackson, Peter

Everett Sargeant III, not to mention everyone in the West Wing."

"I'm not worried about the other staff. They're not on Howard Liss's radar." He ventured a smile. "Please, let's just keep this between us, shall we?"

The minute he left, I headed for the computer. "So that's your mom's boyfriend?" Cyan asked.

I didn't think it was a good idea to look up my Internet question while Cyan stood next to me. "Just while she's in town."

From behind us, Henry grunted. We both turned.

"He's here to stay," Henry said.

"What do you mean?" I asked.

Henry stopped chopping scallions to look up at us. "He's got the look."

"What look?"

My former boss waved his knife at me. "You're not going to get rid of him very easily."

"Great," I said.

Cyan patted me on the shoulder. "He's very good-looking."

"So was Ted Bundy."

Cyan laughed, but at least she headed over to the other end of the kitchen. I was free to surf the 'Net. Sargeant's inquiries — with Kap at his sleeve — were too suspicious to be the routine questions he claimed. The first thing I typed into my browser was "Puffer fish," then, "Enter."

And there it was.

Tetrodotoxin. Extremely deadly. Could cause death in as little as twenty minutes. This *had* to be the toxin Kap and Cooper were discussing at lunch today.

Puffer fish was considered a delicacy, but much too dangerous for me to consume myself, let alone serve to the president. But if my hunch was right, it was this toxin that killed Minkus.

I signed off and sat there for a minute, closing my eyes against the fear. Puffer fish poisoning was serious. No wonder they suspected the kitchen. I had no idea how to deal with the onslaught of publicity this revelation was certain to generate.

All day, with this new tetrodotoxin information floating around, I had expected the Secret Service to swarm the kitchen and kick us out again. That hadn't happened. Instead, the eggs arrived just as Craig had promised; preparations moved forward for the following day's holiday meal; and Cyan, Henry, and I made great strides on the Egg Roll preparations.

When I finally left the White House that night, it was late. The Metro was still running, fortunately, so I set off for the Mac-Pherson Square station, hoping the brisk walk would help clear my head. Just outside the East Gate, I pulled out my cell and was surprised to see I had two missed calls. The first one was from Tom. "Call me when you can." I looked at the phone, waiting for more. But that was the extent of the message. Time-stamped about two hours ago.

The second call was from Liss. Of course. My new buddy. Despite Kap's best efforts, Liss had probably gotten wind of the ME's report and wanted a news scoop for tomorrow morning's edition, about how often we served puffer fish to the president. I listened to his message. "Olivia — I understand that the two men we discussed have indeed had their audience today. You may be interested to know that when they left their meeting, they went straight to visit the 'late agent's' office." He paused, as though allowing me time to let the information settle in. "What do you think they are looking for?"

He'd made it sound like one of his scandalous headlines. The lunatic. I ignored his call and instead steeled myself before dialing Tom. He answered right away. But rather than say hello, he asked, "Why did you tell Craig we had broken up?"

"He *told* you?"

"Why did you do that, Ollie?"

"So he could no longer hold you responsible for my actions."

Tom made a noise of complete exasperation. "You didn't think I could handle it?"

"I didn't think you should have to."

He was silent a moment. "Let me guess: You're running your own investigation."

I shook my head, even though he couldn't see me. "I'm just trying to clear the kitchen's name."

"Well, you can quit right now. You've been cleared."

"What about Bucky?"

He didn't have an answer for that.

I pressed my luck. "Can I ask you something?"

"Shoot."

"They know what killed Minkus, don't they?"

He hedged. "This is a discussion for another time."

"Was it really tetrodotoxin?"

"Where did you hear — ?" Agitated, he nearly shouted, "How do you know that? No one knows the name of . . ." His voice trailed off but his anger was still palpable.

I was at the mouth of the MacPherson Square station, but I didn't head underground, where my signal would be lost. "I just heard some things, okay?"

Tom's irritation manifested itself in a series of restless noises. "My God, is nothing safe from your damn snooping?"

I started to answer, but he cut me off.

"We're on cell phones. Stop talking. Now." He blew out a breath. "Where are you?"

"Just about to get on the Metro to go home."

"You're at the station?"

"At the top of the stairs."

"Wait there," he said and hung up.

I didn't much care for the idea of hanging around waiting for Tom, especially when he sounded so aggravated. It was dark out, and standing alone outside a Metro station made me believe I was asking for trouble. But he arrived in less than five minutes. Pulling up in a government-issue sedan, he popped the locks and waved me in.

"First of all," I began, even before my butt hit the seat, "I work in the White House. I hear sensitive things all the time."

He pulled away the moment my door was closed. "Do you usually broadcast them over your cell phone?"

"No one is listening in on my cell phone."

"You sure about that?"

I shrugged.

His mouth was tight as he asked, "You

ever think they might be listening in on mine?"

"I thought yours was secure."

He made an exasperated noise. "You and I work in the White House. *Nothing* is as secure as we'd like it to be."

"Second," I said, "if this puffer fish toxin is what killed Minkus, why in the world is the kitchen cleared of suspicion? I would think this would make us look more guilty."

"Puffer fish isn't the toxin's only source," he said.

"I know that. But that doesn't mean the kitchen should be cleared."

I had no idea where we were going. From the arbitrary turns Tom took, it appeared he had no idea either. "You don't want to be cleared?"

"Of course I do. I just don't understand it."

There was a parking spot open, just a few cars ahead of us. Tom was silent as he pulled into it and shut off the engine. "Why do you need to understand? Why can't you just accept the facts as presented to you?"

"Because they don't make sense."

He stared out the windshield for a long moment. We were on a deserted street not far from the expressway, and I could see the lighted Washington Monument in the distance. At least I recognized where I was, in case he made me get out and walk.

I took in his profile, and knew that would never happen. For all our miscommunication and differences of opinion, Tom was an honorable guy.

"Now, listen carefully, Ollie," he said, still staring straight ahead. "I am going to tell you something that is not classified information. But it's close. This may not answer your questions, but if you listen . . . carefully" — he turned to face me as he repeated the directive — "you should be satisfied. And maybe then you'll be able to stay out of the Secret Service's business. For once."

I was about to protest that I hadn't actually done anything wrong this time, but the look in his eyes warned me to keep quiet.

"Hypothetically," he said, "special agents who have done field work . . ."

"Like Minkus?"

He held a finger to my lips. Despite my resolve to distance myself, I felt a familiar tingle at his touch.

"Special agents who have done field work," he repeated, "may, and I repeat — *may* — have acquired the necessary means to . . . dispatch . . . hostile individuals who intend to harm the agents."

"Dispatch meaning . . . kill?"

He nodded.

I thought about that. At dinner on Sunday Minkus and Cooper were the only two present who had ever done field work. "Okay."

"Tetrodotoxin," he continued, assuming a bit of a teacher-tone, "which can be extracted not only from the puffer fish, but from the blue-ringed octopus, and several other species as well, is very effective in killing humans." He raised his eyebrows. "Because tetrodotoxin is an unusual substance, a medical examiner would not know to test for it. At least not initially."

"I'm with you," I said.

His eyes registered sadness. I wished I'd chosen different words.

"It is not unreasonable to assume that a field agent could have such a substance in his or her possession."

"So you think Cooper did it? You think Cooper spiked Minkus's dinner?"

Tom's eyes narrowed. He didn't answer, but I could tell that wasn't the conclusion he wanted me to draw.

"If we take our hypothetical agent as an example . . ." he said.

Okay, he meant Minkus.

". . . and that agent believed he was being targeted . . ."

"For what?"

"*That* is classified."

I nodded. "Go ahead."

"If the hypothetical agent was under pressure from outside forces . . ." Tom gave me the evil eye. "Strong forces, say from hostile foreign governments . . ."

I nodded again.

". . . we think it is likely that such an agent might have been prepared to protect himself."

"Then how did *he* end up dead?"

He shrugged. "That's the million-dollar question."

"Could he have committed suicide?"

"That is one of several scenarios we are looking into."

I held Tom's gaze for an extended moment. "That's a nice, tidy answer," I said. "But there's more, isn't there?"

He licked his lips and shrugged. "All I can tell you is that agents all over the world — some from other countries — have the same means of killing at their disposal. It's also possible that our hypothetical agent was assassinated by another country's operative."

"China, most likely," I said. "Right?"

Tom leaned back, and it was then I noticed how close he had been. "That's as much as I can say."

"I take it from your reaction over the phone that this revelation about tetrodotoxin won't make the evening news."

He shook his head. "We can't let that out. Not yet. No one knows except for the president, a couple of trusted advisors . . ."

I thought about Cooper and Kap. Were they the trusted advisors Tom referred to?

". . . and those of us on the PPD. I gotta tell you, Ollie: I never expected the chef to be party to this information."

"I overhear a lot."

"Sure," he said, clearly not believing me. "Just don't tell anyone else, okay? We're not even telling the Minkus family, yet. Until we know for certain whether he was targeted — or whether he took his own life — we can't let even a hint of this get out."

We sat in silence for a moment.

One thing still bothered me. "What makes the medical examiner so sure this toxin didn't come from the kitchen?"

Tom shifted in his seat. "Hypothetically, again?"

Could he use that word any more times tonight? "Of course."

"Toxic substances are tightly controlled by the government — as you might expect." He squinted into the night. "But occasionally the government experiences a breach.

And sometimes a breach isn't discovered until an inventory is taken."

"The NSA is missing a supply of tetrodotoxin?"

Tom's jaw worked. "It may have simply been misplaced."

It all made sense now. "That's why the ME knew to test for it."

He didn't answer that. He didn't have to. "Whether an individual acquired it from the government supply, or whether this is a mere clerical error, there are serious issues at stake. And a lack of competence we find unacceptable." He looked at me. "There are already measures in place to discover what happened and to prevent any such mix-up from happening again."

"Wow." There really wasn't much else to say. "This is real, isn't it?"

He looked at me.

"I mean, we hear about espionage . . . but there are real people who use toxins against one another. On purpose." I shuddered. "I don't like it."

"Necessary evils."

"Maybe," I said.

Again we were silent for a long moment. I broke the silence. "What are you doing for Easter tomorrow?"

He shrugged. "Family stuff."

"I'm cooking at my place," I said, by way of conciliation. "At four. In case you're interested."

His eyes were unreadable. "I . . ." His voice made a tiny little catch. "Ollie. I think maybe we need this break."

I felt my heart wrench.

He looked into my eyes. "Can I ask you something?'

I swallowed hard and nodded.

Tom inhaled audibly. "Last night you said that you can't be yourself with me. Do you really believe that?"

My mouth went dry. I wanted to avoid answering, but he stared at me with an intensity that would brook no lie. "I do, actually."

The expression on his face looked like somebody had punched him in the gut, but he nodded and glanced at his watch. "The Metro probably isn't running anymore. I'll drive you home."

"Thanks."

We made small talk as we drove, and I waited until he pulled up to my building to say, "I'm sorry."

He sat in the darkness for about ten seconds, staring straight ahead until he finally shook his head, and said, "No, I'm the one who's sorry."

CHAPTER 23

The First Family had attended services the night before, and had no other official plans beyond entertaining their family for dinner at noon. An easy day, as far as we were concerned, and we planned to start preparations for the Easter meal just as soon as the morning rush was over. Cyan and I finished garnishing the breakfast plates just as Henry strode in. "Happy Easter," I said.

Uncharacteristically grumpy, he pointed at me. "Do you know Howard Liss?"

"I wish I didn't."

"He accosted me on my way in to work." Henry tied on an apron and consulted our schedule as he continued, working and talking at the same time. "The man is stalking the White House. When he saw me, he wanted to know why I had been brought back here to work."

"That's none of his business."

Henry's face flushed. "I wanted to tell him

that, but you know reporters — they'll make it sound like you're hiding something. I just told him that I was happy to be able to help out as we prepared for Monday's big event."

I sensed there was more.

Henry's eyebrows bunched together. "He asked about you. Specifically, he asked if you had any connection to Phil Cooper."

"He did?"

Henry nodded. "Liss seems to believe that Cooper has a hidden agenda. He didn't accuse the man of killing Minkus, but he came close enough for me to smell the suspicion on him. This Liss is a wild card."

"You're telling me. I don't know where he gets his information." I voiced a tidbit that had been bothering me. "Don't you find it odd that he never publicized the fact that Bucky is suspended?"

Cyan shrugged. "Maybe he doesn't know. The newspapers didn't even mention it. I think Paul kept that information in-house."

"I wish all information was kept in-house," I said.

Henry continued, undaunted. "Liss is determined to get Cooper fired."

"He told you that?"

"Close enough. I quote: 'Our country can't afford to clean up any more of Cooper's messes.' "

I shook my head. "We can't worry about Liss. Or anyone else, for that matter. Our job today is simple: Easter dinner for the First Family, then the last-minute preparation for tomorrow. The sooner we get it all done, the sooner we can all get home to our own families. Now, let's do our best to provide our president with the best dinner ever, shall we?"

Henry's smile was wide. "You have become the leader I expected you to, Ollie."

Monday morning I woke up earlier than I normally would. I couldn't sleep, knowing how much we had to do. I had been through Easter Egg Rolls before — but this one loomed large. Short-staffed, behind schedule, and still suspected by the public, we were nonetheless expected to put on the biggest, best Egg Roll event ever. My family must have felt the same charge in the air because Mom and Nana got up with me, and bustled me out the door with good wishes for a successful day.

"You remember how to get there?" I asked them for the tenth time.

Mom sighed. "Yes, and before you double-check again, we do have our tickets. We will be there, Ollie. We wouldn't miss it."

I couldn't take the Metro this early, so I

drove in, trying my best to enjoy the dark morning sky and the promise of possibility. I usually loved early mornings — the air smelled fresher and the world sparkled with newness — but today my worries kept me from being able to enjoy any of it.

Once in the kitchen, there was very little chatter. After preparing the First Family's breakfast, we set to work on everything else planned for the day. My mind was on Tom. And Bucky. And getting everything done just right and on time. The annual Egg Roll was a major Washington affair. I remembered the huge crowd waiting patiently for ticket distribution on Saturday. No one wanted to miss it.

Activities were scheduled — and food provided — all day. In addition to the actual rolling of the eggs, there would be a kid-friendly band playing pop hits; famous politicians reading books to youngsters; tours of the gardens; and, of course, visits from the Easter Bunny and other familiar characters.

By eight in the morning, we were ready.

"Let's roll 'em out," I said.

Henry began the arduous task of getting the hard-boiled eggs out to the South Lawn. Although he had lots of help from the wait staff, it was still a major production to get the eggs out with minimal breakage, and into place in time for the festivities to begin. We'd boiled about 15,000 eggs in total, dyeing a large portion of them. The remaining undyed eggs were set up at tables where children were offered supplies and the opportunity to decorate their own eggs, if they wished.

The pre-dyed eggs were used in the races. Marguerite Schumacher's team not only provided giant spoons to push the eggs down their grassy lanes, her volunteers kept order — inasmuch as that was possible — running and timing the races, and naming winners. On a day like today, however, everybody won.

It was nice not to have to worry about that part. Once the boiled eggs were out of my kitchen, I breathed a sigh of relief. They were a huge responsibility and I was happy to deliver the precious eggs into Marguerite's capable hands. Major hurdle number one: complete.

But then I remembered Bucky. He had worked so hard to get these eggs done — to get them delivered — to make sure everything went smoothly. For all his complaining, the curmudgeon should be here to appreciate the fruits of his efforts. I missed him.

With a grunt, I hoisted a lemonade dispenser onto a wheeled cart. We provided soft drinks and snacks all day. Keeping items cold, and others warm, was one of our biggest challenges. Another important concern was inventory. We wanted to have enough so as not to run out of anything. As Henry and the wait staff wheeled the third and fourth carts of eggs out the back of the White House and toward the South Lawn, I went over the menu again with Cyan. She and I had been alternating outdoor and indoor duty as we confirmed our strategy to replenish the buffet tables at regular intervals. We'd be keeping our runners busy.

On my final trip back to the kitchen, I ran into Cyan on her way out. "We're good to go," I said. "Perfect timing. I was just coming to get you."

Together we headed to our station, just south of the East Wing. The morning was bright, the dew just beginning to evaporate. I wished for a touch more warmth today, and I was hopeful for it. The forecast called for a surge from the south. I rubbed my arms. Five more degrees would do it.

In addition to the official Easter Bunny, who was easily recognized by the massive, beribboned basket he carried, there were at least a dozen other costumed characters strolling the grounds. But most were not ordinary rabbits. Pink-, blue-, and purple-furred, I knew these were actually Secret Service agents in disguise. Cyan and I had seen several of them donning their outfits in the Map Room — the Guzy boys among them. One of the monstrous brothers lumbered by me. With a bulletproof vest and the bright, thick hide, it had to be extra hot in that costume. And no way to even wipe his brow without removing the headpiece. Poor guy.

"The Eagle has landed," Henry said when he joined us. "Or should I say, the eagle's eggs have landed?"

There were two long buffet tables set up in the grass, about twenty feet apart. The way we had it planned, Cyan and Henry would each handle one and I'd float between them, overseeing the entire food service, allowing them breaks when needed. It would be a long day, but we'd been through this before. To be honest, we enjoyed this particular event. No one wanted to miss even a minute of the kids' excitement.

The buffets were set up identically. We offered simple fare — cheese sticks, salads, veggie burgers, and fruit, among other barbecue staples like grilled chicken and hot dogs. We had, in fact, worked hard to keep the menu uncomplicated but sufficient to satisfy as many tastes and dietary needs as possible.

"Here they come," Cyan said.

I looked up at the wave of humanity rolling toward us. Within minutes, the lawns were packed and veteran egg-rollers made their way to the South Portico, waiting for the First Lady to make her appearance on the Truman Balcony.

I wished I could stand up there, too, just for a moment. I wanted to be able to overlook the grounds. There were tents — giant three-pole monsters, and little one-pole pavilions — set up in strategic spots all over the Ellipse and South Lawn. The large exhibition areas would serve as main stages for the featured tween bands, and the small ones for political dignitaries who'd volunteered to read picture books aloud. There were craft tents, too. Some offered egg dyeing, others allowed kids to create cardboard bunny ears for themselves. With flowers and streamers and balloons against the backdrop of the springy green lawns, this was truly a most beautiful event.

We always had a huge contingent of volunteers. Most of them were local teens, some were members of the Egg Board, but all were easily recognized by their white aprons and big smiles. The sun warmed my bare forearms. But I still felt an unhappy chill.

Cyan and I were putting our finishing touches on the buffets when the music strummed to life. I heard the beginning strains of "Easter Bonnet," and looked up to see two full-size yellow bunnies accompanying the First Lady on the Truman Balcony.

Those of us on staff had been told what the visiting public had not. All yellow bunnies were performers. The rest of the "hare" staff, aside from the official "Easter Bunny," of course, were Secret Service agents in disguise. They would keep in character by mingling and interacting with the kids, but in case of trouble, the pink, purple, and blue rabbits were on call.

The yellow bunnies on the balcony were pretending to conduct the band while the families on the ground stared up, enjoying the beautiful music and crisp spring day. When the song ended, Mrs. Campbell stepped to the microphone. She gave a short speech of welcome and reminded everyone that the races would begin when her husband blew the whistle.

From that moment on, it was a whirlwind. My team and I worked the grills, barely getting time to look up and enjoy the show. When we did, during the infrequent lulls, I watched the little kids run around in bouncing bunny ears while happy parents looked on. Next to us, a kiddie band played nursery rhyme songs, and in spite of all I had on my mind, I found myself humming the ditties by early afternoon. Catchy little buggers.

At some point soon, the Marine Band would be called upon to play. I thought how much Mom and Nana would be thrilled to hear them.

I checked my watch. They should be here by now. After a quick confirmation that things had slowed down and everything was under control, I asked Henry to oversee the process while I went to find my family. "I'll be back in a minute."

He waved a spatula at me. "Take your time."

I made my way down the gentle slope toward the Ellipse, where guests were still arriving. I had told Mom that I would be stationed near the East Wing, so I hoped to find them somewhere in the approaching crowd.

"Ollie!"

I turned. Nana was waving — her smile as bright as the day had turned out to be. I changed directions, and was about to ask where Mom was when Nana closed the distance between us and grabbed my arm. "Guess who we ran into?"

"I have no idea —"

"Ollie!" Kap called as he and my mother made their way around a group of stroller-pushing parents. "Wonderful party."

I gave him an auto-pilot response: "Thanks." Then collected my thoughts. "What are you doing here?" I asked. "Do you have grandkids participating?"

He laughed. "No, unfortunately. I have a little business to take care of today." Well, wasn't that cryptic. "It's amazing what events you can attend when you pull a few strings. But I am delighted to see you again." At that he tugged my mom's arm tighter into his. "This has been a most pleasant surprise."

Nana nudged me. What she wanted me to say or do, I had no idea. "Mom, I want to be able to take you inside later," I said, and then turning to Nana, "Both of you." So as not to appear too rude to Kap, I added, "My family has never been inside the White House."

"Then you are in for a treat," he said. He looked about to say more, but his eyes tightened. I followed his gaze. Phil Cooper and his wife had just struck up a conversation with Ruth and Joel Minkus. Why Kap should be distressed by this, I had no idea, but I read his concern as clearly as if there were a neon sign above his head advertising it. "Will you excuse me?" he asked. With that he turned and walked away.

"That was strange," Nana said.

The Coopers and the Minkuses looked to be engaged in lighthearted conversation, but when Cooper leaned forward to say something to Ruth, she instinctively leaned back. Body language rarely lied, and I wondered what vibe she'd gotten from this man that made her want to keep her distance. No matter. I found it more interesting that when Kap approached, all conversation stopped. So, why not join the happy little party to find out more?

"Let's go say hello," I said, and led Mom and Nana closer.

"Good to see you, Ruth. You, too, Joel," Kap said, shaking Joel's hand. Ruth murmured politely.

Kap held a hand out to Cooper and introduced himself. Cooper obliged and both men acted as though they had never met before. What was up with that?

Kap shot me a look that reminded me of my promise not to mention his presence at the White House the other day. But none of this made any sense. D.C. was a small enough town. They could have run into one another any number of ways — and they had both been at Minkus's wake. Their charade made me curious and the hairs on the back of my neck began to prickle.

"It's good to see you, Ollie," Ruth said, placing a hand on my shoulder. "This event is so cheerful. And we needed something to cheer us up. We're very glad we came, aren't we, Joel?"

Joel put his arm around her. "Very glad." He turned to me. "My mom needed a break. She's been staying in the house by herself all the time."

"Look over there," she said excitedly. "Senator Fredrickson. Go say hello."

He shook his head. "I'm here for you today, Mom."

I was close enough to hear her whisper, "And the whole reason we came out was for you to network. So get going. You will never win that senate seat without help." She pushed at him. "Go on."

He obliged, clearly under duress.

"Now that the crowds have died down, maybe you ladies would like something to eat?" Kap asked. "How about we sample these lovely buffets?"

"That sounds wonderful," Mom said. She

and Nana joined Kap. And, much to my surprise, the Coopers and Ruth followed.

"Help yourselves," I said, "while I make sure everything is under control."

I checked in with Henry, who waved me off. "We're doing fine," he said with a wink. "I have done this before, you know."

Cyan called me over. "Henry is enjoying his time in charge again. Take advantage of it. Go enjoy your family. We're fine."

Mom and Nana had gotten in line in the right-hand buffet behind Ruth Minkus and Francine Cooper. Kap and Phil Cooper went to the left. As I passed behind the two men, I heard Cooper whisper, "I told Ruth we were getting close."

Kap's reply was tense. "You didn't tell her what was missing?"

"No, of course not. She still thinks it was an inside job."

"She doesn't suspect?"

Cooper almost laughed. "I think she suspects *you.*"

Kap kept his voice low. "She despises me. But I understand why. And if Joel has political aspira—" He stopped himself when he saw me. "Ollie, what can I do for you?"

"I was about to ask you the same thing. Are you finding everything you need?"

Kap gave me a puzzled look. I could tell

he was wondering whether I'd overheard them. What did Ruth not suspect? That her husband had been poisoned by some missing tetrodotoxin?

Cooper seemed unfazed by my sudden appearance. He smiled, and brought his face close enough to mine that no one nearby would be able to hear him. "Thank you, Ms. Paras, for not mentioning our visit the other day." He glanced around. "At least not to those outside the White House."

"I will be the first to admit I don't understand," I said. "But —"

"Yes, thank you," Kap said, cutting me off.

Just then Mom and Nana joined the group, looking for a place to sit. "When you're finished," I said to them, "I can take you on that tour."

Because I didn't think it appropriate to sit and eat with the guests, I meandered over to watch an egg roll race, reflecting on how this was exactly the sort of family event that our nation was famous for. I talked with a couple of volunteers and then made my way back to the buffets. Ruth was waiting for me. "Why is Kap sitting with your mother?" she asked.

I shrugged, not thrilled about the situation myself. "They've been seeing each other," I said. "Socially."

Her lips tightened into a thin line. "I don't trust him. I don't think you should, either."

"Why not?"

She gave me a meaningful look. "He is not who he seems to be."

Instinctively, I moved closer. "What do you mean?"

"I shouldn't tell you this," she said, her eyes wide. "Because I'm not even supposed to know . . ." Her words came fast, as though she were afraid she might get cut off. "But my husband found out that Kap" — she gestured toward the crowd with her eyes — "was selling U.S. secrets to China."

My heart skipped a beat, then began to race. Ruth grabbed my arm. "Kap only pretends he was my husband's good friend now that he's dead. But Carl saw through him."

"Do you have proof?"

She squeezed my arm hard. "No, of course not. Don't you think I would come forward if I did?" Looking morose, she glanced to where Joel was chatting up a senator from Illinois. "Carl had proof. He told me he did. And Carl was about to blow the whistle on Kap." She swallowed, glancing around yet again. "So Kap had him killed. And Cooper was the one who did it," she said. "Right under my nose."

"Why are you telling me this?"

"I need your help. And Howard Liss trusts you."

Liss, I thought. That's when the light dawned. Ruth was the confidential source he kept talking about.

"Ollie!" Nana called to me from about twenty feet away. "We're ready."

I waved. "I'll be there in a minute." I was trying to process Ruth's revelation. "What does Liss have to do with this?"

"He knows the whole story," she said. "He's the one who figured out the connection between Cooper and Kap. Howard Liss has been following this story from day one and keeping me updated. I help him, too, a little bit. I trust him. And he trusts you."

I shook my head. "I *don't* trust Liss."

"Whether you do or not," she said, "we need your help. We need to uncover their treason before they kill anyone else."

Nana called me again. "I really have to get going," I said, inching away.

Ruth's eyes narrowed as she looked at me. "Don't you care about your country?" she asked.

That irked me. "Of course I do," I said, with more than a little spirit. "But if you're depending on Liss for your information, I want no part of it."

She looked stricken, then resolute. "Listen," she said, talking quickly, "Kap plans to kill Cooper. Did you know that?"

I didn't want to continue this conversation and tried again to make excuses, when she said, "You didn't believe that those two just met today, did you?"

So she knew. Stunned silent, I waited for her to continue.

"Cooper and Kap pretended they didn't know each other. That was for my benefit," she said, pointing her finger hard into her chest. "Cooper killed my husband. Now Kap needs to get rid of that loose end. He's going to do that by killing Cooper."

I waved to Nana and Mom, who were still waiting. Next to them, Kap stared at me with an odd expression on his face. I turned to Ruth. "What do you need me to do?"

CHAPTER 24

Ruth was about to answer, but Kap took that moment to steer my mom and nana over. "We're ready for our tour," Nana said cheerily. "If you have a few minutes."

What I wanted to do, more than anything, was show my family the China Room, the kitchen, and take them into the heart of the White House. But here I was, asking them — again — to wait just a little bit longer. "I'm sorry," I said, "something came up."

"What's going on, Ollie?" Mom asked.

Ruth excused herself, shooting Kap a hateful glare as she left.

Kap watched her leave before speaking. "You were talking with her for quite a long time there."

I nodded. "She's having a tough day. Holidays, you know."

"Anything else?"

"Why do you ask?"

Kap's expression was unreadable. "Just

making conversation."

Oh, sure, Kap. Claim you're striving for inane conversation while the world crashes down on me. Ruth's allegations were nothing short of explosive, and I needed to sort facts from conjecture. "Hang on one minute," I said, and raced over to where a giant pink bunny leaned over to pat an adoring toddler on the head. When the bunny righted himself, I sidled up. I was pretty sure who was inside this suit. "Agent Guzy?" I whispered.

The bulky head turned toward me, blocking my view of anything beyond its fat fuzzy grin. I tried to look behind the screen-printed eyes, but couldn't see inside the darkness. The head moved up and down slowly, nodding. I knew that bunnies were instructed not to talk to the children, but I hoped he could hear. I whispered, "I need your help."

Waving a pink-pawed good-bye to the children who had gathered around him, the Guzy Bunny followed me away. As we walked, I explained what little I could. "Listen, I don't know exactly what to expect, but the gentleman I am about to introduce you to may bear watching."

Guzy Bunny leaned his giant head close to mine. One of the bent ears grazed the side of my face. His voice was nearly inaudible. "What do you need me to do?"

I leaned up, pulling the plaster and fur face closer, hoping to be heard over the high-pitched squeals of children playing tag nearby. Hoping to not accidentally tug his head off.

"Just keep an eye on this guy, all right? I'll hurry back as soon as I can with more information."

The big head nodded again. Guzy Bunny followed me to the table's edge.

"Look who came to visit," I said with forced cheer.

Mom and Nana looked up at me, painfully unimpressed. Detritus from the day's event littered the tabletop, and the other empty chairs were tilted and angled, as though their occupants had just tumbled out of them. Kap sat on the edge of his folding chair and studied the grounds, looking ready to bolt at any moment.

"This is . . ." I thought fast. "Fuzzy. He's going to take you around the grounds and show you the gardens."

Mom shifted in her seat. "We don't mind waiting for you, Ollie."

Nana patted the big pink paw. "No offense, Fuzzy."

Fuzzy Guzy stayed silent, obviously waiting for them to stand and join him. When that didn't happen, he lowered his cotton-tailed bulk into the nearest empty chair — right next to Kap. Without saying a word, the big rabbit patted the table in front of him, and folded his paws one on top of the other. "Thanks," I said. "I'll be right back."

"Ollie." Kap started to get up. "Do you need help?"

"No, not at all," I said and sprinted away before he could argue.

Leaving Mom and Nana with him seemed wrong somehow. Ruth had said that Kap wasn't who he pretended to be, and I believed that. In fact, I'd sensed that from the start. But in this crowd, with all of those kids running around, and with Fuzzy Guzy watching over them, I didn't know how much safer they could be.

I spotted Ruth about a hundred feet away. She was leaning against a tree trunk, in conversation with Phil and Francine Cooper. Damn. Another delay. "Ruth," I called. She turned and waved. I hadn't expected her to be with Cooper. Could she be warning him about Kap's alleged plans?

I slowed my pace, striving to appear casual. "Did you all have enough to eat? How was the food?"

Francine smiled and told me how wonderful everything tasted. Cooper distractedly agreed. Ruth made eye contact with me and raised her brows. What did that mean?

"When you have a few minutes, Mrs. Minkus," I said, "I wouldn't mind a chance to finish our conversation."

"Maybe later," she said. "I'm not feeling so well."

Phil Cooper was instantly solicitous. "Do you want to sit down? Can I get you something?"

The offer seemed to stun her. "No, I'm just a bit unsettled," she said, her voice shaking. "I'm not used to eating — I haven't had much appetite over the past several days. Please don't trouble yourself. I'll be fine."

As though drawn by the tug of a magic umbilical cord, Joel rushed over from out of nowhere. "Mom, what's wrong?"

She smiled up at him. "Nothing, honey. Maybe you should call for the car. Would you, please? I'd like to go home now."

Joel ignored her request and instead grabbed the nearest folding chair, pressing his mother to sit. As Ruth lowered herself onto the seat, she shooed Phil and Francine Cooper away. "I'm fine," she said. Her voice seemed to have regained its strength. "You two don't need to worry about me. Joel is here now." The Coopers left, albeit reluctantly.

One of our volunteers came over and asked if there was anything she could do. Although Ruth tried to assure us all, I knew it was too late. This was the White House. No one got light-headed around here without it becoming a federal case. This little incident — forgettable in most any other environment — had just shattered my hopes for continuing our conversation.

When one of our on-site paramedics arrived "just to make sure," I left Ruth in good hands and decided on the best approach to extricate my mom from Kap's company.

Phil Cooper saw me walking rapidly across the lawn, and changed his trajectory to intercept me. "Is she okay?"

"I think she'll be fine," I said, slowing. "The medic is checking her out. And Joel's there."

Phil nodded. Francine joined us. "She seemed okay five minutes ago," she said. "It's like something came over her all of a sudden."

I turned back to look at Ruth again. All of a sudden? Like . . . Carl Minkus?

Oh my God.

"What was she doing right before I came up?" I felt panic rise up in my chest. Ruth's rantings about Cooper's involvement in her husband's death started to solidify. But I couldn't stop myself from asking, "Did she eat anything?"

Cooper looked at me like I had bay leaves shooting out my ears. "We all ate," he said, clearly confused. "And it was very good."

"Did she complain about tingling in her lips?"

Phil had unscrewed the cap of his water bottle and drained what was left before he answered. "No, she didn't complain about anyth—" In that instant I knew he understood the nature of my question. His face lost all expression and he stared at the area where the medics were now talking with Ruth. "You don't think her food was tainted . . ."

My limited research on the toxin led me to understand that victims had tingling mouths and numb tongues, which quickly spread into paralysis of the diaphragm. Unless the victim was given immediate and constant CPR, the toxin led to death.

"She said she was feeling light-headed. That isn't what Carl Minkus complained of, is it?"

Cooper touched his fingers to his lips. "No," he said. "Carl was different. But . . . I can't help thinking . . ." He scanned the crowd.

"What?" I asked.

From behind us, Kap appeared, deftly moving into the space between me and Cooper. "What's happening?" he asked. Turning to the large pink bunny behind him, he said, "Get away from me. Go find some kids to entertain."

Cooper was pale. "They might have struck again. Let's get over there."

Without a backward glance to me, Kap and Cooper headed toward Ruth Minkus, the pink bunny trotting faithfully behind. Ruth was seated on the grass now, surrounded by her son, a medic, and several volunteers. I heard her protesting that she was just fine and that she and Joel would like to leave.

"She sure sounds better," I said.

Francine's pretty face twisted with concern. "Ten minutes ago she was hurrying around — busy. In fact, I thought it was strange that a woman still grieving for her husband should be shuttling food and drinks for other people."

That got my back up. Guests should not be working at this event. "You mean she fixed a plate for Joel," I said for clarification.

"No," Francine said. "Actually, it was kind

of strange. Phil and I were getting ready to leave and she came over with a couple bottles of water. She said we looked thirsty." Unscrewing the bottle in her hand, Francine took a swig, emphasizing her point.

Francine had used the word *strange* to describe Ruth, twice in the same conversation. The back of my neck and shoulders began to prickle again. Thoughts began to formulate. I excused myself and jogged toward the small group gathered around the woman on the grass. Francine followed me.

"No, really," Ruth was saying in a voice much stronger than I expected. "I'm just fine." Without another glance at those around her, she grabbed her son's arm and stood up. "Joel — let's go. Now. Please. Get the car."

Joel took off like a shot. As soon as he was out of sight, Ruth boosted herself to leave. What prompted me to stop her, I don't know. But I needed to. She had the answers, and there was no time to lose. "Ruth," I said, "just a minute."

She didn't answer. She kept walking. Very fast.

I started to follow, but Cooper grabbed my arm. His empty water bottle dropped next to my feet. Sweaty and pale, he held fingers to his mouth. "My lips," he said thickly. "I can't feel them." He looked around with wild eyes.

Cooper let go of me long enough to grab Kap's arm. "Not China," he said. Then his knees gave out and he collapsed to the ground. "It was her."

In an instant, I understood.

I dropped to the grass next to Cooper and pointed to the direction Ruth had taken, "Stop her," I said to Kap. Then to the medic, I shouted, "This man needs help!"

The medic responded at once, calling for assistance as she closed the distance between us. "What have we got?" she asked.

"Tetrodotoxin," I said. "It's what killed Carl Minkus."

A second medic relayed that information into his radio as he knelt on the ground next to me. "He will go into respiratory failure quickly," I said. "His diaphragm will be paralyzed. You *have* to keep him alive."

I bolted to my feet and ran to catch up with Kap, looking back long enough to see Francine standing terrified next to the emergency response team. She sobbed as she watched them work on her husband. I wanted to be there for her, but I had to follow Kap. I could see him in the distance, looking both ways; it was obvious he had lost Ruth. Behind him, Fuzzy Guzy looked ready to pounce on his quarry. My mom was about halfway between the two, looking both ways as well.

For a moment I wondered where Nana was, but I didn't have time. I ran, full out.

I didn't get far.

"Ollie!"

I turned.

Ruth stood behind one of the abandoned balloon sculpture tents, the right half of her body hidden from view. She peered out around the corner, struggling with something I couldn't see. "You need to get me out of here."

I said the first thing that came to mind. "You killed your own husband? My God, why?"

"Get me out of here. I know you can do it."

Whatever she had behind the white canvas made her recoil.

"Get me out of here now." Her teeth gritted. "Before it's too late."

Several hundred yards away, Kap turned to look around. I started to call to him.

"Don't," she said.

And then she jerked her quarry into view.

I started to scream, but clapped my hands over my mouth. If I drew any attention to the three of us . . .

Nana fought her captor, but Ruth was twenty years younger and ten times stronger. She'd shoved fabric into Nana's mouth, and had her wrapped in a bear hug from behind. "Shut up," Ruth said, but her voice was ragged from exertion. Then to me: "Get me out of here or your grandmother gets dosed."

My mind telescoped to the small vial in Ruth's left hand. She held on to it so tightly, I could see the whites of her knuckles straining her skin. Nana kicked and tried to scream. Ruth rocked sideways, maintaining control of my grandmother's writhing form.

"Don't mess with me, I'm warning you. You have to get me out of here. You *know* how to do it."

Secret Service agents were busy with Cooper and with Kap. No one took notice of three women by this vacant tent. I took a step closer. "Give it up, Ruth."

"You want Grandma dead?"

Nana kicked, and although Ruth grimaced, she didn't let go.

Working to tamp down the panic crawling up my throat, I pleaded. "Listen to me. Let her go — I'll get you out. I will."

"She comes with." Ruth gave the area a quick glance. "No one is going to question us if we're helping your grandmother. She stays with me until I'm out."

My mouth was dry, and I couldn't think — couldn't begin to figure a way out of this one. "Nana," I said.

Ruth tugged Nana in a vicious Heimlich maneuver. Nana's muffled gasp tore at my heart. She slumped, unconscious.

"Nana!" I cried, starting toward her.

"Get back!" Ruth said. "Damn." Tightening her hold around my grandmother, she pulled her hands close enough to start unscrewing the vial. "Get me out now, or I swear . . ."

"Okay." My fear made it almost impossible to breathe. "Keep the bottle closed. Please."

She looked both directions. "Which way out?" she asked. Then, as I started to move toward her, she yelled at me to stop again. "I don't trust you."

At that moment the trees behind Ruth parted and a giant purple bunny emerged. But this one was headless. The second Guzy brother held one finger on his lips as the other reached into the side of his costume. I prayed he was going for his gun.

"You can trust me," I said, talking quickly. "You can. There is a way to get you out. I know how to do it."

Ruth shook her head. When she let Nana's

body go, it dropped almost soundlessly to the ground. My heart dropped with her.

"No," she said. "You *won't* do it. You're one of those bleeding-heart patriots." Her words came fast. "But . . ." She glanced at the vial, then at Nana's prone form. "I can make sure you won't follow me." She bent, intending to pour the liquid onto Nana's face.

I rushed her, just as the Guzy behind Ruth shouted, "Stop!"

Her head jerked up.

The split-second delay was all I needed. I hit Ruth in a full-body tackle, grabbing her bony wrist, dragging it away from Nana as far as I could. Ruth and I twisted together as we fell to the ground. She gurgled her surprise, but recovered quickly and began fighting me, hard.

Her face contorted with effort, she yanked her arm. I felt her wrist slipping out of my grasp but the bottle flew from her hand. Time seemed to move in slow motion as the vial somersaulted about six inches above her face, about six inches below mine. I clenched my mouth and eyes shut until I heard the dull thud of the glass hitting bone. It had bounced off her cheek, spilling its contents all over her face — some in her eyes — with the bulk running down her cheek and into her open mouth. I immediately let go and jumped away from her, feeling my own face for any vestige of the deadly liquid on me. Dry. Thank God. Ruth sat up and spit, crying out for help as she clawed at her eyes.

I whirled to grab my grandmother by her shoulders. "Nana?"

She blinked up at me. "Are we safe now?"

None of the liquid had landed anywhere near my grandmother. I breathed a deep sigh of relief.

"Are we safe?" Nana asked again.

"Yes," I said. "What about you? Are you okay?"

"Help me up," she said.

"Maybe we should wait for the paramedics. You shouldn't move around so fast."

She boosted herself on one arm. "Help me up," she said again, this time forcefully. "You think I didn't do that on purpose?"

"You faked passing out?"

"Dead weight is always harder to work with," she said as she got to her feet. "Figured you needed some assistance on this one, honey. Glad your old nana was here to help."

We gave Ruth and Guzy wide berth as he came behind her, pulling out his handcuffs from within his fuzzy costume. "Careful," I warned. I pointed to the vial and to Ruth, who was sobbing into the soft grass. "Tetrodotoxin."

The headless rabbit spoke into his microphone as he knelt next to her.

The emergency staff quickly surrounded us. Joel broke through. "Mom?" He scanned the crowd before kneeling at his mother's side. "What happened? Who did this?"

Ruth had begun to hyperventilate, screaming about a conspiracy, but I noticed her gasping for air. I couldn't watch. And I didn't want Nana to see any of it either. I walked her away from the crowd. "Let's get you inside," I said. Secret Service agents swarmed the area, and we made a slow trek toward the White House. Within seconds, Mom joined us.

"What's going on?"

"I'll tell you later. Where's Kap?"

She pointed back in the direction we'd come. "He's checking on Mr. Cooper. Ollie, what just happened?"

Nana held my mom's hand. "Corinne, we figured it out. Me and Ollie. We figured out who killed that Minkus fellow." She looked up at me. "I don't understand why, though. Do you know?"

I shook my head. Even if I had suspicions, I wasn't ready to share them aloud.

"See, Corinne," Nana continued, "it's just like I always say. She takes after me." Reaching up to pat my cheek, she said, "The apple doesn't fall far from the tree, eh?"

CHAPTER 25

Craig Sanderson circled my chair for the third time.

This small office in the East Wing — the same one where I'd waited to be interrogated by Secret Service assistant deputy Jack Brewster last week — was cold. I kept my hands together between my knees for warmth, but shivered involuntarily. Craig smiled at my discomfort, and tried to share the enjoyment with the only other person in the room, Agent Snyabar.

Snyabar stared straight ahead. Totally impassive.

Craig started in on me again. "You told the medic on the scene that Agent Cooper had ingested tetrodotoxin."

It wasn't exactly a question, so I didn't answer.

He rubbed his chin, feigning thoughtfulness as he continued to pace around me. "I have to wonder how you knew which toxin killed Carl Minkus."

Still not a direct question. I bit the insides of my mouth.

"Not that we aren't grateful, mind you. Agent Cooper is in intensive care, but is expected to make a full recovery." He stopped and looked down at me. "I'm sure he's very appreciative of your intervention. And your prescience. How did you know what he'd been poisoned with? Oh wait! I forgot just who we're dealing with here — the White House chef who feeds the First Family and saves the world in her spare time." A frown contorted his face as he glared down at me. "Like a special agent in disguise. Talk about delusions."

Silence hung in the air between us. I stared at the walls.

Craig cleared his throat. "Ms. Paras, you made a special effort to inform me that you and Agent MacKenzie were no longer . . . in your words, 'in a relationship.' "

I looked up at him.

His eyebrows arched upward. "Why?"

"I told you why. So that you could no longer hold him responsible for my actions."

He made a sound like, *"Tsk."*

"What?" I asked.

He exhaled loudly. "This is an unfortunate turn of events. However, the ends do not justify the means."

"What are you talking about?"

Craig's smile was just nasty as his frown. I wanted to slap it off his face. "While I'm sure Agent Cooper is indebted to you for saving his life, it is clear to me that you could not have known about the toxin unless Agent MacKenzie breached security by telling you."

I jumped in my chair. "He didn't tell me."

"Oh, I suppose you guessed?"

"Yeah, kind of. I figured it out."

Craig seemed to find that funny. He looked up at Snyabar again. The other agent kept his eyes forward. "And how — exactly — were you able to figure out something so incredibly obscure?"

I bit my lip. I couldn't mention Kap. Late yesterday, I had been debriefed to the extent deemed necessary. Kap was, indeed, not the man he appeared to be. A covert CIA agent, he and Cooper had uncovered Carl Minkus's deep secret. It was Minkus who had been selling intelligence to China for years. Cooper and Kap were on the verge of being able to prove his treason — but then Minkus died. In the White House.

"I hear things, and I can put two and two together." Sitting up a little straighter, I added, "That's a talent that comes in handy,

430

don't you think?"

"Two plus two," he said. "In addition to being a culinary genius, the chef is a math whiz." His eyes narrowed and his jaw tightened. "You will be interested to know that I have taken steps to dismiss Agent MacKenzie from the PPD."

I caught my breath. "You can't do that."

"I most certainly can, Ms. Paras." He lips widened in a mean, straight line. "Unless you care to share any more of your mathematical skills with us . . ."

I waited. I had no idea where he was going.

"For instance, if you tell me specifically how you 'deduced' the name of the toxin . . . if," he continued, raising his voice, "you were to cooperate — fully — I *might* be convinced to refrain from transferring Agent MacKenzie to the uniformed division."

During yesterday's debriefing, which had not included Craig, I learned that both Cooper and Kap had suspected Chinese operatives from the start. They were, however, stymied as to how the assassination had been carried out. Never did they suspect Ruth of slipping the toxin into her husband's dish.

I wasn't supposed to talk about it. I had given my word. But I thought about Tom —

he had worked his entire career to become a member of the elite PPD. And now Craig, with no justification, planned to strip him of that. "I can't talk about it," I said. "But I can tell you that Tom did absolutely nothing wrong. He did not breach security." I sighed. "He never does, even when it costs us both."

"Not good enough. Who else could have possibly told you about the tetrodotoxin?"

Desperation ran through my mind. Then, I had it. "I did get the information from someone here at the White House."

Craig's eyebrows raised again. "Who?"

I took a deep breath. "Peter Everett Sargeant the Third."

"The sensitivity director?" His face contorted. "How would he know anything?"

I shrugged. "He came in and started grilling me about puffer fish on Saturday. He asked, repeatedly, if I'd ever served it to the president. It wasn't much of a leap after that. Like I said, two plus two . . ."

"Nice try, Ms. Paras, but —"

The door opened. Craig's boss, Jack Brewster, walked in, followed by one of the Guzy brothers and Tom. "Excuse us, Ms. Paras." He gestured me out. I stood, making eye contact with Tom, but his expression was unreadable. Just as I made it to the doorway, Brewster added, "You are released."

I stood still as the door closed behind me.

It had been suggested — strongly — that I take some personal time. And now that I had agreed, I had no responsibilities in the kitchen until late next week. Bucky was being reinstated, and I knew that my team, especially with Henry there, would handle everything just fine. Although I longed to go down there to see my staff, I knew it would be best if I went home and spent time with Mom and Nana.

But something made me stay. Exhaustion? Fear for Tom? Whatever it was, I stopped at a chair in the hallway and sat down.

The last I'd heard yesterday, Ruth was in intensive care. No word on her condition today. But she had talked — some. From what the authorities discovered, she had known about her husband's treasonous activities for a long time. He had even shared with her his fears about being found out. He knew Kap was onto him and he planned to take Kap out.

Aware that Carl's treason would be brought to light at any moment, Ruth could no longer take the pressure. Worse than her husband being a traitor was the effect Carl's arrest might have on their son's political aspirations. Reasoning that Carl would be put to death for his actions anyway, she did her best to prevent him from ruining their son's life by squelching the ugly truth before it came out. When Carl revealed his plan to kill Kap, Ruth saw an opportunity to save her son's career. She used Carl's own supply of toxin to kill him, in effect hoisting him by his own petard.

All to save Joel from the stigma of being the son of a traitor.

I thought about Nana's observation at the wake. No happy family pictures on that digital slideshow. My guess was there were more issues in Ruth's life — but those we might not ever know.

So deep was I in thought that I didn't hear the door opening until Craig emerged. He shot me a look that would kill a less sturdy woman. But I stood.

He stormed down the hall.

I scrambled to get out of the way when Jack Brewster came out a moment later, talking genially with Tom. Brewster saw me and walked over. "I don't condone your involvement in sensitive activities, Ms. Paras. Remember that." He turned to Tom and shook his hand. "I'll see you later."

Guzy and Snyabar followed Brewster, but as they passed, Snyabar turned to me and winked.

"What happened?" I asked Tom.

His eyes held a look I hadn't seen before. Excitement tinged with sadness. "I've been promoted." He looked down the hall where Craig had gone. "I've got Craig's job. He's been assigned to a field office."

It took me a moment to find my voice. "How?"

"Someone — a high-ranking someone whose name I have not been provided — came to your defense. Craig tried very hard to get you fired and to get me reassigned. Instead, it backfired on him."

I thought of Craig's gloating smile as he was grilling me. "Good."

Again Tom looked down the hall. "He was just trying to do his job, Ollie. Protect the president."

Suddenly I felt very small. Craig *had* just been doing his job. I shouldn't be taking any glee in the fact that he'd been demoted. "Yeah, you're right. I'm sorry."

He turned toward me. "I am, too. This is not how I wanted to be promoted. If Craig hadn't tried so hard to get rid of you . . ." He gave me a look that I didn't understand. "You have friends in high places and you came out on top. Again."

"Then why do I feel just the opposite?"

"That I can't answer. But I feel it, too."

Our eyes locked for a few seconds. He didn't smile. Instead he mumbled that he needed to go, and left me standing in the hall.

I stared after him for a long moment, before heading home.

CHAPTER 26

"How did it go?" Mom asked the moment I came through the door.

"Confusing." And far too much to discuss just now.

"You still have a job?" Nana asked.

Mrs. Wentworth and Stanley were in my kitchen, looking up at me with anticipation. I said hello. "I still have a job," I answered. "Although I don't know how I managed it."

Nana patted my hand as I pulled up a chair to join them. "You did good," she said.

There were cookies in the middle of the table, and within seconds of my sitting down, my mom had poured me a cup of steaming coffee. I glanced at the clock. "It's still morning," I said. "I feel like I've been gone for days."

"Why do you folks have all the fun?" Mrs. Wentworth asked. "Your grandma's been here for a few days and she gets all the excitement. Just once I'd like to be involved in one of your adventures, Ollie."

I shook my head. "Believe me, they're not all they're cracked up to be."

"Did you see the morning paper?" Mom asked. She must have known I hadn't, because she pulled it out and folded it to Liss's column. "Read this."

Today, *Liss Is More* gives credit where it is due.

I glanced up. "Oh no. Am I in it?"

"Keep reading." Mom said with a smile.

Yesterday's fun-filled extravaganza on the White House South Lawn — the annual Easter Egg Roll — was marred by two unhappy incidents.

"He shouldn't be reporting this!"

"Keep reading," Mom said again.

Not one, but two attendees were stricken by illness and had to be taken to nearby hospitals. Agent Phil Cooper suffered a massive heart attack. He is expected to make a full recovery thanks to the quick intervention of medics on the scene. Not so lucky was Ruth Minkus, widow of the recently deceased Carl Minkus. She was believed to have suffered from a ruptured aneurysm in her lung. Although she was rushed to emergency surgery, she did not survive. Our sympathies are with Joel, who has now lost both parents in little over a week.

In the middle of it all, once again, was White House Chef Olivia Paras, who appropriately gets in more hot water than a tea bag. (This reporter made several attempts to reach Ms. Paras for comments, only to be rebuffed.) This time, however, she is credited with alerting paramedics and is to be thanked for her presence of mind as well as her heretofore unknown ability to triage.

"I can't believe this."

Nana chuckled. "You shouldn't. Most of it isn't true. Except for the part where you should be thanked."

My family and neighbors knew part of the truth, though not all of it. They didn't know about Minkus's treason. They knew Ruth killed her husband, but they didn't know why. They didn't know Kap was an undercover spy — although I believed my mother suspected as much. All they knew, and cared about, was that we were all safe, here, and in one piece. And I still had my job at the

White House.

I turned my attention back to Liss's article.

It is too bad that Mrs. Minkus died before the medical examiner released his findings. She would have discovered that her husband died of natural causes after all. Unfortunately, she went to her grave believing someone had murdered him. I am sad for her, but even more so for Joel Minkus — this week has been the worst of nightmares.

And today I announce my vacation. An extended vacation. Effective immediately, I am suspending this column. Indefinitely. This week has been too much. Even for a crusty old newsman like me. As they say, Liss Is More, but sometimes less Liss is better. At least for the moment.

Carry on.

"Wow." That was about the only thing I could say.

"Yeah," Mom said, folding the paper neatly. "I'm keeping this."

"What for?"

Nana slapped my hand playfully. "Souvenir, what else?"

■ ■ ■ ■

The phone rang while Mrs. Wentworth and Stan were still at my kitchen table. It was Suzie and Steve calling, this time with happy news. Apparently the FBI had cleared them, just as the Bureau had cleared Bucky. They were grateful to me for the reprieve, despite the fact I insisted I had nothing to do with it.

Later that afternoon, I offered to take Mom and Nana anywhere they wanted to go, but they insisted I relax. "Too much excitement," they said. "You need a break."

I had just dozed off on the couch with my family reading and watching TV next to me, when the apartment phone rang. I rose to answer it and sucked in a breath when I saw the Caller ID — "202."

This was exactly how this whole ordeal had started a week ago.

My heart pounded, but I answered.

It was Marguerite Schumacher.

Mom and Nana stopped what they were doing to watch me. I listened to Marguerite, answered in the affirmative several times, and with a great sigh, hung up.

"What was that about?" Nana asked.

Mom had gotten to her feet. "Is everything okay?"

For the first time in days, my heart was light. "Remember that White House tour I promised you?" I asked.

They nodded.

"We're on tomorrow at noon."

I watched relief flood their faces.

"Oh, and wear something nice," I added.

They both looked at me in puzzlement. "Why?"

"The president and his wife," I said, "have invited *us* to lunch."

EGGCELLLENT EGGS

Eggs are one of the most basic ingredients in the kitchen. They're great on their own, whether coddled; scrambled; fried; boiled; or simply accented in omelets, quiches, and custards. They serve to bind savory ingredients together, as in meat loaf, meatballs, croquettes, and so on. They make baking possible, forming a protein base for everything from cookies to cakes to pancakes to crepes to soufflés and beyond. Eggs are probably the single most versatile ingredient a cook works with. They're also fast-cooking, full of nutrients and easily digested protein, and delicious. What more can any chef ask for?

I work long hours, so I frequently fix myself breakfast for dinner after a long day in the kitchen. There's just nothing better than a fried egg sandwich for a late-night meal when I don't feel like rustling up something complicated to eat. I refuse to apologize for it these days. Whenever I mention my little secret of eating breakfast food at night, my friends all confess to loving breakfast for dinner, too. It's even become something I deal with in my job, because the First Family actually asks for breakfast for dinner about once a month, so I've added it to the official White House First Family Meal Rotation. I never thought my secret fetish for breakfast at night would become a job requirement. But eggs are comfort food, so I can see why they remain perennial favorites, especially in the White House.

Here are a number of good egg recipes to try for yourself, ranging from the simple to the refined. Eggs don't have to be confined to breakfast or brunch. Try them for dinner. I bet you'll find, as I have, that the people you're feeding will love them. Happy noshing!

Ollie

EGGS BENEDICT

8 eggs
4 egg yolks
2 tablespoons cream
Juice of 1/2 lemon (around 1 tablespoon)
1/2 teaspoon kosher or sea salt
Pinch cayenne pepper or paprika (optional)
1 cup (2 sticks) butter, melted and still hot
4 English muffins, fork split, buttered and
   toasted
8 slices warm Virginia ham (or Canadian
   bacon, if you prefer) cut to fit the muffins
Chopped parsley to garnish (optional)

Serves four.

Bring a medium saucepan full of salted water to a rolling boil. Reduce heat to a gentle simmer. Crack 1 egg into a small bowl, taking care not to break the yolk. Gently slip the egg into the saucepan filled with hot water, and repeat with 3 more eggs. (You can usually fit 4 eggs at a time in the hot water. Too many, and the eggs won't poach correctly.) Gently coddle to doneness, about 3 minutes, until the whites are set and the yolks remain runny. Remove the eggs from the hot water with a slotted spoon. Set on warmed plate to hold. Repeat with remaining 4 eggs.

Make Hollandaise Sauce: This blender recipe takes a lot of the angst out of the process of making the sauce the traditional way, which is over a double boiler with a wire whisk. I find it's a lot easier for home cooks to get perfect hollandaise sauce this way. Place egg yolks in a blender container. Add cream, lemon juice, salt, and a pinch of cayenne or paprika (optional, but it adds a nice bite). Cover and pulse on low until blended. Remove the middle insert from the lid, and while continuing to blend on low, slowly and gently add the hot butter to the egg mixture, in a gradual stream. The sauce should thicken and smooth about the time the last of the butter goes in. (The hot butter cooks the egg yolks and the blender emulsifies the lemon juice and melted butter with the yolks.)

On warmed serving dish, top each toasted English muffin half with a warm slice of Virginia ham. Place a poached egg gently on top of the ham. Pour hollandaise sauce over eggs. Sprinkle with paprika and chopped parsley to garnish. Serve warm.

This recipe sounds a lot more complicated than it is, and it's a restaurant favorite because it used to be a lot harder to make at home. In fact, eggs Benedict used to be a bear to make — especially getting the sauce right. Doing it on the stove, the sauce had a tendency to curdle in inexperienced hands. Thanks to the wonder of modern blenders and a good stove, you should be able to have this on the table in less than 20 minutes.

HERBED SCRAMBLED EGGS

Six eggs
2 tablespoons olive oil, divided
3 tablespoons chopped chives
1 clove garlic, smashed, peeled, and minced (see note, below)
1 teaspoon fresh thyme leaves, or 1/2 teaspoon dried thyme leaves
1 cup fresh spinach, washed, de-stemmed, and patted dry
Kosher or sea salt and pepper, to taste

Serves two.

Break eggs into a bowl. Stir with a fork or whisk gently to break up, but not to blend totally. Set aside.

Heat a large skillet over medium heat. Add 1 tablespoon olive oil and gently rotate the pan to coat the bottom. Add chopped chives, garlic, thyme, and spinach. Stir until spinach wilts and the garlic cooks through and softens, about 2 to 3 minutes.

Transfer mixture to warmed serving plate.

Add remaining olive oil to the same skillet. Gently rotate the pan to coat the bottom. Pour beaten eggs in oiled skillet. Allow bottom to set. Bring in the edges to the center, letting the remainder of the uncooked eggs pour across the pan to cook. Add cooked herbs and greens. Stir slowly until eggs are cooked and the greens and herbs are roughly incorporated, 1 to 2 minutes. Top with salt and freshly grated pepper, to taste. Slide onto warmed serving plate. Serve warm.

The easiest way to deal with fresh garlic is to place a clove on a cutting board, place the broad end of the blade of a chef's knife over it so the blade is parallel to the cutting board surface, and smash your fist against the smooth metal of the knife — carefully! Don't let your flesh get too close to the knife's cutting edge — kitchen accidents are bad. The pounding will smash the garlic and burst the clove free of its papery wrapping, which you can pull off and discard. You can then chop the clove easily.

CINNAMON FRENCH TOAST

4 eggs

1 cup half-and-half

2 tablespoons brown sugar

1 tablespoon cinnamon, plus extra for serving

1 teaspoon vanilla

1 small loaf French bread, raisin bread, or whole wheat bread, sliced

1/2 cup (1 stick) butter

Maple syrup

Confectioner's sugar

Fruit to garnish (optional)

Ice cream or whipped cream (optional)

Serves four.

Preheat oven to 200 degrees F.

Break eggs into a flat-bottomed square casserole dish. Whisk until uniform and yellow. Stir in half-and-half, brown sugar, cinnamon, and vanilla. Whisk till blended. You will need to whisk lightly before each dip; the cinnamon tends to float.

Dip slices of bread into the egg mixture, one at a time, on both sides.

Heat griddle over medium-high heat. Place

pats of butter on griddle, one for each space on which you plan to cook a slice of toast. Place dipped bread slice on top of each pat of butter. Cook until browned, about 2 minutes. Top with another small pat of butter. Flip slices onto butter to cook other side of toast until browned. Remove to warmed serving plate. Place completed toast slices in oven to keep warm while you continue cooking.

Place slices onto a small pool of maple syrup. Sprinkle with cinnamon and confectioner's sugar. Add a side of fresh fruit to garnish. Serve with more maple syrup on the side.

For true decadence, serve with ice cream or whipped cream.

SCOTCH EGGS

This is a hearty recipe that is the old Scotch equivalent of a modern breakfast sandwich — portable, easy to eat on the run, and filling enough to see a working person through a busy morning. This is not diet food, but it is amazingly tasty.

6 eggs
1 pound breakfast sausage, thawed

1 cup seasoned bread crumbs

Serves three.

Preheat oven to 350 degrees F.

Hard-boil the eggs: Place the raw eggs in a saucepan with enough room-temperature water to cover about 1 inch over the top of the eggs. Bring the water to a boil over medium-high heat. Remove from heat and let sit for 15 to 20 minutes. When the pan, water, and eggs have cooled enough to safely handle, pour off water. Rattle the eggs in the pan to bash the eggshells against the side. This will break them and leave the eggs easy to peel. Peel off eggshells and discard.

Divide breakfast sausage into 6 pieces. Roll each piece into a ball and flatten it. Put the sausage patty on your hand, place a hard-boiled egg on the sausage and gently roll the sausage around the egg with both hands until it is covered in an even layer of sausage. Roll the sausage-covered eggs, one at a time, in seasoned bread crumbs. Place the crumb-covered eggs on a cookie sheet or in an uncovered casserole dish and bake until sausage is cooked through, about 25 minutes.

To serve, cut each egg in half lengthwise.

Lay the two halves on a plate, side by side, cut side up, to show layers of crumbs, sausage, egg whites, and egg yolks.

Serve warm.

A FAT-FREE, CHEESE-FREE, YOLK-FREE, HIGH-FIBER OMELET

Given that almost every recipe in here is likely to send a cardiologist into palpitations, here's the exception.

1/2 cup broccoli florets, cleaned and chopped
1 cup fresh spinach leaves, cleaned and de-stemmed
1/2 cup fresh mushrooms, thinly sliced
1 plum tomato, chopped
1 green onion, rinsed and thinly sliced
1/4 cup fat-free ham, cubed
1 1/2 cups egg substitute
Salt and pepper, to taste

Serves two.

Coat a nonstick skillet with nonstick cooking spray and place over medium heat. Add the vegetables and the ham to the skillet. Sauté until the veggies are cooked through, the spinach has wilted, and the broccoli is tender, about 3 to 5 minutes. Remove from heat to a warmed plate and set aside.

Rinse and dry the skillet. Spray again with nonstick cooking spray. Add egg substitute to pan. Roll the pan around, spreading the egg substitute evenly across the skillet surface. Reduce heat. Cook over medium heat until bottom is well set, about 2 to 3 minutes. Flip egg in pan to cook other side. Place vegetable-ham mixture on half of the egg's surface. Fold cooked egg round gently over veggies. Slide out of skillet onto warmed plate.

Season with salt and pepper, to taste. Serve warm.

DEVILED EGGS
6 hard-boiled eggs
3 tablespoons Dijon mustard
1/2 small onion, very finely minced
1 tablespoon white wine
2 tablespoons mayonnaise
Paprika, for garnish
Chopped chives, for garnish

Serves four.

Cut hard-boiled eggs in half lengthwise.

Scoop out yolks into a medium bowl. Set whites aside on serving tray. Refrigerate. Whisk the egg yolks with Dijon mustard, onion, white wine, and mayonnaise. When well blended, pipe or spoon the egg yolk mixture back into centers of cooked whites. Sprinkle with paprika. Top with chopped chives. Serve chilled.

AIOLI (GARLIC MAYONNAISE)

3 egg yolks
4 cloves garlic, smashed, peeled, and very finely minced
1 tablespoon Dijon mustard
3/4 cup olive oil (not extra virgin)
1 teaspoon white wine vinegar
1/2 teaspoon kosher or sea salt
1/4 teaspoon white pepper (You can use black pepper if you don't have this, but you'll see the flecks of it in the finished product. It gives it a rustic look, which isn't all bad.)
Juice of 1 lemon

This is a blender recipe, to take all the stress out of getting it to emulsify. Place the egg yolks, garlic, and the mustard in the container of a blender. Cover and pulse to blend completely, about 1 minute. Remove the center of the lid, and begin to pour the olive oil into the container in a thin stream, still running on slow. When the mixture comes together and looks like mayonnaise (usually about when half the oil is incorporated), stop pouring oil and add in the vinegar, salt, and pepper. Blend. Add in another thin stream of olive oil while blending. Stop when about 2 tablespoons of oil are left to add. Add a splash of lemon juice. Blend. Adjust seasonings to taste. Add the rest of the oil if needed. The sauce should be thick, creamy, and rich, with a lovely tang of garlic.

If you don't want to use raw eggs for this, don't worry. Start with a cup of good-quality regular mayonnaise. Whisk in 1/2 cup olive oil, 3 cloves finely minced garlic, and the juice of 1 lemon. It won't be as good, but it's close, and you won't have to worry about using raw eggs.

SPINACH QUICHE

1/2 cup butter

3 cloves garlic, smashed, peeled, and finely minced

1 small onion, trimmed, peeled, and finely chopped

1 pint fresh mushrooms, cleaned and thinly sliced

1 (10-oz.) package frozen chopped spinach,

thawed and drained
4 ounces herbed feta cheese, crumbled
8 ounces good-quality cheddar cheese, shredded, divided
1/2 teaspoon kosher or sea salt, or to taste
1/4 teaspoon ground black pepper
1 deep-dish pie crust, unbaked
4 eggs
1 cup milk

Serves six.

Preheat oven to 400 degrees F.

Melt butter in a large skillet over medium heat. Add minced garlic and onion. Stir gently and cook until onion is soft and slightly browned on the edges, about 5 minutes. Add mushrooms and stir until warmed through and reduced, about 3 minutes. Add spinach, feta cheese, and half of the cheddar cheese. Add salt and pepper, to taste.

Place mixture into unbaked pie shell.

In a medium bowl, whisk eggs until blended, add milk, whisk to combine well. Pour into pie shell over vegetable mixture.

Place filled pie shell on cookie sheet to keep

it from overflowing.

Place into preheated oven. Reduce oven heat to 375 degrees F. Bake for 20 minutes. Top quiche with remaining cheddar cheese. Return to oven and bake for an additional 30 to 40 minutes. Quiche is done when the eggs are set and firm in the center.

Remove from oven and let sit for 10 minutes. Serve warm.

CHOCOLATE SOUFFLÉ

Soufflés, by definition, are temperamental. If something goes odd, or somebody bumps the oven wrong, or the phone rings at the wrong time, the thing can deflate like a kid's balloon. So go into this knowing that it will taste good, even if it doesn't look good. But it's actually pretty easy to make — it just isn't always goof-proof.

But it will usually look fantastic, and it will impress your guests like almost nothing else will.

3 tablespoons unsalted butter, softened
1/2 cup sugar, divided use
6 egg whites
4 ounces best-quality dark chocolate,

chopped
1/2 cup very cold water
1/3 cup cocoa powder
Confectioner's sugar, for garnish (optional)
Berries, for garnish (optional)

Preheat oven to 350 degrees F.

Coat the insides of 6 individual soufflé dishes completely with 1/2 tablespoon butter. Refrigerate until the butter is set, about 3 minutes. Place a teaspoon of sugar into each dish. Shake and turn the dishes until sugar completely coats the butter. Tip out any excess. Add more sugar if needed.

Place prepared dishes on a baking sheet and set aside.

In a very clean mixing bowl (any fat will keep the eggs from whipping well), beat the egg whites on medium to high speed until foamy. Gradually add the remaining sugar a little at a time, and beat until eggs are glossy and soft peaks form when beaters are lifted. Set aside.

Place a large metal mixing bowl over a pan of simmering water. Place the chocolate into the bowl, and stir until melted, glossy, and smooth. Remove from heat. Add the water and the cocoa powder. Stir until smooth. Let cool 1 minute.

Add about 1/3 of the egg-white mixture to the cooled chocolate mixture, folding together gently.

Add the folded mixture to the remaining egg whites. Fold together gently.

Spoon into prepared dishes. Using a straight-edged knife, level the egg mixture in the dishes even with the tops of the dishes. Wipe the edges of the dishes with a dampened towel to clean them.

Bake until soufflés puff up and are cooked through but still moist in the center, 12 to 14 minutes.

Sprinkle with confectioner's sugar and garnish with berries, if using, and serve immediately.

PASTA PRIMAVERA

6 ounces bow tie pasta
2 tablespoons olive oil
2 cloves garlic, smashed, peeled, and minced
2 chicken breasts, de-boned, skinned, and

chopped into 1-inch cubes

1/2 pound of asparagus, trimmed, washed, and sliced into 1-inch pieces

1/2 pound cherry or grape tomatoes, rinsed and halved

1/2 pound baby squashes, rinsed, trimmed, and halved

1/4 cup fresh basil leaves, julienned

Kosher or sea salt, to taste

Black pepper, to taste

1/4–1/2 cup freshly grated Parmigiano-Reggiano cheese, or to taste

Serves four.

Bring a large saucepan of salted water to a boil over high heat. Add bowtie pasta and cook according to package directions.

While pasta is cooking, place olive oil in a large skillet over medium heat. Add garlic and chicken to the pan, cook until garlic is soft and chicken is browned, about 5 to 8 minutes. Add vegetables and cook until vegetables are warmed through and beginning to soften but still retain a little bite, about 6 to 8 minutes.

Stir in fresh basil and remove mixture from heat. Season with salt and pepper, to taste.

Drain cooked pasta. Toss chicken and veggie mixture with pasta. Top with cheese. Serve warm.

WARM BRIE TOPPED WITH WALNUTS, MAPLE SYRUP, AND BERRIES

This looks great, tastes better than it looks, and takes almost no effort.

1 small round Brie, at room temperature
1 cup peeled, chopped walnuts
1 cup good-quality maple syrup, divided
1 quart rinsed berries, any type
Assorted crackers

Serves four.

Preheat oven to 300 degrees F.

Cut the top rind off a small circle of Brie. Place on an oven-safe serving platter. Top with walnuts and 1/2 cup maple syrup. Turn oven off. Turn broiler on high. Broil cheese until nuts are toasted and cheese is soft. This is something you'll have to watch closely — the nuts can burn quite quickly. Remove from oven.

Add remaining syrup. Surround Brie wheel with alternating pools of berries and crackers. Serve immediately.

ABOUT THE AUTHOR

An award-winning author, **Julie Hyzy** also enjoys writing short stories, many of them mysteries and science fiction. Like Ollie Paras, Julie was born in Chicago, but loves the history and grandeur of Washington, D.C.

The employees of Thorndike Press hope you have enjoyed this Large Print book. All our Thorndike, Wheeler, and Kennebec Large Print titles are designed for easy reading, and all our books are made to last. Other Thorndike Press Large Print books are available at your library, through selected bookstores, or directly from us.

For information about titles, please call:
(800) 223-1244

or visit our Web site at:
http://gale.cengage.com/thorndike

To share your comments, please write:
Publisher
Thorndike Press
295 Kennedy Memorial Drive
Waterville, ME 04901